I0621143

When Sean Loves Rusty
A Bayou Boys collection

Includes

Meant To Be (Bayou Boys #1)
Moving On (Bayou Boys #2)
Tricked Up for Treats (Bayou Boys #3)
Jingle My Bells (Bayou Boys #4)
For Better Or Worse (Bayou Boys #5)

Chris Cox

This is a work of fiction. Names, characters, places and incidents are the product of the author's imagination or are used fictitiously and any resemblance to actual persons, living or dead, business establishments, events or locales is entirely coincidental.

All rights reserved.

No part of this book may be reproduced, scanned, or distributed in any printed or electronic form without permission.

When Sean Loves Rusty
Copyright 2014, Chris Cox

ISBN: 978-1-940601-11-3

To Dakota, a shooting star

To Kim, who dreams about Sean and Rusty just like I do. You're a fantastic editor and wonderful friend. Thanks.

Bayou Boys series

Meant To Be (Bayou Boys #1)
a Sean and Rusty short story

Moving On (Bayou Boys #2)
a Sean and Rusty short story

Tricked Up for Treats (Bayou Boys #3)
a Sean and Rusty short story

Jingle My Bells (Bayou Boys #4)
a Sean and Rusty novella

For Better Or Worse (Bayou Boys #5)
a Sean and Rusty novella

When Sean Loves Rusty (Bayou Boys #6)
a collection of Bayou Boys stories (#1 through #5)

Down To The Studs
A Levi and Clint novel
available Summer 2014

Meant To Be

CHAPTER ONE

"How do I look?" Sean stood looking into the vanity mirror, wearing his crisp pink and white pinstriped oxford shirt, cherry pinstriped suspenders and tailored gray pants. On the white bathroom rug, his feet were still bare, his toes curled under. The New Orleans humidity popped tiny beads of condensation along his forehead and neck.

Standing so close behind his lover, Rusty could see the fine baby hair curling at Sean's nape. He breathed in the scent of uniqueness Sean gave to Happy for Men cologne and let a smile surface on his kiss-swollen lips.

Rusty wanted to nuzzle Sean in that tender spot between his earlobe and shoulder. Wanted to sink his teeth in just enough to cause Sean to shudder with desire. Wanted to whisper into Sean's ear that he was beautiful.

But that's not what Sean needed to hear right now.

"Perfect." Rusty gave in to temptation and put his hands on Sean's shoulders, squeezing tight enough to emphasize the words he didn't need to say. *I've got your back. I always will.*

Sean's gray-blue eyes met his in the mirror. "Fourteenth time's the charm, huh?""

Worry had completely washed out the dreamy look of passion that had been there only an hour and a half ago. It had only been a blow job, but it had been the best one Rusty could offer.

Sean had been too anxious to make love.

Rusty swallowed back his sorrow and his memories. There had been a time... But that had been before...

Now was not the time to think of that. Sean would see the pain in Rusty's eyes and he would think of that time, too. Not that either of them would ever be able to forget.

With a need greater than desire, a need to protect, a need to wipe away the fear in Sean's eyes, Rusty wanted to take Sean back to bed and make his lover's world soft and safe.

Safe from failure. Safe from disappointment. Safe from the prejudice that cut into Sean's soul, reinforcing the damage done from the moment his father first suspected his only son wasn't like most of the other boys, making Sean feel less than okay because of who he was.

Rusty gave into temptation and leaned in close to whisper into Sean's ear, "They'd be fools not to hire you."

While Sean's GPA was decent, he came across as incredibly shy. And incredibly gay. Either one could be the reason behind his unsuccessful job interviews for an entry level mechanical engineering position.

Sean responded to Rusty's nuzzling by leaning his head back, ear to mouth, caressing him, soaking him up.

Most people thought Rusty was the stronger of the two. Physically, he topped Sean by an inch or two and fifteen pounds. Not much, really, but he looked sturdy. Sean looked delicate. Always had. But he was so much stronger than Rusty. Rusty could never have survived intact after enduring what Sean had endured.

"Then I've met a lot of fools, lately." Sean tried for a grin, but failed. "I'm so sorry, sweetie. I'm really trying."

"No sorry to it." Rusty wrapped his arms around Sean's waist, tightening hard enough to feel Sean's ragged breath. "We've got each other."

Sean turned to face Rusty, his arms reaching up to wrap around Rusty's neck, seeking the comfort he never verbalized.

"If we have no other place to live, we can always share a box under the bridge." Muffled in Rusty's neck, it sounded more like a sob than a forced laugh. ""Who knew my graduation would make us homeless?""

Rusty had caught Sean staring so often at the letter giving them two weeks' notice to vacate student housing that he had finally ripped it from the refrigerator door, tore it into strips and took it out with the trash.

He thought about not reminding Sean about their bittersweet safety net. But it made him feel better to know it was there and he thought, underneath Sean's pride, it would make Sean feel better, too.

"Mom's got our rooms all ready for us. She's really excited that we might be moving in. You've seen the sitting room she's made out of Jolie's old bedroom so we would have our own little corner of privacy along with our bedroom."

Sean nodded. "Maybe it won't come to that. There's got to be someone who wants me."

"I want you." Rusty trailed featherlight kisses along his neck.

"And I thank God daily for that."

Rusty knew Sean did. His deeply spiritual lover was grateful for everything good that came his way, things that most of the world took for granted.

"So you think this will do?" Sean squinted critically into the mirror, picked up his eyeliner and frowned at it.

Rusty had advised him to dress however made him feel best about himself. With Sean, that would include eyeliner and mascara. The eye makeup was a sign of defiance. A sign of vanity. A sign of wanting to be beautiful for Rusty, knowing Rusty loved the way the dark lines and lashes accentuated Sean's light eyes.

Those eyes.

Rusty hadn't even known what gay was when he'd fallen into those eyes and fallen into love all those years ago.

For people who scoffed at the idea of soulmates, Rusty knew they were wrong. He had known he was meant to be with Sean since he was eight and Sean was nine.

Best friends to lovers. There had never been anyone else for either of them.

That first year in high school, Sean had tried dating a girl or two to get his dad off his back but it had done nothing but make Rusty sad and angry and jealous and made Sean more aware than ever that he couldn't be straight no matter how hard he tried.

How a man could throw away his own son—a person he'd made—because his son had been born gay was a concept Rusty couldn't wrap his mind around.

But Sean's father was another thing Rusty didn't need to think about right now. With that deep connection he and Sean shared, Sean would pick up on it. Depressed was not the best way to go into a job interview.

Seeing the vulnerability in Sean's eyes, the inevitability that who he was would lead to disappointment broke Rusty's heart. His biggest hope was that, during their lifetimes, he could find a way to show Sean how truly perfect he was just the way God made him.

Sean put down the liquid eyeliner tube without unscrewing it. The tube bumped the big zirconia stud that lay on the bathroom counter. "Probably not, huh?"

"Tonight, baby." Rusty caught sight of his own matching zirconia stud in his earlobe. "Tonight we'll dress. We'll be exactly who we are, okay? And we will party like there is no tomorrow."

Working for his family, the family that believed gay was as much a righteous part of him as being green-eyed was for his oldest brother and musically talented was for his younger sister, Rusty had never had to be anyone but himself.

He resisted the urge to kiss the tiny white scar too close to Sean's eye that still bore the reminder of his coming-out confession to his family.

Yes, Sean was the stronger of the two.

"Tonight, we'll go out or stay in. Your choice. Either way, we'll have fun," he promised, trying to give Sean hope that today would end well, no matter what.

"We need to start packing up."

"We've got another week." Rusty didn't remind Sean he had already started to cart a few things over to his mom's whenever it was convenient or that he'd already arranged with his dad and brother to come over the weekend before their last day to help with the furniture.

He glanced at the watch on Sean's wrist. "You need to get going, sweetheart."

Slowly, Sean unclasped Rusty's arms from around him. "Those who are about to die—"

"—salute you." Rusty gave him a hard kiss on his cheek, knowing if he tasted Sean's lips they would have a harder time pulling apart. He caught Sean''s hand and put it on his heart. "We'll be okay. We have all we need right here."

Sean left the interview trying not to get his hopes up like he had the other thirteen times he'd shaken hands and plastered on a smile as the recruiter promised to get in touch soon. If Rusty had been interviewing, he'd have companies competing for him. He had that kind of dynamic personality, even if his math skills were so poor he couldn't keep his own bank account straight.

Still, losing this one would hurt more than the others. It was his dream job. Sean had been fascinated by underwater robotics ever since his dad had been stationed in Hawaii when he was seven. That's where his dad had taught him to snorkel— where they'd actually spent time together— before the transfer to New Orleans, before his dad started to watch him closely. Before his dad made him feel like he was doing everything wrong, telling him to toughen up and be a man every time he had the chance.

Why did his mind always wander in this direction when he was under stress? Sean pushed away thoughts of his father and of home. Six years. Long enough to let it go.

Just like he needed to let go of any hope that he'd get a call for the job he interviewed for.

He'd done horribly, even worse than usual. His palm had been sweaty when he'd shaken the interviewer's hand and mumbled his introduction. Despite his determination to maintain friendly eye contact, he'd caught himself staring past the interviewer or looking down into his clasped hands at least a half-dozen times. His monotone answers to the interviewer's questions wouldn't impress anyone. And he'd stumbled, tripping on his own feet as he got up to leave the interview room.

The weight of his student loans, of Rusty's sympathetic smile, and his own crushed confidence pulled his shoulders down, making his neck ache.

Sean shook off his suit jacket before he climbed into Rusty's old Toyota Corolla. *Their car*, Rusty always corrected. When he'd first begun interviewing, he'd dreamed of buying something new, replacing Rusty's ride with a more reliable car that would look good in Rusty's parents' driveway when they went for Sunday dinner.

One that would tell Rusty's family that their baby boy wasn't making a mistake by loving Sean.

Too aware he was wallowing in the self-pity he had been unsuccessfully hiding from Rusty, Sean made himself take the stairs two at a time to their third floor apartment. The physical exertion felt good.

He hadn't run in over a week. Then again, the apartment needed packing up. Student housing was only available for students, not for newly graduated, unemployed mechanical engineers.

Standing in the bedroom he and Rusty had called their own for the last four years, Sean wasn't sure what he should do next. No more exams to study for. No more resumes to send out. No more plans to make about sharing the car. After this last interview, he had nowhere he needed to be.

In a burst of anger, he kicked an empty packing box, venting until the hapless cardboard lay torn and flattened on the floor.

Ashamed of his outburst, he neatly and methodically finished off the job, bending and folding the box smaller to take up less room in the dumpster. After changing into running shorts, a T-shirt, and and his battered running shoes that he would replace with his first paycheck, he took off for a last run around the campus housing that had been his and Rusty's first home together.

The last time Sean had nowhere to live, Rusty's family had taken him in. It seemed history was about to repeat itself, only for a different reason this time.

Only three miles into his run, he was gasping for breath. The stress of the last few weeks had cut his wind. He slowed as he reached the campus pool, not even realizing where he'd been headed until he got there.

The water always soothed him. Rusty said it was the Pisces in him that made him part fish. When they'd lived in Hawaii his dad had taught him how to swim and then how to dive. The whole family had spent most of their time on the beach. Sean remembered being happy there.

When he'd asked for diving lessons for his tenth birthday, he had thought he could recapture those times with his dad. But it had been too late. His father had already recognized something in him that he hadn't yet understood in himself.

The pool was mostly deserted except for the bored lifeguard sitting on the stand. A sign on the pool fence advertised open positions for the summer. Sean had done that job since his teens. Maybe he should apply.

That's what five years in college and in debt got him. A job he was qualified for at sixteen.

Still, he went in, hung around the snack shop counter, then asked for a locker key instead of a job application, knowing his pride was standing in the way of making an honest living.

Pride. He would always associate that word with the word gay.

Gay pride. Yeah, all that had ever done for him was make him homeless.

"What's wrong, Rust Bucket?"

Rusty settled into his older brother's work truck and buckled his seatbelt. "Sean has another interview this morning. I'm just worried about him."

His brother sent him a disbelieving glance. "Uh-huh. Wanna tell me the rest of it?"

As if he were dumping a pallet of landscape pavers off his back, Rusty took a deep breath and unloaded on his brother. How did Sean survive without family? "It's not that I want Sean to fail. Really, it isn't."

He waited for confirmation that the judgment and condemnation he heaped onto his own head was justified. Instead, his brother simply turned on his blinker and slowed to hang a right and cut through a residential neighborhood, avoiding mid-morning traffic.

"I know you wouldn't hurt Sean for anything in the world. What's the problem?"

"I don't want anything to change." Rusty winced as it came out as more of a whine than a statement. "I even suggested he apply to graduate school, not because I thought he would like to go but because I like the life we have right now. I want it to always be like this."

"And if he gets a grown-up job, it won't be."

Rusty nodded. "It won't be."

He stared out the window with a landscaper's eye, automatically taking in the selections of plants and their arrangements as they passed by the tiny front yards in the older neighborhood.

"Is it wrong that I'm looking forward to moving back in with Mom and Dad? But Sean thinks it's a step backward."

"Isn't it?"

Rusty hated the juvenile reply even as he voiced it. "You don't understand."

His brother, married for over a half-dozen years, hadn't lived in their parents' house since he'd turned eighteen.

His brother smirked. "All of us Duchenes are momma's boys. Those first months I was on my own, I ate supper every night with Mom and Dad. We're still over there every Sunday for dinner. Thankfully, Amanda puts up with my need to be so close to my family, but it took a lot of discussion— a lot of fighting, if you want to know the truth— for me to understand that we needed to build our own family ties, too. We almost didn't make it."

"I didn't know that."

"It's not something I'm proud of." By the tightness of his jaw, Rusty could tell how deeply this still bothered his brother.

"But Sean loves Mom and Dad."

"And they love him." His brother grinned. "Wanna know a secret?"

"Sure."

"It was Mom's bread pudding with praline rum sauce that won Amanda over. Mom promised to make it every Sunday just for Amanda. It made her feel special."

"I can't even figure out what *I* can do to make Sean feel special. Much less what Mom and Dad can do."

His brother gave him a sympathetic smile. "The boy does have some issues, but he's definitely got his reasons. You've got a good heart, Rust Bucket. He"s lucky to have you."

Sean tried so hard to make Rusty happy. To please him. To be everything he thought Rusty might want or need.

"I'm the lucky one."

CHAPTER TWO

The pool manager handed back the application form Sean had carefully completed once desperation had trumped ego. "Sorry, Sean. The lifeguard position is a campus job and since you've graduated..."

Great. He couldn't even get hired for a part-time, minimum-wage position he had years of experience in.

"Thanks for checking for me." He shrugged away the sympathetic look trying to hide his own disappointment that bordered on dread behind a look of stoicism.

Head down, he headed straight for the door before his mask cracked.

His student loan repayments would start next month. He had applied for an extension, but that would only make the interest pile up.

Graduate school, Rusty's suggestion, would only dig them deeper into debt— assuming he could actually get into graduate school with his GPA.

"Sean, wait," the pool manager called. "Did you see the notice on the bulletin board? The Dive Shop is looking for help.""

"Thanks. I'll check it out," he said without turning back. Rusty always said Sean didn't need to talk much. Everyone could read what he was on his mind by looking into his eyes.

But then, Rusty had special privileges to look as deeply into Sean's eyes as he wanted to.

Or he always had. These last few months, Sean had pulled back, trying to protect Rusty from the direness of his worries.

Reversing direction, Sean headed to the community bulletin board and scanned the flyers stuck there.

"Upper right corner," the pool manager said.

There it was. Black print on white paper when most of the other flyers were Day-Glo orange and neon green.

Counter help needed. See George.

Sean's diving certification card lay heavy in his wallet.

He reached out to grab the job notice but then clenched his fist.

This was so not how everything was supposed to turn out.

He and Rusty had talked and planned for hours about how Sean would get a decent job, then they would get a nice condo and save for a house. They would buy a second car— used until they paid off the student loans— then celebrate with something better.

Modest dreams. Affordable dreams. Not anything extravagant, although Rusty always threw in a vacation to Hawaii where Sean would teach him to surf.

And now...?

He grabbed the flyer, tearing it from the pin.

Fine. It was a job, right? And it paid something, which was more than he was making now.

Moving in with Rusty's folks was bad enough, but knowing he had nothing to contribute to the added expense of two more bodies in their household was beyond damaging to his self-esteem. He'd already lived off of them those two last two years of high school. He couldn't add to the debt, no matter how hard the Duchenes insisted he was family, as much for being himself as for being Rusty's partner.

But, at twenty-three, most men were moving out of their mother's house instead of back in.

Rusty pushed open the truck door, grabbed his gloves from the side pocket and pulled them on as he walked back toward the trailer full of Formosa azaleas.

Levi Graham, of Graham Contracting and the general contractor for this job, loped toward them. Dark sunglasses hid his eyes and a baseball cap shielded his face and made his hair curl up in the humid temperatures. "Rusty, got a minute?"

"Sure. What's up?" He tried to give Levi a strong look without being too obvious. He and Sean had an ongoing discussion on whether Levi was straight or gay. All they could figure out was that he was presently unattached and they had a friend...

Under his loose tank top, Levi shrugged his shoulders to stretch them then reseated his cap before rubbing his earlobe as if the empty piercing there bothered him.

Levi was one of the most laid-back men Rusty knew but now his twitchiness made Rusty uneasy.

"The client wants a rock garden with a fountain in the backyard, but she wants some greenery, too. Can you give me some ideas and an estimate?"

One of those clients? Rusty raised his eyebrow, showing he understood Levi's unspoken message.

Levi gave him a nod.

Rusty grinned at the challenge. "Show me."

This was the part of the job Rusty loved. His grandfather said he was a natural at assessing the micro-environment and coming up with the right plantings for both effect and long-term viability.

He'd been told the humid subtropics of lower Louisiana were different than any place on earth. He wouldn't know, having been nowhere else, except for the rare family vacation spent mostly in their SUV as they traveled to the mountains of Arkansas where the terrain was definitely different than his home turf.

Unlike Sean, who had been everywhere, living in exotic places like Hawaii and Germany and Japan. But Sean wouldn't know a boxwood bush from a bay tree.

Then again, Sean could talk diving depths and underwater caves for hours.

If only the corporate recruiter spoke his language, Sean would have no trouble acing his interview.

For the first time since he'd lain in Rusty's arms that morning, he felt the tension leave his shoulders and neck. Dive shops did that for him.

There was something about the smell of neoprene that settled him.

He found his way to the counter, partly hidden by a display of sunglasses and a rack of fins. Laying the flyer on the counter, he cleared his throat and said, "I'm here to see George."

And smiled when his voice didn't break.

The girl at the counter gave Sean a nonchalant shrug, said okay, and sauntered off to the back room behind the counter.

After several minutes of hovering near the counter, feeling uncomfortable near the unattended cash register, Sean decided to look around instead.

He fingered a mask before wandering over to the board advertising guided dives. Staring blankly at them, he took a deep breath, readying himself to talk to George, should he ever make an appearance.

We'll be okay. We have all we need right here. Rusty's parting words had sustained him all morning.

The bell above the door rang, and Sean looked up to see Bill Frazier, the interviewer from this morning. And there went all feelings of being okay.

The man saw him, did a double take as he recognized Sean, then said, "Hi."

Sean nodded, and managed to say, "Hi," back.

Bill moved toward the board. "Planning a dive?"

"No." It was short and clipped. Not what Sean had intended, but he didn't want to tell the guy he was applying for a counter job. That he was giving up on using his degree. That he was settling for a paycheck of any size from anyone.

His terse answer didn't seem to bother Bill, though. "See anything here you recommend?"

Sean looked through the list. "How experienced are you, Mr. Frazier?"

"Call me Bill. I'm Master Scuba Dive Instructor rated." He peered over Sean's shoulder. "I remember from your resume that you're Rescue Diver rated, right?"

"Yes, sir." From the corner of his eye, Sean noticed a man coming around the counter toward them. George, no doubt.

How was he going to handle this?

"Our waters are pretty murky around here. Lake Pontchartrain is popular if you want a quick dive that doesn't require a lot of travel time."

"Which one would you go on this time of year?"

"I think I'd pick Al Hernandez's dive at Manila Village. For one thing, I know the crew. They're safe, but won't smother an experienced diver. And the ride out to the site will give you a taste of our marshes and wildlife."

"Great. Thanks." He patted Sean on the shoulder. Sean was proud of himself for hiding his flinch at the contact. If only he could be the outgoing touchy-feely type like Rusty, or at least comfortable with a stranger's friendly gesture, he might have a job by now.

Instead, he took two steps back before he could stop himself.

Bill gave him a nod, acknowledging the boundaries Sean had just put up between them, then turned to George.

"I'd like to sign up for a dive."

"Sure. Step over here and I'll get you fixed up." George ambled toward the counter gesturing to both of them.

Not knowing what else to do, Sean trailed them.

George pulled a notebook from under the counter. "Got your card?" he asked Bill.

"Right here." Bill pulled out his wallet and sorted through his various credit and identification cards. Fumbling for his dive card, he dropped his PFLAG card on the counter.

There goes that excuse for not getting the job. Immediately, Sean mentally kicked himself for his pitiful attitude. Sure, prejudice existed, but he wouldn't be a victim to it.

"And you?" George asked, his pen poised over the notebook entry he was making.

He forced his chin up, ready to confess. "I'm not here to sign up for a dive." Words failed him, so he gently touched the flyer still lying on the counter. ""I was hoping…"

George studied him, then shook his head. "Sorry, kid. I've hired my niece for this job." He looked up into the shoplifting mirror at the girl who thought she was hiding among the swimwear, texting. "But check back in a week or so, in case it doesn't work out."

"Okay, thanks." Under Bill's scrutiny, he wanted nothing more than to disappear into thin air. Instead, he gave both men a nod then controlled his steps along with his breath, using all the willpower he could gather to leave the shop with dignity.

As soon as he slid into the Corolla's worn seat, he realized his phone had been buzzing for a while.

Pulling it from his pocket, he checked, seeing Rusty's smiling face on the text message.

Thinking of you. Love you.

He texted back,

Love you, too.

And in the end, that's what mattered, right?

CHAPTER THREE

"Rusty Duchene? It's been awhile since I've seen you. How are your mom and dad?"

"They're just fine, thank you." With a happy grin, Rusty let Mrs. Filler trap his palm between her two beringed hands. Levi, standing slightly to his left, gave him a relieved nod.

"How is Julie, Mrs. Filler?"

"Doing well. You know she's engaged, don't you?"

"No, ma'am, I hadn't heard."

"We miss you at church." She turned to Levi. "Rusty and Julie always sat next to each other in catechism class. They made their First Communions together at St. Anne's."

"Our family is going to St. Andrews Episcopal now."

"Episcopal? The Duchenes have been Catholic ever since I've known them."

"A few hundred years."

Curiosity overcame good manners when she asked, "Why...?" before letting her invasive question trail off.

Rusty gently pulled his hand free, feeling his grin turn to plastic. "It's the gay thing."

It seemed Mrs. Filler was suddenly fascinated by his earring.

To break her stare, Rusty turned and gestured toward her rock garden. "What mood are you wanting to create here?"

A half-hour later, in the privacy of Levi's truck, he finished drawing out his ideas and making a list of plants to purchase.

"I've added fifteen percent to the overall price because I have a feeling we're all going to earn that much and more in time spent reassuring Mrs. Filler that she made the right decision before this project is done."

"I'll leave the reassuring up to you. You had her giggling like a teenager before you were done."

Rusty blew out his breath, trying but failing to hold back his frustration. "She only got giggly when she found out I was gay. Now she'll feel politically correct because I'll be her token gay landscape designer, like her hair stylist. How many times did she tell me she wanted to introduce me to him, even though I told her I already had a boyfriend? I hate being typecast."

Levi smirked, "It's better than hiding who you are, huh?"

Something sharp in Levi's voice made Rusty pause. He'd wondered a few times about Levi, but the man didn't obviously ping his gaydar. Maybe a slight ghost echo? Maybe Levi was bi?

And now who was typecasting. Rusty rolled his eyes at himself.

Levi shrugged. "As long as it pays the bills, right? To tell you the truth, Rusty, I think you got her soothed more because her family has known yours for centuries, and not because of your sexual orientation. And your skill did the rest. Your ideas are brilliant."

"I guess." Rusty thought of Sean, trying so hard to get a job on his own merits. But Levi was right. The job market was mostly about *who* you knew, with a bit of *what* you knew thrown in.

"Talking of paying the bills— my boyfriend just graduated in mechanical engineering and is looking for a job. Is Graham Contracting hiring?"

"Mechanical, huh? If he were a civil engineer, I might be able to help."

"The job doesn't have to be in his field. He's good with math and paperwork." Rusty signed the design and handed it off to Levi. "I wish he would just chill and wait for the perfect job but he's driving himself crazy about being unemployed."

Levi noted the hefty profit margin, knowing Mrs. Filler would agree to the price solely because of the Duchene influence. "Let me see what I can come up with."

Precariously balancing a box of textbooks on his hip, Sean pulled the door to their apartment shut for the last time, wishing Rusty was here. Rusty always knew what Sean needed. If he were here right now, he would wrap his arm around Sean's neck, pull him close, and growl into his ear that it would be okay.

Instead, Rusty was working on-site at a cabin on Lake Pontchartrain, working with Levi to put in spring plantings for a new vacation home.

Sean still fumed and felt ashamed that Rusty had used family influence to practically coerce Graham Contracting into offering him a job they had clearly made for him. But he couldn't afford to let ego get in the way of a paycheck.

He'd asked for time to think about their offer, but he already knew he would be calling them on Friday to accept the job.

As he pushed on the door to make sure it had locked, his phone vibrated his pocket and he couldn't help but smile.

Before he even dropped the box to fish out his phone, he knew it had to be Rusty. Rusty always knew when Sean needed him. He'd use the excuse to call to remind Sean about meeting him for lunch, but they'd both know he was calling because Sean needed to hear his voice.

But the display showed an area code and phone number Sean didn't recognize.

Great. He'd dropped that heavy-assed box for a wrong number.

"Hello?"

"Sean Delahunt?"

"Yes."

"Bill Frazier, from Oceanic Mariner, Incorporated. You interviewed with me a little over a week ago."

"Yes?"

"We are prepared to make you an offer for an entry level mechanical engineering position."

"Yes?" Sean cringed at his inane reply, pacing because he couldn't stand still.

This was it. He'd done it. He would not only be pulling his own weight, but actually be able provide for all the things he and Rusty had dreamed about.

"I'll give you the details then follow-up with an email, okay? The position pays industry standard and comes with a moving package and a signing bonus to help you relocate."

One word stood out above the rest. "Relocate?"

"Yes." Mr. Frazier paused, then said, "The job is in our corporate office in Boston, Massachusetts."

"Oh."

"Will that be a problem?"

He wanted to blurt out "no", but Rusty— family meant everything to him. And Rusty had his own career, also tied to family. This was his home.

Sean tried to think of a diplomatic reply, but finally had to go with blunt honesty when nothing else came to mind. "Uh, I don't know."

He heard a strained clearing of throat on the line. "We have a new hire orientation starting in two weeks. We'll need to know by next Wednesday, at the latest, to start processing your paperwork and get you moved up here in time. Can you get us an answer by then?"

"Yes, sir. I'll have an answer by then."

"You are a strong candidate for this position. We really hope the answer will be yes."

"Thank you, sir." Flipping the phone off, Sean squeezed his eyes shut, trying to breathe through the chaos zinging every nerve ending.

Pure peace. That's what Rusty felt as he sat on the grassy bank of Lake Pontchartrain. A breeze kept the humidity at bay while waves set a soothing rhythm for his soul.

New Orleans. Everyone who had ever traveled said there was no other place like it on earth. All Rusty knew was that New Orleans was home.

No matter what life handed him, he knew he could handle it as long as he had his roots firmly planted here.

He was halfway through his sandwich when he felt that certain awareness that told him Sean was nearby.

"Hey, you." He searched Sean's face, seeing pain there. Leaving the apartment was bad for both of them, but especially for Sean. The apartment had been the first place where he'd felt at home, like he had a right to belong there, since he'd been five or six.

"Hey you, back." Sean's forced smile stabbed through Rusty's heart.

Rusty would do anything to keep the world from hurting his lover. If only he had that power.

As Sean came into range, Rusty reached out and pulled him tight into his chest with an arm around his neck. "I started eating without you. I was starving."

"It's okay. I'm not hungry."

Getting Sean to eat was one of Rusty's hardest trials. With relief, he realized he would soon have his mother to help him out. Nobody, not even Sean, could resist her cooking especially with her insistence to have another bite or two to please her.

The way Sean burrowed into Rusty meant he wanted to be held tight and Rusty obliged.

"Rusty?" Sean's muffled voice sounded unsure. "I gotta tell you something. We've got a problem."

Rusty smiled into Sean's hair. His partner always seemed to think problems were bigger than they were. "Okay."

The gulp of air Sean sucked in sounded watery before he cleared his throat. "I got a job offer."

"What?" Not what Rusty had expected to hear. He wanted to push Sean back to look into his face, to read his eyes, but Sean clung too tightly to peel away. Instead, he squeezed the shaking shoulders tighter. "Fantastic, baby!"

"It's in Boston."

It took two full breaths as Rusty's brain tried to wrap around Sean's words until he got the big picture.

Softly, feeling Sean's pain, he whispered to the most important person in his life, "I'm so sorry, baby. But there'll be other jobs. The right one will come along. Until then you've got Graham Contrac—"

Sean stiffened, trying to break the bonds Rusty hadn't even realized he'd tightened so much. "I think I want to take it.'"

CHAPTER FOUR

Five days. Five tense, horrendous, gut-churning, painful days of indecision.

Sean awoke from his uneasy sleep with Rusty snoring on the other side of the bed in the room that had become so familiar to him those last two years in high school. How could two men put so much distance between them on a queen-sized bed?

But then, the arguments that had preceded this worried him even more.

"What about all the debts I've accumulated, Rusty? The years I've put in for us, for our future."

"Our future? Don't you mean your future? I never asked you to go to college or to become an engineer. And don't worry about the debts. Dad"s already said—"

"I don't want your father paying my debts. They've already given me room and board since I was sixteen. And I know they slip you money all the time. Don't you get it, Rusty? This is about us becoming our own men. Standing on our own feet. Being independent. I *need* to do this."

Rusty had looked at him like Sean was out of his mind.

Sean took a shaky breath, trying to find the words to reason with Rusty. "Don't you understand? I've finally got my chance. Things have always been easy for you. You've never felt indebted like everything you own is from charity. You've never had to fight for every scrap of self-respect you could scrape together."

"What are you talking about? Charity? My family loves you just like they love me." The way Rusty looked past Sean's eyes instead of into them proved he wasn't listening. "Damn it, Sean, don't you realize what you're asking me? You want me to give up my career to move to a place I don't know anything about. I don't even know what grows in

Boston's environment. And what about my family? I know it's no big deal to you, since you don't even talk to your folks, but it's a big deal to me. Do you know what you're asking of me?"

"Family? I thought I was your family. I thought I was enough."

Rusty had clenched his fists, bitten his lip, and turned away.

Moving to Boston would mean Rusty would be giving up his family— a safe harbor for both of them— as well as his own career where he was working hard to build a respected reputation.

Passing on this job would mean Sean would be giving up his chance for his own self-respect, his opportunity to be his own man, the ultimate climax of all they'd worked for and sacrificed for as he went through school earning his degree.

They'd hurled barbed insults. Both of them were selfish. Neither of them listened to the other. And then Sean had stopped talking, not able to bear another agonizing exchange that ended up with him fighting the urge to cry and Rusty fighting the urge to hit the wall.

Maybe he should have called Mr. Frazier back immediately and turned down the job. Or just packed up his stuff and left.

Or—

He didn't know what he should have done to avoid all the hurtful things they'd said and left unsaid between them. After all these long, torturous days of heated words and cold silences, he still didn't know what to do, and he had to give his answer to Oceanic today.

In his sleep, Rusty rolled over, reaching for Sean. When his flailing hand found Sean already sitting up, Rusty blinked and Sean watched the awareness of pain wipe the dreamy sleep from those beloved brown eyes.

"Hey." Rusty's voice was growly from sleep, his hand frozen in mid-reach.

"Hey, back." Sean gave him a tight smile, but couldn't hold it in place as Rusty let his hand drop.

"I've got something for you." Rusty reached over to his nightstand, pulled open the drawer and came up with a small box.

He gripped it tightly in his fist while he scooted closer to Sean in the bed.

Slowly, carefully, he trailed a finger down Sean's cheek then across his lips.

Sean couldn't stop himself— didn't want to stop himself— as he kissed at those fingers.

He wanted to lean into Rusty, be wrapped in his arms, lose himself in Rusty's heat and hear everything was going to be okay.

Instead, he held himself firm.

If he lost himself this time, he might never find himself again.

Rusty swallowed hard enough Sean saw his throat convulse, then said, "You know, extended family is still family, even if they're thousands of miles away."

What was Rusty saying? The tone of his voice— soothing, placating, loving— made more sense than his words.

Rusty fidgeted with the box in his hand. "And with your new job, you can carry all the bills for a while until I get work, right?"

Sean blinked, trying to see past that earnestly intense gaze Rusty was giving him to the message underneath. Could he let himself hope?

"And Sean," Rusty shoved the box at him, "the best thing about Boston is we can be married there."

Sean opened the box to see two matching copper rings inside. Each band had a continuing pattern of fleur-de-lis around it.

"Will you?"

Sean gulped in enough air to answer. "Yes."

Then he was gasping for breath again as Rusty lunged toward him, tackling him and pinning him to the bed.

Raised over him, his weight pressing Sean into the mattress, Rusty said, "I love you. I'll love you forever."

And Sean felt the truth of that in every cell in his body.

"I know." He pulled Rusty down close. "I'll love you forever, too."

Moving On

CHAPTER ONE

Rusty paced back and forth in baggage claim, alternately looking at his phone, which updated him that Sean's plane had landed at least fourteen minutes ago, and searching the crowd that rushed to grab their bags.

The only thing he wanted to grab was Sean.

God, these two months apart had been torture.

Phone sex sucked. Sadly, not literally.

Then, the nightly phone calls started to get shorter and shorter. Sometimes Rusty got nothing more than a quick voice mail message, or worse, a text, telling him not to wait up for a real call because Sean was going out after work with his new friends.

New friends.

He tried to squash his jealousy by thinking of how happy Sean sounded. How excited he was in his new job. In his new world.

The times he had gotten to talk to Sean, he'd tried to match Sean's tone as he'd sat on his mother's well-loved living room couch, or crouched on the lonely queen-sized bed they'd shared for so many years—except for the last two months.

Sean hadn't even come home for Rusty's twenty-fourth birthday last month. Saving the plane fare had been the sensible thing to do to make their plan work.

The plan, which Sean had mostly engineered, was that as Sean's training was over and he'd passed his probationary period for his new job, Rusty would move up to Boston to join him. No sense in Rusty leaving his solid employment in the family business if Sean washed out of the new hire program. Like that was going to happen. Sean never failed at anything.

Sean would move out of the apartment where he'd sublet a room with another guy. He and Rusty would find an apartment to move into, and Rusty would start his own job hunt.

The days had crawled. But now, Sean had passed his probationary period and his job was secure. No, not a job. A career.

Engineers didn't have jobs. They had careers. Unlike landscape designers whose only qualifications were that his daddy owned the business.

Because they were saving money, Sean had found an apartment without him. With the way Sean waxed on and on about it, Rusty was certain it would be perfect. At a perfect price for their single-income budget. In the perfect part of the city. Among perfect friends.

He still had a hard time understanding that Sean had made good friends without him. He was trying really hard to be glad about that.

Sean promised they would be Rusty's close friends, too.

Since when were friends an intimately shareable commodity like towels and toothbrushes?

These last two months, Rusty had felt as if he'd only been going through the motions of living. But now that they were in the moving part of their plan and Rusty's life could begin again.

Rusty put behind him all the heartache that had gone with packing up his possessions. Deciding what would stay and what would go. Looking through tear-filled eyes to see his mother's tears flowing freely down her face.

Her baby boy was moving, far, far away.

Into the arms of his lover, if he wanted to be melodramatic about it. But right now, his arms held nothing but himself as he scanned the crowd. Only one bag circled the carousel and it didn't look like Sean's.

Once again he checked for texts.

Nothing.

In the airport restroom, Sean brushed his teeth with his finger one more time. His stomach still lurched but at least he'd stopped dry heaving. His only saving grace was that he'd held off until they'd touched ground.

He and air travel did not mix.

As the son of an air force pilot, his airsickness had always been a source of embarrassment for his father. But then, his father had found bigger things to be embarrassed about.

Rusty.

Sean needed him so much. He ached for him. Not just his body, but his heart. This time apart had been so painful.

He'd worked hard at keeping himself busy, even though without Rusty every effort had been challenging. Just like Rusty's mom had advised him, he'd gone out often and made friends. His only other option had been to sit alone in the room he shared with another guy who dropped his clothes all over the room, including on Sean's side, and had never learned to fart only in the bathroom.

Sean would never again complain when Rusty left his shoes in the living room.

But spending every minute he could away from that hated apartment had given him time to explore the city.

He'd found the perfect apartment for him and Rusty and had started hanging out in their community room even though their lease hadn't started until yesterday.

A few of the guys did theater and gave him free passes to the shows. Not only did those shows take care of a couple of hours that he didn't have to spend in the company of his awful roommates, but the afterparties had been great for meeting new people.

Rusty would be so proud of him.

Everyone knew that Sean was the shy one, waiting for Rusty to pave the way for him. But he'd tried, really tried to put himself out there. To make his way in this brave new world. To pave the way for Rusty to join him.

His mind and heart stayed heavy knowing he was taking Rusty away from his tight-knit family. Having a set of new friends ready and waiting for him was the only thing Sean knew to do to ease the pain.

He splashed water on his face, drew in a careful breath and waited for his gut to gurgle. When it seemed to stay right side up, he shouldered his backpack then made his way to baggage claim, trying not to jar his stomach too much.

Rusty would make it all better. He always did.

Rusty scrolled through his phone, checking for texts, checking for messages, checking for anything that would tell him where the hell Sean was.

Then a spidery feeling came over him and he looked up.

Sean.

His heart swelled so big it hurt his chest.

Sean came running at him, hurtling himself at Rusty.

Wrapping his arms around his Sean felt so good, so right. So—.
Damn. Something was off. In Sean? In him?

Yeah. In him.

Ignoring whatever it was—he'd figure it out later—he lifted Sean
off his feet and swung him around, feeling the warmth of Sean's breath
on his neck, the beat of Sean's heart against his chest, the clutch of
Sean's hands in his hair.

Sean wrapped his legs around Rusty's waist and clung to him so
tightly Rusty could barely breathe. Not that he needed air now that
Sean was home.

Home. Not anymore.

Even as he thought that, Sean slid his feet down to the floor and
loosened his grip.

The air between them cooled too quickly.

The display of affection was new for Sean. Rusty had always wanted
to put his hand on Sean's shoulder, wanted to bump knees under the
table, wanted to twine his fingers through Sean's as they walked
together.

But Sean always shied away in public, although in private he soaked
up Rusty's touch.

But now, out in the middle of the airport, Sean was clinging to his
hand as if someone were threatening to rip them apart.

Rusty blinked through the moisture in his eyes. "You got your hair
cut."

"I thought it might make me look older."

It didn't. Still, why hadn't Sean mentioned he was trying a new look?
It was something they always talked about.

The new tattoo around Rusty's bicep itched, reminding him that
they didn't always talk about everything.

He'd done it as—what? An act of defiance? A sign of protest? An
anchor to the home he'd never imagined having to leave?

Anger rushed through him, even when he tried to hold it back.
Anger and something else he couldn't name.

Why ever he'd done it, it hadn't been for Sean.

Sean pulled him close, still not kissing him, and said into his neck,
"God, I missed you."

His tone was raw, cutting through the uncertainty.

Sean *had* missed him.

"Me, too, baby. Me, too." He nuzzled Sean on his bare neck. "Let's
go home."

Wrong thing to say. He knew it as soon as he had escaped his lips.

Sean pulled back to look him in the eye. "You're okay with this?"

As he had done from the moment he'd first agreed to the move, Rusty nodded his head in a lie. "I'm okay."

"You'll like Boston. I can hardly wait to introduce you around."

"Umm-hmmm." Rusty turned his attention to the lone bag circling the carousel. "Is that yours?"

"No. I only brought this." Sean turned, putting his backpack between them as he headed for the doors leading to the parking lot. "Just shower stuff and a change of clothes for tomorrow. I figured that tonight we could wash what I'm wearing right now and that will get me two days of clean clothes."

Two days of driving stretched in front of them. Two days with plenty of time to talk.

Or two days of long silences.

"We're never doing this again." The torment Rusty had felt during the last two months came out in a growl. "We're never going to be apart this long again. No matter what."

Sean nodded, his eyes filled with wetness. "No matter what."

Seeing if this new *Touching in Public is Okay* rule still held, Rusty threw his arm around Sean's shoulder.

Sean snuggled in as if he wanted to climb inside Rusty's shirt. Turning his face into Rusty's shoulder, he breathed deeply. "The scent of you. There's nothing on earth that even comes close."

Finally, Rusty's emotions went into overload. He had to lighten the mood or shatter apart. So he laughed when he answered, "So, I smell? I'm hoping that's a good thing."

Sean pulled back enough to send a solid fist into Rusty's stomach. "Dork."

Then he rubbed the place he'd punched. "And yeah, it's a very good thing."

Almost, Rusty said, *Welcome Home, baby.* But he caught himself in the nick of time. "I've already loaded our car onto the dolly, so I brought my brother's truck."

"You haven't started loading without me, have you?"

Rusty had a sinking feeling that what had started off as a good thing was now not so good. "All done, baby."

Beside him, Sean did that thing where he pulled back without moving or saying a word. He was gone a good two or three seconds, moving automatically under Rusty's direction, but not really being there.

Wherever he went, when he came back, he seemed to have uneasily settled something inside himself. "Okay."

"Okay." Rusty started to explain. To apologize. To try to make it better. But he'd done nothing wrong. His parents, brothers and sister had all wanted to pitch in. It had helped them all cope with the reality that he was moving away. He was the first of the Duchenes to leave Louisiana ever since his ancestors had come from France via Acadia during the great exile five hundred years ago.

"Okay." Sean echoed again. But his tone held disappointment.

"Talk to me."

Sean stalled by walking to the driver's side of the big truck and holding his hands out for the keys.

Rusty dug them from his pocket, but didn't hand them over. "Are you sure?"

Sean wasn't the best at driving bigger vehicles. In fact, Rusty had already resigned himself to being the sole driver of the moving van with their car piggybacking on the two-wheeled dolly behind.

"I'm sure." Sean had that stubborn set to his jaw, the one that told Rusty an argument would be long and messy. Not what he wanted after two months apart.

He clicked open the doors with the remote before dropping the keys into Sean's open hand.

"Control freak." He'd meant it to sound more teasing than it came out.

Sean just gave him a sharp glare before he climbed into the driver's seat. After a few seconds of dead air space, Sean dropped some of the challenge in his voice when he said, "I haven't driven in two months. Public transportation just isn't the same."

"Makes sense." Rusty would have agreed with any excuse Sean gave to see that tightness ease from the corners of Sean's mouth.

He'd have given Sean a blow job right then and there if Sean would just let him drive. Okay, truth was, he'd have given Sean a blow job with no strings attached if he thought his shy lover would agree to it.

From the passenger seat, he tried not to wince or be too obvious about grabbing the door or stomping on the imaginary brake as Sean jockeyed the truck back and forth to clear the tight parking space.

It had taken Rusty only one try. But then, he'd been driving heavy equipment around the nursery grounds since he could use a phone book to see over the steering wheel.

Sean hadn't learned to drive until he was seventeen and Rusty's oldest brother had practically forced him to learn.

Rusty had cleaned off the bench seat just so Sean could sit there and snuggle up on the drive home. But he didn't scoot over and use the space himself. Sean needed no distractions.

Sean pulled up to the airport parking attendant's hut and stuck out the slip along with the money needed to raise the wooden arm blocking their exit. As he pulled forward too soon, barely clearing the moving arm, he said, "So, everything's already packed and on the truck?"

"Uh-huh." Rusty pried his fingernails from his palms.

"What all did you pack?"

"Everything."

"I was going to sort through some stuff. Maybe clear out some of the junk."

"You said you were going to do that when we moved from student housing into Mom's house and you never did."

"I was going to this time around. No sense in hauling junk up to Boston if we don't need to."

"Well, it's all packed and loaded onto the truck." Rusty was ready to get off this endless loop. "We can sort through it together when we get to the new place, okay?"

"Together." Sean slowed too slowly for the red light, almost putting them in the middle of the intersection. He blew out a breath. "Okay. Together."

It had been stupid to insist on driving. Sean hated driving this huge truck. Every car braking in front of him made him nervous he would run into it.

He wished Rusty would reach over and rest that warm callused hand on his thigh. Rusty's touch always grounded him. But Rusty sat, quiet and tense, wincing at each red light or lane change.

Rusty was right. Insisting on the keys had been a control issue. Sean had felt so out of control from the moment he'd accepted the entry level engineering job from the college recruiter.

Then he'd been on pins and needles all throughout his two month probationary period, worried he'd screw up and be unemployed once again.

With student loan payments coming due—Sean didn't want to think about it anymore.

He breathed a sigh of relief as he turned into the neighborhood where he and Rusty had been living with Rusty's parents for way too long. Now to make it down the narrow streets without sideswiping a mailbox.

Soon. Soon they would have a place of their own. They would have their own choice of artwork on the walls. Their own colors of towels in the bathrooms. Their own set up for pots and pans in the kitchen.

Not that Sean wasn't grateful to Rusty's parents. They'd opened their doors and their hearts ever since Sean had been kicked out of his parents' house, his answer to coming clean about being gay.

Taking in a needy sixteen-year-old along with their household of teenaged and college-bound children had to have taken a toll on both their finances and their nerves. But Mr. and Mrs. Duchene had done it. They'd accepted Sean, every inch of him inside and out, made sure he graduated from high school, helped him enroll and get student loans for college and celebrated every success he'd had along the way.

But grown men didn't live with their mothers. Or in this case, with their fiance's mother. In the last two months, Sean had developed the habit of rubbing his ring whenever he thought of Rusty's proposal. Maybe they should have saved their wedding rings for the wedding, but engagement rings just weren't done for guys—even if Rusty or he had found the extra money to buy an additional set of rings.

February, after Mardi Gras season, when the work slowed down for New Orleans landscapers, that's when Rusty's family would come to Boston to witness their legal official union.

He got a big knot in his stomach whenever he thought about marriage.

It's not something he wanted to think about right now. Instead, he used all his concentration to weave through the winding neighborhood streets to the house that had kept him from being homeless. Cautiously, he parked in the street close to the curve, although Rusty would have had no problem pulling into the narrow driveway next to his mother's car.

As he turned off the truck, Rusty reached for his door handle, clearly ready to escape the truck Sean's driving had turned into a death trap.

But Sean grabbed for Rusty's hand. "Wait."

It came out like a barked order. Sean winced when he realized he sounded like his father. When Rusty looked over, Sean forced his sweetest smile. "Please?"

Rusty ran his free hand down Sean's arm. "What's wrong, baby?"

"Hold me." Sean swallowed down the lump in his throat. "Please."

Rusty opened up his arms and Sean slid over to the middle seat of the truck. Twisting to plaster himself as close as he could against Rusty, Sean buried his head in Rusty's neck. "I'm taking you away from your family. What if I've really fucked up?"

"We, baby, not you. If we fucked up, we did it together."

That shouldn't have been reassuring, but it was.

Sean nuzzled into Rusty's shoulder. "Together."

Rusty rubbed circles into Sean's back as he nodded. "Together."

CHAPTER TWO

As soon as Sean's foot touched the driveway, the front door of Rusty's house swung open.

The door was decorated with a big gauzy ribbon wreath, just like the first time it had swung open for Sean all those years ago. Warmth spilled out along with Mrs. Duchene, just like then, too. Her arms were open as she half-ran, half-skipped toward Sean.

"You're home. Our baby boy is home, Papa."

She wrapped him up, her head coming to his shoulder, and held him tight.

Although he'd never called them Momma and Papa out loud, he'd done it inside his head ever since he'd moved in.

They didn't push. They never pushed. Just accepted.

He gave her an extra squeeze that she returned in kind.

The tension in Sean's neck released, making him feel light-headed. He'd carried that knot ever since he'd accepted the engineering job in Boston.

Before the hug became awkward, Mr. Duchene hovered over them, patting him on the back.

"My turn, Momma."

They'd done this transition so often for their children and grandchildren that they didn't even jostle Sean as Mrs. Duchene unwrapped her arms and Mr. Duchene took her place.

Sean knew how fortunate he was to have felt the love in those arms six years ago.

Now, like then, he felt so safe.

But he was leaving this voluntarily and taking Rusty away from it, too. What had he done?

"Leave some for me, Dad." Rusty's sister Jolie added her clench over the top of Mr. Duchene's. "Welcome home, Sean."

At his knee, Rusty's three-year-old nephew started tugging on Sean's shirt tail. "Me! My turn! My turn to hug Uncle Sean."

Mr. Duchene dropped his arms and Sean let loose of Jolie with one arm to scoop up the nephew he'd known since the day the kid was born. He'd always been Uncle Sean to Tommy, loved as equally as Rusty.

Unconditional love. He didn't take it for granted.

"You've gotten so heavy. Have you been eating all my pecan pie?"

"Not yours. Mine!"

It was a game Tommy never tired of playing.

Mrs. Duchene rubbed her hand across the part of Sean's shoulder not covered by hugging arms. "Not this time, Tommy. The whole meal is for Sean."

Tommy studied him, a crease between his eyebrows that made him look just like Rusty. "You'll share, right?"

"Well." He drew the moment out, just like Tommy expected him to, "Okay."

A couple Sean had just met had a kid. He'd never thought about it, never thought it was possible. But Rusty would make such a good daddy. So maybe someday?

"But," Mrs. Duchene broke in, "the pies are for tomorrow, after church."

Sunday Dinner—moved to Saturday to accommodate them. Sean thought he and Rusty would be on the road way before then. Over his shoulder, he saw Rusty shrug.

Sean gave him an accepting nod. What was a few hours when he was taking Rusty away from his family?

"Wanna stay with Uncle Sean."

"No, Tommy. We talked about this already."

"Don't wanna go out to eat. Wanna stay here."

Tommy's mother scooped him up and blew on his tummy. "Wanna take you with me." She cast a quick look at her husband behind her as she carried the giggling three-year-old with her. "We'll be in the car." She planted another raspberry then commanded over her shoulder, "Hurry."

That put everyone in motion as Mrs. Duchene scurried back into the house for the handbag that held everything anyone would ever need and everyone else made quick strides toward all the cars and trucks in the driveway.

Rusty put his arm over Sean's shoulder. "They're giving us tonight alone."

Sean wanted to say something, to thank someone, but the thickness in his throat made speaking impossible. He would *not* cry. He hated that weakness in himself.

Instead, he purposely thought of undressing Rusty.

Sentimentality warred with passion.

Passion won.

Sean gave up his effort to speak. Instead, he grabbed Rusty's hand, rushing past Mrs. Duchene who dodged neatly, and pulled Rusty up the stairs.

The bedroom was bare, except for their queensized bed. Thank God not *everything* had been packed up yet.

That bed had never looked so huge. Or so seductive.

Rusty's skin prickled. Wanting, needing Sean's touch.

All those nights. Those horrible, awful, lonely nights sleeping alone all came to a head, literally.

His hands hovered over Sean's hair. "Baby, we can't ever do this again. I felt so lonesome."

He waited, but Sean didn't say, 'Me, too.' Instead, he only nodded, not meeting Rusty's eyes. Rusty could hear his own breath in and out. Too harsh.

To soften the silence, he pulled Sean's mouth into his. He knew his lips were hard, bruising, devouring. His fingers scrubbed through the short buzz of Sean's hair where they used to thread through the longer silky length. Right now, it didn't matter. Nothing mattered accept that Sean was home.

Sean's lips parted, letting Rusty in.

Toothpaste over the unique flavor of Sean. Nothing in this world could compare.

At least that's what Rusty had always thought. Had Sean compared?

Sean's hands pushed between them, diving under the hem of Rusty's shirt.

The circle of tiny fleur-de-lis inked around Rusty's bicep itched like it hadn't done in weeks. He pushed down his worry about what Sean would say.

It wasn't like he had to ask permission. It was his body, after all. But they'd always talked about stuff like that. Like haircuts and stuff. Just because it was fun to, it was reassuring to. It's what they did.

His hand ran over the sides of Sean's new cut, feeling the bristles under his palm. Sean hadn't bothered to tell him about this, or even text him a picture.

Then his lovers' palms were running along his stomach, up over his chest pausing on his nipples. Rubbing, rubbing and sending signals straight to his cock which was already straining against the zipper of his jeans.

Sean pulled his mouth away.

In Rusty's ear, Sean breathed out, "God, I missed you."

Rusty was done with kissing, done with words.

He grabbed the tab of his zipper and yanked. Sean took over, pushing down the waistband of jeans too tight and too thick to be between them. Anything that kept Rusty away from Sean was too much right now.

As soon as his jeans cleared his ass, his cock sprang as free as it could within the bounds of his boxers.

It ached so bad. Worse than he could ever remember it aching. He pushed his boxers down to join his jeans.

"Touch me," he begged.

"I will, baby," Sean promised.

Sean backed him up in a soft shuffle. Rusty didn't even bother to look behind him. Wherever Sean wanted him was just fine with him.

When the backs of his knees bumped into the edge of the bed, he sat.

Sean stripped his jeans down to his ankles while Rusty toed off his running shoes. Then Sean was freeing him of his jeans and socks, exposing him to Sean who still stood fully dressed.

His vulnerability sent shivers through him.

"Take the edge off, please. Take care of me."

"Always." Sean dropped to his knees, cupping Rusty's balls in one gentle hand, squeezing with the perfect pressure. His lips wrapped around Rusty's cock, engulfing the head as his other hand wrapped around the base, just holding him.

Rusty thrust forward and Sean obliged, taking him deeper, sucking harder, holding firmer.

"Can't hold back."

Sean's eyes met Rusty's. They sparkled as he gave a short nod and took Rusty even deeper, deeper than he'd ever swallowed him down before.

And Rusty let go. Let go of all those nights he'd muffled his cries in his pillow. Of all those nights he'd dreamed of a warm leg thrown over his and woken up twisted in the sheets. Of all those nights he'd stared at the ceiling wondering if Sean had met someone new and wouldn't need him anymore.

His moan ended deep in his chest as the smell of sex surrounded him.

He just floated, fuck-dumb and hazy, not thinking. Just feeling the moment. This perfect moment in time that was the best moment of his life.

And then he was lying back on the bed, blinking the moisture from his eyes so he could see Sean more clearly instead of in the fuzzy haze Sean's mouth and hands had put him in.

Slowly, he became aware of the here and now despite his best efforts not to.

Sean lay next to him, entwining his hand in Rusty's. His cock pressed against his still-zipped chinos. A wet spot showed Sean's need.

Disappointment in himself coated Rusty's feel-good. "I didn't take care of you."

Sean lifted his head and gave Rusty a crooked smile with that hint of sadness he always tried to hide. "Not yet." He squeezed Rusty's hand. "But you will. I'm sure."

If only Rusty could be that sure.

Reality burned through his cum-induced mind fog.

He'd been looking at the want ads online. Nothing he was qualified for. He hoped he would do better once he was up there.

Boston. It sounded so big. So cold. So scary.

But Sean had made friends, so how scary could it be?

He'd always been the one. He'd been the outgoing one. The funny one. The bold one. It had been his job to pave the way for his shy Sean.

Sean had been their deep thinker. The cerebral one of the two.

And now Sean had it all going on. He'd made friends, possibly more than friends, all by himself. He was everything and Rusty was nothing.

Rusty reached over and rubbed Sean's swollen cock. He was good at something, right? Good at giving Sean pleasure. Good at making Sean scream.

The only person he'd ever slept with was Sean. They'd both been virgin lovers and they'd learned together.

Maybe he wasn't so good. Maybe Sean knew that now.

All those nights when Sean didn't answer his phone. When he texted that he was out and to not wait up for his call.

Beside him, Sean wiggled. "Don't stop."

"No. I won't stop." He reached for Sean's belt buckle.

Giving head when Sean was so big wasn't Rusty's favorite thing. He didn't like feeling like he couldn't breathe. But he'd do it, knowing how much Sean loved it.

For Sean, he'd do it and pretend it was okay, even though Sean knew how he felt. Sean knew everything about him.

But now, there were things he didn't know about Sean.

Thus the condoms in the bathroom along with the lube. He'd never bought condoms before. There had never been the need.

He prayed there was no need now.

But Sean had been gone so long and had made new friends and—

Oh, God. He was making a mistake.

No job. No family. No friends.

Sean traced across Rusty's abs, tickling him and making him suck in. An obvious bid for more attention.

He realized he'd been absently running his fingertips along Sean's waistband.

Now, he brushed his palm over Sean's full cock through the thickness of the chinos.

Sean bucked under Rusty's hand. "Fuck me."

That's not the way they usually did it.

"Okay." Anything for Sean. And this was a good thing. A loving thing. Not even a hardship. Just not what he'd imagined Sean's homecoming to be.

Sean leaned up and raised an eyebrow, making Rusty feel all inferior. "You don't have to sound all enthusiastic about it or anything."

Sarcasm out of that beautiful mouth always sounded so jaded. Sean only used it when he was feeling threatened. And never, ever against Rusty.

He forced a smile to cover his hurt, to force everything to be all right. All that effort gave him a piercing pain in his chest.

But for Sean, he'd do anything, take anything to make it all okay.

Wouldn't he?

Sean bit his lip, wishing he could take back what he'd just said, especially the way he'd just said it.

He'd snapped at the one person he loved most in the world.

Just all his frustration, physical, mental and emotional had reached its peak.

He'd thought being back with Rusty, being home even though it would soon no longer be their home, would put his world right. Instead, he felt like he was about to explode.

Lifting his hips, he tugged off his chinos leaving on the new underwear he'd picked up to give his lover a thrill. They'd never been able to afford the big name brands, but now, for Rusty, for his homecoming, he'd splurged a bit.

As he revealed his bright yellow and blue Diesel boxer briefs, he watched Rusty's eyes, hoping the hurt and the puzzlement over Sean's piss-poor mood would change into that laughing, sparkle Sean needed so badly.

Instead, he saw a flash a anger followed by sadness.

Which he fully deserved. He was taking Rusty away from everything good in his world. A good fuck couldn't make up for that. He'd offered to bottom, thinking that giving Rusty his submission, his control, would help. But he should have known better. Nothing could help.

His shiny new underwear didn't look nearly as appealing with his deflated dick.

Rusty, still in his T-shirt, just nodded. "Be right back."

He disappeared into the bathroom through the connecting door, which made sense. No bedside table to hold the lube.

Sean shed his clothes, trying to shed his sad attitude with them.

When Rusty came back, he was determined to be propped up on one elbow, leering for all he was worth.

Only seconds later, Rusty stood framed in the doorway, hesitating and biting at his bottom lip.

The air conditioner's fan started to whir, giving a reason for why the room felt cold. Without meaning to, Sean shivered. But then, he was buck naked, totally exposed to the chill in the air.

Sean ignored the ball of scary worry expanding in his stomach and tried his most seductive whisper. "You're wearing too many clothes, don't you think?"

His usually chatty lover gave a sharp nod of his head. Then he transferred something from one hand to the other holding the lube.

A condom? Rusty had bought condoms?

The worry ball grew so big it bumped Sean's throat, burning like dry ice and threatening nausea.

Rusty peeled off his shirt, revealing an inked armband circling his left bicep.

"What the hell, Rusty?" Sean realized he'd pulled his legs up and circled his arms around them. Now, he was freezing.

Rusty held out his full hand as if it held a snake. "You were gone so long."

"So you cheated on me?" In an instant, Sean felt the fires of hell burn through him, burning through that icy ball and turning his blood to boiling lava.

"No!" Rusty dropped to his knees, right there in the doorway. "No, not me."

"Me?" Sean rose on his knees on the mattress, needing the height, needing the movement, needing this moment to have never happened. "You think I cheated?"

Rusty looked down, then jerked his head up to stare. Full accusation was in his eyes. And pain. And— God, Sean couldn't be mistaken, but hope? Hope that his accusations were wrong.

Fear turned Sean's righteous indignation into something else. Something he had no name for, but it had sadness and desperation and fear and disappointment--and hope all bundled together.

He had to swallow twice to get past the tears. "How could you even think that?"

"You were out every night. You never go out—not without me. And even then, I usually have to talk you into it." Rusty opened his hand and let the condom and lube fall to the floor. "And you talked about all these friends you made. Mostly about this guy named Carter. It was Carter this and Carter that. And I called, at like, three in the morning and Carter answered your cell."

"When? When did you call?"

Rusty sat back on his heels. "Does it matter?"

"Not if you don't trust me, it doesn't." Sean realized he was strangling a pillow. Now he buried his face in it. "Oh, God, Rusty. Oh, God."

Although he didn't hear Rusty move, he felt Rusty stand over him. He'd always felt safe with Rusty. Loved. Now he felt intimidated, like he should cower and be ready to dodge a blow.

He made himself meet Rusty's eyes. Rusty had never made a move against him, not even in play. And the wetness threatening to spill in Rusty's eyes said he wouldn't now, either.

Rusty looked so young. So vulnerable. So lost.

Sean's lips felt too stiff to move but he persevered. "I did nothing wrong."

"I didn't say you did." Rusty sat on the edge of the bed, careful not to touch Sean, and dropped his head in his hands. "We never talked about—about being exclusive."

Was this guilt talking? What was Rusty telling him.

It had always been just them, just the two of them. Sean had never needed anyone else, never wanted anyone else. But he'd been gone two months. Two months when Rusty had plenty of opportunity to wonder how it might be with someone else. To wonder what he was missing all this time being only with Sean.

Sean fought the nausea that rose in his throat. He had to concentrate to get his clenched mouth to move correctly. "No, we never have."

"We have friends who are in relationships, but still sleep around. They view sex and lo-." He couldn't bring himself to say the word right now. "-as two different things to them."

"Which friends?"

"You know, some of the guys we've hung out with at the clubs."

"Acquaintances, then."

"Yeah, I guess." Rusty scrubbed his fingers into his scalp. "You're trying to get this conversation off track."

Sean blew out a breath. "Yeah, I guess I am. I'm just trying to buy some time to think." He slammed his fist into the pillow over his stomach. "I can't think, damn it."

"This isn't about thinking. It's about feeling." Rusty's hand hovered over Sean's shoulder, ready to give comfort when it came to emotions Sean had trouble dealing with. But this time, he didn't touch Sean, didn't rub away the worry, didn't rub in his concern, his stability, his groundedness.

Sean felt like he was diving in the dark where there was no up or down. Where was the surface? Would he be swimming deeper and deeper until his air ran out? This desolation. This confusion. This blackness. Was this what it felt like to drown?

Unable to stop himself, Sean reached up and rubbed a finger over Rusty's new tattoo. "Is that what you wanted? To see how it was with other guys?"

Rusty pulled away from Sean's touch. In all the years they'd known each other, in all the years they'd been together, Sean couldn't remember that ever happening before.

"What the fuck are you talking about?" Rusty pushed himself off the bed then stalked to the doorway and stood with his back to Sean.

Was this it? Was this the end of them?

No. It couldn't be.

He bit his knuckles using the pain to clear his tears. "I have loved you since the first time you scooted over to let me sit with you at lunch. Do you remember, Rusty?"

Please, remember, Rusty. Please remember who we've always been to each other. Who we are to each other. Please be my lover. My love. My soulmate. My completeness.

Magnificent in his nakedness, Rusty nodded once. His dark curls tracked down the nape of his neck. Sean knew that whispering kisses right there, right where that bottom curl rested, drove Rusty wild.

"I was the new kid and nobody would let me sit with them. But you did. You pushed Toby McClellan off his chair and told me to sit."

Rusty's shoulder blades tightened. "You looked so sad. So lost. But you had this look in your eye, like you dared anyone to pity you."

"So you did."

"No. I didn't pity you. I admired you. I admired your courage. Your bravado." Rusty hugged himself.

Sean wanted to go to him. To wrap his arms around the boy who always included him, to the man who always comforted him.

Instead, he squeezed the pillow tighter and willed Rusty to turn around. If he would just turn around.

"Bravado. It was all bluff. I was scared shitless. Every time we moved, I was scared shitless."

"What were you afraid of?"

"Of being alone."

"Is that why you're with me?" Rusty unfolded his arms and scrubbed both hands through his curls. "No, of course not. You would never have to be alone if you didn't want to be. With the way you look, with the way you *are*, you'd just have to give a guy one of those sideways looks and he'd follow you anywhere."

"No, Rusty. No. They wouldn't. *I* wouldn't."

"You did. You said you really wanted to go to Boston." Rusty turned around. The tears streaking his face broke Sean's heart. "And I said I would follow you anywhere."

"And now you don't want to."

"I can't bluff like you. I'm afraid." He crossed his arms, hugging himself. "I'm afraid of being alone."

Sean found himself plastered against Rusty, holding him so tight his arms ached. Sean couldn't lose him. "You can stay here, baby. We'll figure something out. I should have never asked you to give up your family. Just because I don't have one—"

God, he loved his job and the independence it gave him. He loved Boston and fitting in. But—he swallowed hard—he loved Rusty more.

"I'll give it up. I'll give up the job. Boston. All of it."

Rusty started shaking, as he buried his face in Sean's shoulder. "I'm going with you. I'm going to be a big boy. A grown-up. I need this. I need to know I can do this. Just—"

"Just what, baby?"

"Don't leave me. Don't ever leave me alone, again."

"I promise, baby. We're in this together. We'll never be alone again."

Weak, dizzy, Rusty let Sean hold his weight. Little Sean, that he outweighed by fifteen pounds. Maybe more now. Sean never ate unless Rusty coaxed him into it.

"You need me." Saying it made it so. He shifted so he was the one holding up Sean.

Sean took the shift easily, not fighting it like he sometimes did.

"Yes, Rusty," his voice broke, "I need you."

"Show me." In a dance made graceful through years of practice, Rusty waltzed Sean backward to the bed.

Together, they settle on the mattress, on their sides facing each other.

Sean's pupils gleamed huge and dark in his blue-gray eyes. Bruised. Skittish. The small white scar beside his left eye stood out even against the paleness of his face.

Rusty wanted to erase the distress in those eyes. Sadly, he knew it would take more than a night to undo what they'd done to each other.

"We're going to be okay."

Sean nodded, but the bleakness clenched into the corners of his mouth said he wasn't sure he could believe that just yet. Then he reached out, his fingertips hovering near Rusty's face, hesitating as if he expected Rusty to jerk back.

Instead, Rusty leaned into that unsure hand, putting his lips against Sean's touch and left kisses on those tentative fingers.

So slowly, so carefully, as if Sean would startle at the slightest suddenness, Rusty ran his hand over Sean's bare shoulder, down his arm to his elbow, then along his ribs caressing the slight curve of his hips.

Sean slipped his hand to Rusty's hair, twining his fingers in the curls that brushed against the nape of Rusty's neck. The gentle searching touch made Rusty shiver.

He whispered into Sean's stillness, "You are my only love. Forever. We're meant to be, remember?"

Again, Sean nodded. But this time, he closed his eyes, leaving Rusty to guess what emotion he was hiding.

"Look at me, please."

When Sean shook his head, Rusty leaned forward to kiss each of those closed lids. "Please. I need to see you. I need to see inside you."

Sean opened his eyes at that. Sadness had been replaced with desire. "I need to be inside you."

Without his conscious direction, Rusty's hand drifted down to Sean's cock, at half-mast. Years of knowing Sean took over as he circled one callused finger around the swelling head. His thumb rubbed the underside, tracking movement as Sean's cock lifted higher and higher toward his belly. He watched as the color deepened into that unique shade of red-purple that belonged on Sean and Sean alone. "This always fascinates me."

Sean drew in his breath as his cock jerked. "Still?"

"Still." Rusty cupped Sean's balls, loving the weight. Loving that he could still hold Sean's vulnerability in the palm of his hand. That trust, even after the hurt they'd just flung at each other, made his breath ragged. "Always."

Sean clenched into Rusty's curls, pulling enough to get Rusty's attention. "I'm sorry."

"You did nothing wrong."

Sean stared, breathing heavy. "I flirted."

Rusty worked hard to keep his hand open, his fingers loose. "Yeah?"

"Yeah. I didn't know what else to do except sit and stare into my drink. So, I flirted a little."

"What else?"

"That's it. No kissing. No touching. Just—" Sean looked down at Rusty's hand cupping his balls. "—just words."

Rusty took a deep breath. "Like the flirting I usually do when we're out?"

Sean nodded. "Like that. But I'm always there when you do it. We both know it's just for fun. We both know you're always going home with me."

Yeah, that's how it always happened. Rusty liked to laugh. Liked to flirt. Liked to be outrageous, especially after a drink or two. Sean had always been by his side, smiling at his silliness. Making sure everyone knew Rusty was taken. Making sure Rusty knew he was taken care of. Giving Rusty the safety to disengage his mouth from his brain every now and then.

They'd get each other home and have super-wild-assed sex, as if the meaningless flirting loosened something up in both of them.

"Did you intend to go home with anyone you flirted with?"

"No. No, never." He hesitated, then tore his attention away from his balls and looked straight into Rusty's eyes. "I went home with Carter a few times, but only to sleep on his couch. My roommate at that shitty co-op apartment always had a girl over in our room. And Carter's apartment is within walking distance from this bar...."

Rusty used all his willpower to keep his hand still and relaxed.

"Carter?"

"Yeah, he lives in our building, the one with our new apartment. He's working on getting his engineering degree so I've tutored him a little. So, in payment, we've had guys' night out a few times. He and his husband have a baby and I've babysat for them a couple of evenings, too."

"You never told me that over the phone. About his husband or his baby."

Sean looked down, then up again. "I wanted to make you jealous. I wanted you to miss me."

"That was pretty stupid, wasn't it?"

"Yeah. It was." Sean drug his fingers across Rusty's chest, circling a nipple.

Rusty fought hard to keep the ploy from distracting him. "You're supposed to be the smart one in the family."

Sean looked down at his balls cradled in Rusty's hand. "Not this time around, huh?"

"It's not nearly as stupid as my thinking—what I thought."

He wanted to let go of Sean's balls. Wanted to curl into a ball himself to brood about Sean trying to make him jealous, to stew about the pain he'd felt when he thought Sean cheated on him. But he wanted more to feel Sean's hands on him, to feel Sean's love inside him.

Teasing Sean's taint with his pinkie, he blew out a breath. "I think we've just survived a pretty big fight."

Sean squirmed, accepting Rusty's provocative fingerplay, accepting Rusty's combination of apology and forgiveness. "Yeah?"

"Yeah."

"So now what?"

That's it. Rusty was done with high emotional drama. "Wanna fuck?"

Sean withdrew his hand, and shifted up on an elbow. "No, baby. I don't want to fuck."

Rusty tightened his hand just enough to make Sean wince. "No?"

"No." Sean's hand wrapped around Rusty's cock with equal pressure. "I want to make love."

Not able to help himself, Rusty had to have the last word. "Yeah. We can do that."

Then he lay back and pulled Sean's mouth to his own, putting an end to coherent talking.

EPILOGUE

Rusty hoped his family attributed his and Sean's twitchiness during their Going Away dinner to their anxiousness to be on the road and not to the sore asses they both had.

Sore asses, warm hearts? That's not how the phrase usually went, but that's how it went for them.

Setting off later than they had expected meant Sean had to drive at least a few hours while Rusty slept. Not that Rusty really slept.

Rusty had to admit that the drive up to Boston was scary as fuck whenever Sean took the wheel, which took precedence over any lingering fear Rusty had of moving away from home. Rusty only let him drive on the interstate and they traded places at rest stops where Sean only had to pull straight in without backing at all.

They slept in the truck both Saturday night and Sunday night to save time and money and rolled into the apartment in the early hours of Monday morning.

Trying to navigate the streets of Boston's South End had kept Rusty's exhaustion at bay until they rolled up to their apartment.

Then Sean tested the bonds of his new friendships when he called them all to help unload.

At two in the morning, they showed up. By three thirty, the truck was empty and their apartment was full.

The studio apartment was small, even smaller than their old college apartment. For what it cost, it should have been at least four times larger in Rusty's opinion. Sean had warned him about sticker shock, but really? This cost half of Sean's monthly paycheck?

Rusty would need to find a job fast. That thought made exhaustion crash down on him.

When Carter offered to follow Rusty to the rental place to turn in the truck, to get it out of the street, Rusty was too tired to protest, even if he wanted to.

Carter was older than Rusty had expected. Recently home from Afghanistan, he was going to school on military assistance while his husband worked in the theater district, helping with set design and acting when he could win the part.

Thankfully, Carter was quiet on the way back to the apartment complex letting Rusty wind down from the last whirlwind days he'd survived.

As Carter walked Rusty to his door, he said, "That box you wanted is on the kitchen counter."

"Thanks." It was clear why Sean liked Carter. He was the kind of guy you couldn't help but like. The kind of guy who remembered at four in the morning that a certain box was important to you and reminded you where to find it.

Sean was still up. Barely. Obviously waiting on Rusty as he smoothed the sheets on their reassembled bed.

Sean gave him a bleary smile. "We better get to bed. I've gotta get up and go to work in three hours. Sorry I can't show you around."

"No problem. I plan on sleeping until noon. Then Carter has already offered to help with the rest of the unpacking after his classes tomorrow." Rusty spotted the box he needed and ripped off the packing tape. "You okay with that?"

"Yeah, sure." Sean stretched. "That thing about me being upset about your family loading the truck was just stupid on my part."

"My family? We, you and me, we are family—don't break out in song."

Sean grinned and starting humming which made Rusty hum, too. Yeah, they were punch drunk. Crawling under the covers sounded like heaven.

Instead, he cracked open the box flaps. This needed to happen now.

"Come help me with this, okay?" Rusty carried the box to their front door, opened the door and set the box on the hallway floor.

Sean gave him a puzzled yawn, but said, "Okay."

Rusty dug into the box and felt around through the packing paper.

"Center this, please. About eye level." He handed Sean a sticky hanger.

Sean's eyes squinted in confusion, but he did it anyway.

"Perfect." Rusty pulled the big bow wreath from the box and centered it on the hook. Then he straightened the little plaque swinging from it.

"There's no place like home, baby," he said as he wrapped his arms around Sean's shoulders.

Sean leaned into him and echoed, "No place like home."

This time, he let Sean have the last word because there was nothing more to say.

Tricked Up for Treats

CHAPTER ONE

Sean slapped for the alarm, turning it off before the annoying screech could wake Rusty. He should have gotten up a couple of hours ago, when he'd woken up. Instead, he'd stared at the ceiling, adding and re-adding, trying to figure out a way to make the money stretch a little bit further.

As a new engineer, he made decent money. Not a boatload full, especially for an expensive town like Boston, but industry standard.

It was those student loans that were killing him. Five years of college had been damned expensive.

Rusty stirred, making sucking sounds in his sleep which always made Sean grin.

Early light was kind to the deep circles under Rusty's eyes. He'd been out late—again, trying to make a few extra bucks taking down sets at one of the local playhouses after their last show.

He'd probably hit an afterparty or two, too. Free food and drink. Who could blame him? And people to talk to. Socializing was part of Rusty's nature.

Sean wished he could have joined him, but his eight to five schedule couldn't handle three a.m. bedtimes.

Even with the dark shadows, Rusty was beautiful. His long dark lashes and olive skin that always looked tan, his big, loopy dark curls and full lips always made Sean hot.

He resisted the desire to run his hand along Rusty's heavy stubble. At twenty-five, his long-time love was growing into a twice a day man. Unlike Sean, who was more the twice a week variety.

"Hey." Rusty blinked open his eyes.

Sean gave into temptation and leaned down to rub his cheek against Rusty's.

"Didn't mean to wake you. Go back to sleep," he whispered, as if that would make a difference in Rusty's state of consciousness.

"'kay." Rusty snuggled deeper into his pillow, a half-smile on his lips.

That smile gave Sean the impetus to climb out of bed. Time to go to work to make a paycheck for his man. Especially since his man had given up everything—family, friends, his own career—to follow Sean from New Orleans to Boston so Sean could have his dream job.

The job was great. But Rusty was so lonely. For the thousandth time, Sean questioned himself, *was a job worth the sacrifice?*

The warmth of being with Rusty under the covers turned quickly to chill. They were trying really hard to keep the heat off as long as possible. In New Orleans, October was just getting pleasant without the heat and humidity.

Not so in Boston. They'd need real winter coats, not the jackets they were used to.

Mentally, Sean added two more line items into the budget.

In the bathroom, he automatically turned on the hot water before he stripped. It took a few seconds to warm up, then lasted about twenty-two minutes before it started cooling off again. He'd timed it once.

With the bathroom properly fogged, he stepped in, pulled the shower curtain tight, and let the water run over his head. Water always made him feel better.

As soon as they could afford it, he intended to take advantage of the company discount to join a gym with a full-sized pool. Rusty would like the weight room.

He jiggled figures in his head. Nope. No way they could add another monthly note to the mix.

Outside the curtain, he heard Rusty say, "Hey, you." A warning before he joined Sean in the tub to keep from startling him. Rusty wouldn't need a warning. He had sense enough to feel secure in his own home.

"Different personality types," Rusty had said, dismissing Sean's apology when Sean had lashed out in surprise, punching Rusty in the stomach hard enough to make his breath catch.

Sean was fully ready for Rusty's big hands sliding down his ribs, cupping his butt, pulling him close to snuggle into his morning wood.

"Decided to get up?" Sean murmured as Rusty reached around to caress Sean's cock with both hands.

"It decided to get up." Rusty wiggled his own stiff cock into Sean's butt crack.

Sean pushed back, groaning. "We should have gotten up earlier."

"Sh! Baby. It's okay." Rusty slipped around to face Sean. He put Sean's hand on his cock then resumed his hold on Sean. "Just like we used to, huh?"

The tenderness in Rusty's eyes made him look fourteen again. That's when they had started to explore themselves and each other. It had been exciting. Scary and so very, very loving.

Like now.

Rusty held out the conditioner tube and squirted some into Sean's hand and then into his own.

Slowly, thoughtfully, gently, Rusty closed his fist around Sean's erection. The pressure was perfect. Experience had replaced clumsy experimentation a decade ago. Rusty knew just how to pulse his fingers, how to run his thumb over Sean's slit, just when to lean close and whisper in his ear, "I love you."

Sean breathed hard, increasing his grip and pace on Rusty's cock, giving a slippering twist from base to tip. "Love you, too, my beautiful man."

Rusty went first, his grip on Sean tightening, cum spurting onto Sean's hips, his thigh, over his own hand holding Sean's cock as he sank to the bottom of the tub to sit with his knees spread wide.

Mindlessly, Sean followed him down.

The ecstasy on Rusty's face pushed Sean over his own edge of total euphoria as he knelt on the cold hard surface of the tub, water falling into his face, running into his mouth as a desperate groan escaped from deep, deep inside him.

Sean found his hands gripping Rusty's shoulders. He held on as Rusty cradled Sean's balls in his hand. Sean felt safe. Secure. Comforted.

He worked his thighs around Rusty's waist, pulling Rusty closer with arms and legs until there was no space between them. Like a life raft, the tub cradled them, pressing against their thighs, keeping them close.

Rusty held him, humming deep and low so Sean could feel it in his chest more than hear it over the falling water.

"You're my life," Rusty told him. "I have no joy without you."

Sean nodded, rubbing his face into Rusty's shoulder, knowing Rusty would hear the words Sean couldn't find to speak.

Time floated past him. No ticking clock. No obligations. No worries.

For this one blissful moment, his world was okay.

Rusty held tight as Sean shivered in his arms. At times like this, he felt like the strongest man in the world, keeping his baby together.

After feeling like the biggest freeloader on the planet for the last month or so, this confidence was a nice change.

Twenty times a day, he bit his tongue to not complain about his lack of employment prospects. Picking up the odd job at the theater didn't even pay well enough to buy a nice meal out for the two of them most times. But discussing his frustration with Sean would do nothing but make Sean feel more guilty about dragging Rusty away from New Orleans.

At least his parents still sent him money. His grandmother had just sent a check for two hundred dollars. Said she won it at the casino and was sharing the wealth with her grandchildren. Rusty didn't question it. He just cashed the check and wrote a handwritten thank you note, something that seemed to delight her each time she got one.

His dad said he'd forward Rusty's commission from the holiday designs he'd done for their clients as soon as the Christmas season kicked off, the week of Thanksgiving. Rusty hoped he could hold out enough from that money to buy a few gifts, although his parents had already expressly forbidden them to give gifts this year.

Sean gave a big shake and Rusty realized the water that cascaded over them was barely lukewarm.

"Come on, baby. Time to get dried off and dressed."

As he'd worried, Sean immediately tensed in his arms. Couldn't be helped. Life had to be faced.

He reached behind him and felt for the knobs to turned off the water, then untangled himself, stood and gave a hand to Sean.

Grabbing a towel, he started rubbing Sean down before himself. Temperatures, hot or cold, had never bothered him that much. Then again, he had a lot more body fat than Sean. If he didn't start running or something, he'd have a *lot* more by the time he found steady work.

He didn't realize he'd gotten too rough with the towel until Sean twisted free and took a step back.

"Leave some skin, okay?" Sean forgave him with a quick kiss which he returned just as quickly.

Those smiles and kisses, that's what made his mornings, his life, complete.

Life without Sean wasn't a life he wanted to think about.

When Sean held out his hand, he gave him the towel and snatched the other one for himself. Two towels. It was enough, especially since he did laundry every other day to keep himself busy.

He slipped on clean sweats and a T-shirt as Sean started his morning work ritual.

Breakfast. Pancakes, not only because Sean needed the calories but because it was one of Sean's favorites, and Rusty had a confession to make.

He shouldn't have done it without discussing it with Sean first. They always made money decisions together. But the opportunity wouldn't wait.

Please, let this be okay.

He decided to scramble the last of the eggs, too. He and Sean and already decided that Grandma's money would make an extra trip to the grocery store feasible.

"Breakfast in twenty," he called from the kitchen, barely needing to raise his voice. That's how small their apartment was.

"Okay." Without a warning prompt or three, Sean would primp until he was running too late to eat. Vanity or food avoidness, Rusty wasn't sure.

He poured the last half-glass of milk into Sean's glass, noticing there was a new carton behind it. Probably a gift from their upstairs neighbors, Carter and family.

Whenever Rusty borrowed their vacuum, he cleaned their apartment, too, both as a thank you and to stave off boredom. In turn, gifts like half gallons of milk and fresh fruit would often appear in their kitchen afterward.

Exchanging keys had been a good thing. When he'd moved up from New Orleans, he'd been concerned about making friends, but he'd been wrong to worry. Carter and Jody were becoming very good friends.

He set the table, putting the flyer for the Halloween contest obviously next to Sean's plate, and took a deep breath.

"Come eat."

Sean in dress shirt and tie always made Rusty's heart beat faster.

"You are so hot." He rubbed his stubby cheek against Sean's clean-shaven one. Sean rubbed back.

"You, too. Love the way you smell." Sean sniffed, like Rusty's shampoo was the world's strongest aphrodisiac.

Sweats and a T-shirt. Unruly hair drying naturally into curly disorder. Extra pounds creeping around his middle. He didn't think so.

But protesting would put Sean in the wrong frame of mind for the big reveal.

He put two pancakes and half the eggs on Sean's plate.

"Too much."

"Just eat it." Rusty turned down the volume on his glare. "For me? Please?"

Even though his goal every morning was to get a decent breakfast into his lover, he had to remember his special goal this morning.

Sean took his first bite under Rusty's watch, then sipped the milk.

He worried with his fork, stirring his eggs, before he hesitantly asked, "Got plans for today?"

The question had set Rusty off last week when he couldn't keep his frustrations inside anymore.

Rusty had shouted in plain language that he had no fucking plans other than filling out another dozen applications and channel surfing for eight straight hours.

The big blow up had left them both feeling emotionally bruised.

But he pouted when Sean didn't ask. Yeah, Sean really couldn't win that one.

"Gonna clean up around here." He looked around the spotless apartment. "Might do a little cleaning upstairs, too."

Sean nodded. "I know they appreciate it."

Rusty took a deep breath. No better time.

He touched the flyer Sean had glanced at and ignored.

"The Cabaret is sponsoring a costume contest."

"Yeah?"

"They have a lot of prizes. Good ones. Cash and gift certificates. Local businesses have donated stuff for the advertising opportunity."

Sean just nodded as he chewed so Rusty continued.

"The cost to enter is forty bucks."

"Kind of expensive."

Gotta do it. Gotta come clean. "I entered us."

Sean kept chewing but put down his fork. Then he swallowed as he ran his finger down the side of the flyer. Other than that, nothing but tense silence.

Yeah, Rusty had really fucked up.

"Will you look at me, please?" From Rusty's tone, he knew how this affected them. How this expense—and the lack of discussion beforehand—impacted them so heavily. Sean wanted to make this all right.

But he couldn't. He couldn't look.

Forty bucks? That would have bought a good used coat at one of the resell places. Maybe not designer label or even fashionable, but reasonably warm.

Rusty shifted, foot to foot. "We can skip date night."

Their one extravagance, date night. Fun once a week with friends, or just the two of them. They'd both agreed they needed that one indulgent splurge as much as they needed food or electricity.

"Forty bucks." Sean looked at him. "We've still got twenty-five in the weekend entertainment budget. We'll just have to have a cheap one. Cover charge, a few beers, walking home instead of a taxi." He tried to smile. "Which will be do-able since we'll only be able to afford a couple of beers a piece."

Rusty got up to scrape the remainder of their meal into the trash. His plate was even more full than Sean's. With his back turned, hunched over the trash can, he said, "Forty each. I entered both of us."

He continued to stand there, dirty plates in hand, and stare at the wall like a little kid caught stealing.

Why? Why did Sean have to be the bad guy? Have to be the grown up? Have to be the practical one?

"Sounds like fun." He picked up the flyer, but couldn't focus on it.

All he could focus on was the brilliant glowing face of Rusty, looking less worried, but still pensive.

"I'll take care of costumes. We can borrow from the theater troupes I've worked for as long as we don't damage anything."

Sean nodded, letting go. "Whatever you think, babe."

That look still didn't leave Rusty's eyes. "Love me?"

Uh-oh. "You know I do."

"It's drag."

"What?" *Oh, shit.*

"Drag. All the guys have to dress in drag."

"Rusty, how could y—." The apprehension, verging on fear on Rusty's face stopped him. Instead, Sean buried his head in his hands.

"I'm sorry." Rusty dropped to his knees next to Sean's chair. "It's just that there are a lot of prizes, nice ones. And entries are limited.

That's why I had to enter without asking you first. There were only four slots left. So the odds are really high. And you dress up so pret—" He faltered as Sean looked out at him from under his armpit.

Rusty looked down, the penitent on his knees. "I'll see if I can get the money back."

Prideful. That's what Sean was. Nothing but prideful. Rusty had given up so much for him without complaint but Sean couldn't wear a silly wig for his lover and best friend?

"I'll do it."

"Yeah?"

"Yeah."

"You won't be alone. We'll all be dressed in drag. And I'll okay the costumes with you first."

Sean shook his head. "Nope. Whatever you decide for me will be fine."

Rusty gave him a doubtful look.

"Just one thing, Rust Bucket."

At the pet name, Rusty gave him a feeble smile. Much better than that desolate expression he'd had earlier. "What's that, baby?"

"Don't hold back. If we're going to do it, we're going to do it to win."

"Yeah? Sean, you're sure?"

"Have you ever known me to throw a competition?" The light in Rusty's eyes returned Sean's ability to grin. "Yeah. Let's do this right."

"Thanks, love."

Although Sean couldn't really imagine it happening that way, he said it any way. "It could be fun."

"It *will* be." Rusty jumped up from his knees and danced around the kitchen chanting, "We're gonna wi-in. We're gonna wi-in."

Damn. What was Sean getting himself into?

CHAPTER TWO

Rusty dragged the huge garment bags into the apartment minutes before Sean got home from work. Over his shoulder, in two huge duffel bags, he carried accessories. *Lots* of accessories.

Thursdays at midday weren't usually so crowded on the buses, but the Halloween crowd had started to emerge shortly after noon. So going down to the theater, waiting around for his friend to unlock the door so he could pilfer the costumes, getting them packed and boxed so he could carry them, then fighting his way back onto the first of the buses and the two bus changes after that had him exhausted.

Plus the worry.

Sean had said he was in it to win it. But winning would take a big effort, a big transformation, a big change of attitude as well as clothing. Dressing in drag wasn't just an outside change, something Rusty was fast learning by hanging out with a few of the theater guys who were really into it.

Wouldn't his momma be surprised about the company he was keeping? Then again, nothing had ever surprised his mom, at least that she let on.

Bigger than that, wouldn't Sean be surprised? It's not that Rusty hid his friends from Sean, it's just that the opportunity to introduce them hadn't really come up. The after-parties at The Cabaret had just sort of happened. Not that Rusty had ever dressed up, but—

It was Halloween. That made everything okay.

Rusty lay the bags across the bed and set the duffels next to them.

Now the wait.

Rusty had known what he was asking of Sean when he'd done it. If questioned, he would tell anyone he'd signed them up because the prizes were so enticing but the real truth was that he thought this would be good for Sean so he could feel okay about letting his femme side out.

When Sean was having a good time, just a little bit drunk, when he forgot to censor himself, Sean wiggled when he walked and he moved his head or gestured a certain way. Relaxed, not thinking, his body would go liquid instead of that stiffness he tried for most of his waking hours.

It was so damned sexy. The real Sean. The Sean most people rarely got to see. Rusty rarely got to see that side of Sean himself. Sometimes after making love....

That shitass father of his. The things he'd said to Sean. Rusty had heard some of them, things like Sean was no more of a man than their spade bitch poodle. Things like Sean might as well wear a bra and a dress since he walked and talked like a girl. The sneer in Mr. Delahunt's voice when he said the word *girl* made Rusty worry for Sean's mom and sister.

But he hadn't stopped there. He'd told Sean not to cower. To stand up to him. If he didn't like the things he was saying, Sean should try to stop him—if Sean had the balls to stand up to him.

Sean's father was over six feet tall and weighed at least two hundred pounds. Sean hadn't even been thirteen when his dad had made that challenge.

If the man said that in public, what had he said in private? Sean never talked about the things his father had done but Rusty had seen bruises too often not to guess. And that had all been before Sean came out.

Of course, all the abuse had stopped the day Sean had stood up to his father, all five foot eight, one hundred forty-five pounds of him and said, "Dad, I'm gay. I love Rusty. There's nothing you can do about it."

Even though Rusty punched in 911 at the first swing, it had taken the police too long to arrive. Sean's ribs hadn't been broken, only bruised. After three days of intensive headaches, his concussion had healed. The scar beside Sean's eye had faded from red to dark purple to white. He could barely see it now.

But sometimes, Sean still cried out in his sleep.

"Hi, honey, I'm home." Sean sounded normal despite the upcoming fun and games. That was a good start to the evening.

Rusty looked at the bags on the bed. *Here's hoping it stayed that way.* "In here."

Eying the garment bags and duffels on the bed, Sean put his backpack on the dresser then gave Rusty a one-armed hug around the waist.

"Well, let's see them."

"Don't you want to eat, first?"

"That bad, huh?"

"I think you'll look hot."

Sean snorted. "What's for supper?"

"Spaghetti." Sean's favorite comfort food, but not on Rusty's top ten, or even top fifty.

"A bribe to behave?"

"More like a thank you for doing this."

Sean poked at one of the duffels. "It's gonna be fun, right?"

Rusty overlooked the cynicism that leaked through Sean's voice. Instead, he overcompensated for it by saying way too enthusiastically, "Yeah, it is."

"What time is Jody coming downstairs?"

"In about forty-five minutes, as soon as Carter gets home to watch Elizabeth."

Sean looked into Rusty's eyes so long and so hard, Rusty had to force himself to keep from looking away. But Sean wasn't really focused on Rusty. He was doing one of his staring-into-nothingness things and Rusty happened to be the anchor for it.

Finally, his eyes flashed fiercely then he blinked and he was Sean again. "Let's eat, then."

Shaking off the chill that tingled down his spine, Rusty draped his arm over Sean's shoulder. "It's gonna be fun, babe."

"Just remember. You're driving."

Rusty grinned. "I've got our taxi on speed dial."

Then he pulled Sean close to him, whispering in his ear. "Tonight, you can let go. I've got you, babe."

Rusty nipped the lobe of Sean's ear for emphasis before turning Sean for a kiss.

He loved when Sean's pupils went big and black like that.

"Love me?" he breathed into Sean's mouth.

"Mmhmm." Sean returned his kiss, complete with tongue sweep. When he broke off the kiss, he leaned back to meet Rusty's eyes. "I wouldn't do this for anyone else."

"I know." Keeping his arms around Sean, Rusty walked him backwards toward his chair at the table. "Sit."

They usually fixed their plates from the stove, but tonight, Rusty wanted to make this all about Sean.

When Sean tried to resist, Rusty ran his hands down Sean's shoulders. "Please. Let me."

He wanted to say, *let me take care of you*. Maybe, someday, after they'd been together fifty years or so, he would be able to say it and have Sean accept it. But for now, he could dish up Sean's spaghetti, pour him a glass of milk and slide a piece of French bread, sans garlic but heavy on the butter onto his plate.

For now, it would have to do.

Sean wiped out the pot Rusty had boiled the spaghetti in, pulled the drain plug out and dried his hands. As he bent to put the pot in the cabinet, he called over his shoulder, "Let me see."

The swish of fabric told him Rusty was complying quickly.

Rusty, in a dress. Soon, he'd be in a dress, too. He really wasn't ready for this.

"Well?" Rusty said impatiently.

Stalling, Sean precisely folded the dish towel and hung it over the sink faucet while he took a deep breath to settle his stomach. Soon, he'd be in skirts, too.

Not looking forward to it. No, that was an understatement. He was dreading it with every quivering inch of his skin.

He reminded himself of the sparkle in Rusty's eyes when he'd proposed this drag competition. It had been one of the few times Rusty's eyes had sparkled since the move.

So Sean had promised. He would always keep his promises to Rusty.

"Well." Sean turned to see, realized he had his arms crossed too tightly and propped them on his hips instead. He took in the dark green velvet neck-to-floor dress with the lace collar, biting his lip to keep from smiling.

Rusty struck a pose, with one hand held against his chest in what Sean assumed was an attempt at demure but just came out awkward instead.

Rusty just couldn't do feminine, not even a little bit.

"Uh, Rusty? I don't think Scarlet O'Hara had a five o'clock shadow. And wasn't she famous for her small waist? They made her hold onto the bedpost to tighten her corset."

Rusty picked at the lace on his sleeve. "You know a lot about her."

"Well, the beard thing was an easy guess. The rest I remembered from the movie when you had to watch it for drama club."

"I must have already been asleep by that part."

"Good thing for you I remember how to pull corset strings. Grab hold of something and I'll get that waist into shape in no time." Sean hoped to God he was bluffing. Surely Rusty didn't expect them to wear corsets.

"Okay. But can we wait until the last minute for that?"

Shit. "Really? I was just teasing. I don't think—"

Smoothing his hand across the heavy velvet, Rusty looked up under his lashes. "It's the only way this thing will close in the back. I tried on everything. This was the only dress that I wouldn't have to shave my chest for that came close to fitting."

"And mine?"

"I had a bigger selection since we don't have to worry about the fur problem."

Sean rubbed his hand over his shirt across his hairless chest. "I guess not.

With a swish and a swoop, Rusty enveloped him in a musty velvet and lace hug. "I love your gorgeous chest and the abs that go with it. Those swimmer's muscles are so lean and tight. In fact, I think I want to take a look right now."

Rusty started unbuttoning Sean's shirt and Sean let him. He could use Rusty's touch because right now, the thought of putting on a corset was making his skin scrawl.

Rusty leaned in close as he pushed Sean's shirt off his shoulders. Whispering close, the way that always made Sean shiver, Rusty said, "Thank you for this."

Sean nodded, not trusting himself to answer. If he were to open his mouth, nothing would come out but *not gonna do it.*

Rusty took care of that worry when he covered Sean's lips with his own. Sean opened and Rusty complied, tasting Sean, then devouring him, while pulling Sean's bare skin against the prickle of the velvet dress.

Sean allowed his horniness to take over. A good fuck and he'd be able to make it through tonight.

His hands wandered over Rusty, searching for a way to touch him, skin to skin, but the damned dress covered everything except for the open slit down his spine.

Instead, Sean went for his own belt buckle. With quick fingers, he unzipped and stepped out of his pants, kicking them out of the way.

Rusty stood and watched, still dressed and grinning. He cocked an eyebrow and asked the obvious, "You ready for me, babe?"

"Take off the damned dress."

"You're so hot when you growl." Rusty bent and grabbed the bottom of the skirt, starting to wrestle it over his head but laughing too hard to make much progress.

To help, Sean caught a handful of material and tugged.

"Wait!" From the folds, Rusty yelled between gut-deep giggles. "Hold on. My arm is stuck."

So, of course, that's when Jody would knock on their door.

As Sean freed Rusty from the tangle of velvet and lace, the light in Rusty's eyes reminded him of the man he'd dragged from New Orleans to Boston with a promise that Sean would make it good for him.

That light. That laugh. That was why Sean had agreed to dress in drag.

He would do this with good grace—for Rusty. Anything for Rusty.

After all Rusty had done for him, what was one night of humiliation disguised as fun?

Rusty volunteered to go first which earned him a smile from Sean.

But the smile was too wide. Too fake. Too brave.

Why did I think this was a good idea? How could I ever have been this stupid?

Too late to do anything differently now. For Sean, anything but carrying through would be failing. And Sean never quite recovered from failures.

So Rusty smiled, just as wide, just as fake and just as bravely has Sean did and vowed he would do whatever he could to get through tonight. And he would never, ever do anything to mess with Sean's psyche again, no matter how good of an idea it seemed at the time.

After a close shave, Rusty let Jody and Sean squeeze him with the corset until the dress buttoned up the back. His posture had never been so straight. Strapping on the fake boobs felt like wrapping his chest with an ace bandage. Between the corset and the boobs, he would swear he was only sucking in enough air to keep the spots from swimming before his eyes. His only relief was when Sean said he'd wait in the den, playing on his laptop until Jody was ready for him.

Keeping up his reassuring front while trying to catch his breath was really getting to him. Letting that fake smile slip seemed to make breathing a bit easier.

Then he tried to walk. The hoop skirt under the dress knocked into everything and threatened to pop up whenever he sat.

Even though Rusty tried to swallow most of his complaints, Jody told him he wasn't doing that great of a job at it and that at least the hoop skirt meant he didn't have to tuck.

Then Jody painted his face, smearing on creamy foundation, coating his lips with deep red lipstick followed by gloss, adding layers and layers of eyeshadow, then eyeliner and mascara until his eyes looked like they were so big they took up most of his face.

And then the wig. The big black synthetic curls got stuck in his shiny lip gloss as they tried to crawl into his mouth. Between the thing Jody stuck on under the wig and the wig itself, his whole head was sweating. He hadn't sweated in a month and here it was October in Boston and he was dripping underneath all this velvet and lace and hair.

Rusty stared at himself in the bathroom mirror. No doubt about it. He made one butt-ugly looking woman.

His drag queen and cross-dressing friends said a guy either had it or he didn't. Rusty definitely didn't.

But his admiration for the guys who elevated this to an art form went through the roof.

Once Jody declared him as good as he was going to get and they did the grand reveal for Sean, Rusty felt like he was carrying around a lot more than ten pounds of velvet on his back.

With grave concern, Sean inspected him.

"So we're going to walk down the street in broad daylight dressed like Southern belles from an incredibly politically incorrect movie."

Rusty had no answer for that. They had decided they would walk the four city blocks to the party to save cab fare so they could afford to have a couple of drinks then do the safe thing and take the taxi home.

But then he thought about what he would do should anyone try to give them any shit. No bits of string and plastic boning was going to keep him from keeping Sean safe.

Jody spoke up before Rusty could suck in enough breath. "You'll be fine. It's Halloween. Everyone is expecting to see people in costume. And you're on the right part of town to be okay dressed in drag, especially tonight."

So Sean put on his brave face and Rusty put on his fierce one, though it probably looked a little less fierce with the false eyelashes and the long dangling earrings. Then again, maybe that made it even more so.

Concurrently, Sean pretended to be reassured.

Faking and pretending. They definitely had the perfect attitude for a costume party.

Jody told Rusty to seat himself on the couch and practice being elegant and graceful.

Not happening. Being still and unfidgety was the closest he could come, and he was mostly failing at that.

To distract himself, he looked at the photos his sister was posting across social media, the photos Sean had been looking at. His nephew was Toto this year, going with the family theme from the Wizard of Oz. Mom was the wicked witch, like usual, while his dad was a tree, like usual. Sister-in-law got to be the good witch and his brothers were the the Tinman and the Lion. He and Sean were usually scary monkeys.

A video popped up of his sister scanning his parents' front yard, transformed into the yellow brick road. Holidays were a big deal for the Duchene family. Through his velvet sleeve, Rusty rubbed his band of fleur-de-lis inked around his bicep.

No sense in being homesick. This was home. His and Sean's home. Happily-ever-after and all that shit.

In the other room, he heard Jody, say, "Stunning. Absolutely stunning, Melanie."

He winced, knowing that wasn't what Sean would want to hear. Once again, Rusty kicked himself for this boneheaded idea. What sounded good after a long night of breaking down sets and chasing the hard work with a couple of beers had never sounded so great after his buzz had worn off.

"Thanks, Jody." Sean sounded okay. Maybe a little stressed but not mad or anything. "I can do my own eyeliner."

Rusty heard the bathroom drawer slide as Sean dug around for his own makeup.

Even though Sean had always loved the look on other guys, it had taken a couple of years to convince him to wear eyeliner out. When a friend of theirs started working the MAC counter, Rusty had drug Sean over partly on pretense but partly in good faith, to help the guy out by giving him his first commission. Rusty had ended up with some kind of moisturizer he gave to his mom and Sean had ended up with guyliner.

By the way Sean preened when he had his eyes made up, Rusty knew he'd done the right thing. And Sean did look so very hot with those shining blue eyes ringed in black, a little smudged from a night of dancing.

Jody popped out from the bedroom and clapped his hands for attention. "May I present, Mrs. Melanie Wilkes."

Then Sean rounded the corner. In a white, off-the-shoulder dress with a big blue sash, lace gloves up to his elbow and matching blue hair ribbon, the outfit was summer to Rusty's winter. Innocence to vamp. From a distance of just a few feet, anyone would mistake Sean for a girl. Okay, from close inspection, a lot of people would still mistake him for a girl.

Rusty looked close. Under the hoops and lace and blond sausage curls was Sean. His Sean who, by his expressionless stillness, showed his anxiety.

Jody had been a lot more subtle with the makeup. But then, Sean didn't need as much.

His eye shadow and false lashes made the cool blue-gray of his eyes intense and piercing. The blush was a bit heavy, standing out on Sean's too-pale cheeks, but the chilly night air would even out the color soon enough. Pink lip gloss outlined the natural bow of Sean's mouth, emphasizing his natural pout. His bottom lip looked especially full, as if begging to be sucked into Rusty's mouth. Pretty didn't begin to cover it.

Jody had called Sean *stunning*. Stunning didn't cover it.

Rusty was surprised to realize he thought Sean looked really hot right now. Good thing he hadn't had to tuck. He might have been crippled for life.

Sean looking everywhere but at Rusty.

Clearing his throat, Rusty tried to think of the right thing to say. "As many prizes as they're giving out, we're sure to win something."

Sean smiled, stiff and hesitant. "You think?"

"Yeah, I think." Before either of them lost their ability to see this through, Rusty stood and held out his arm. "Come on, Miss Melly. We've got a party to attend."

Clinging to Rusty's arm, Sean tried to make himself stop shaking. He hadn't been able to keep from staring at himself in the mirror as Jody transformed him. Hadn't been able to stop his father's words the first time he'd come home wearing a pink shirt in support of breast cancer research. Words about trying to be prettier than his sister. About how he should be ashamed of himself. About how his father was ashamed of him, for not being the man he should be.

"Cold?" Rusty readjusted the blue Pashmina over Sean's shoulders.

"A little." Sean fought to keep from shrugging away.

He wouldn't hurt Rusty for anything. Not any more then he was already hurting Rusty, anyway. He'd heard the sadness in Rusty's voice when he talked to his mom last night about their annual neighborhood Halloween party, the first one Rusty had ever missed. They'd be missing Thanksgiving and Christmas with the Duchenes, too.

They passed a scarecrow and a Catwoman on the street. The Catwoman gave them an appreciative wolf whistle that made Rusty laugh and twirl his parasol in double time.

Rusty had been excited about tonight for weeks. If dressing in drag made Rusty happy, then that's what Sean would do.

"You know, we owe a lot to the drag queen culture. Stonewall Inn and all."

"Yeah, I know. The birth of gay rights." Sean had helped Rusty with the research paper that had almost gotten Rusty expelled his senior year. If not for Rusty's dad….

What would it feel like to have a father who had your back?

"Shoes fit okay?" Rusty asked.

"Fine." Actually, the ballet flats were pretty comfortable. "Yours?"

"A little weird. I can feel the pavement under my feet. I thought that might be why you're walking the way you are."

"How am I walking?"

Rusty squeezed Sean's arm. "Kinda stiff. Like you're walking on glass or something."

"Just getting used to this." Sean pushed on the hoop skirt, sending it swaying.

Rusty strutted a bit, making his sway on purpose. "Fun, isn't it?"

Fun wasn't the word Sean would have used. But the worried smile on Rusty's face had him echoing, "Fun," to put Rusty at ease.

To emphasize the point, Sean forced out, "This is going to be great fun. Lots of prizes."

At the end of the block, as they waited for a crossing signal, Rusty leaned down and said into Sean's ear, "You got a purty mouth."

Sean made himself grin then pressed a careful kiss onto Rusty's painted lips. "You, too."

As the light turned green, a little hybrid squealed tires as it accelerated.

"Burn in hell, faggots," yelled the driver out the window. The kids in the back seat stared as they zoomed past.

Burn in hell, faggot. That's what Sean's dad had yelled as the police put him in the back of their squad car. The medic trying to get Sean to lay down on the gurney had moved between them to block Sean's view, to protect Sean from his own father. The woman had looked like she wanted to say something, but there had been nothing to say.

Just like Rusty looked right now.

Hell. Sean had a voice. He had something to say.

He would do this for Rusty.

"Ready, Miss Scarlet?" He loosened his grip on Rusty's arm so that his lace-covered fingertips barely grazed the velvet sleeve. Taking the lead, he strode across the intersection, deliberately letting his hips swing to make the hoop skirt sway.

CHAPTER THREE

Rusty wasn't sure what happened but he was damned sure glad it had.

At first, Sean's flippy, flirty, femme-ness had an edge of hysteria to it, which had been a big worry. But the third screwdriver had toned down the hysteria even as it cranked up the swish and sway of Sean's skirt.

Sean leaned over, almost laying across Rusty's lap. Rusty was envious of his mobility. Sean hadn't needed a corset and the strapless bra holding his falsies in place apparently didn't threaten to shift around like Rusty's shoulder-strapped super-duper-sized bra did.

"Time to check the makeup, loverboy." Melanie Wilkes had just been written on the chalkboard for the next group. "Girls always go to the bathroom in pairs. Come with me?"

They were being called on stage for the judging five at a time then interviewed individually.

How serendipitous that tonight's interview questions were all about the Stonewall Inn riots. Could this night get any better?

Scarlet O'Hara had already done her best to saunter across the stage and answer the randomly drawn question in a sulky Southern drawl. Thanks to his high school research project, he'd correctly answered that June 28, 1970, which just happened to be his oldest brother's birthday, was the first Gay Pride marches commemorating the Stonewall Inn riots. But demeanor and attitude counted as much as costume and correct answer. Rumor said it wasn't only attitude on stage, but off as well. He knew he was far outclassed.

But Sean had helped him with that paper and he'd really gotten into being Melanie, or at least her modern-day vodka-and-orange juice swilling version. So, at least Sean had a chance.

Rusty followed Sean into the unisex bathroom then stood back while Sean used his elbows against the other queens to claim mirror space.

From his little purse, his reticule Jody had called it, Sean took out a lipstick. He leaned close to the mirror and outlined his lips, smacking them together before he put the lipstick away.

Seeing Rusty watch behind him, Sean gave him a wink of those thickly lashed eyes. "Okay?"

Lovely. Beautiful. Exquisite. Rusty went with the safe, neutral, "Okay."

While this new sassy version of Sean might appreciate a more extravagant compliment, Rusty wasn't sure what tonight was all about.

Tonight. Tonight when they were home and they'd stripped off the skirts, washed off the makeup—maybe before they washed off the makeup—, and the smell of sex rose from their warm bed, maybe then he'd figure out some answers. Until then, he wasn't going to question. He was just going to enjoy the hell out of tonight.

Once done, Sean gave Rusty an air kiss then pranced—pranced!— up the stairs to the stage.

With hoops swaying, Mrs. Melanie Wilkes sashayed across the stage, batted eyelashes at the judges, correctly answered "Six" when asked how many days the riots had lasted, then flounced off the stage, snapping her fan with a gesture so gracefully self-confident, the judges, all professional queens, raised their eyebrows in envy as someone in the crowd yelled, "Work it, girl!"

Once off the stage, Sean met Rusty's wide eyes with, "I said I was in it to win it."

This was the man Rusty loved.

The sparkle in Rusty's eyes made tonight worth it. All the self-talk he had to continuously force through his head, deliberately putting his father's words behind him, all the constant reminders to loosen up, he would be okay, was worth it. Rusty was worth it.

To see Rusty smile with his eyes as well as his mouth was worth anything.

The list of prizes was impressive. Sean was smart enough to know he had a shot. Being pretty had never been so lucrative. Being okay about being pretty had never been so important. As long as he remembered to flaunt it, he could win something, maybe even one of the top prizes.

He slugged back a swallow, almost choking on an ice cube, then rapidly blinking his eyes to keep them from watering, saving his mascara from running. As a judge looked his way, he turned the blinking into flirty fluttering and flipped his fan. There was no doubt that something in the aqua vitae made flaunting easier.

When Rusty held a pastry-wrapped cocktail weenie to his lips, Sean took the hint and ate it, deliberately sipping his drink instead of gulping it to wash the dry weenie down.

"Want to switch to straight orange juice?"

"Straight? I thought tonight was all about *not* being straight." Sean heard himself giggle at that. *That's right, Dad. Giggle.*

Rusty changed the glass in his hand for a full one, decorated with a plastic sword skewering an orange slice. "I'm hoping you're sober enough when we get home to show me how unstraight you are, baby."

If Sean wasn't worried that Rusty's skirt would bop up and give them both black eyes, he would have scooted onto Rusty's lap like a couple of dozen partiers had already done with their ladyloves.

"Bent. That's me. Totally bent." Through his alcohol haze, Sean realized it didn't hurt to say that. Would it hurt in the morning?

Somewhere, in the part of his brain that wouldn't quietly drown, he didn't think the word would cause him pain. Not anymore.

Victory.

"What was that, baby?"

He must has said it out loud. "You know what, Rusty?"

"What?"

"I'm gay." He looked into Rusty's deep, dark, safe eyes. He had a voice. And a body. And a mind and a heart and a soul to be proud of.

He was Sean Delahunt and he was okay just the way he was put together. "I don't think I'll ever swallow it down again."

Hoop skirt or not, Rusty gathered him up and half-dragged him onto his velvet lap. "That's good, baby. Real good."

Rusty's big warm hand rubbing on Sean's bare shoulder made him purr. "Like a cat," he said out loud.

Rusty leaned in and laughed. "No pussy in my bed."

Sean licked up Rusty's throat, loving the bristle of Rusty's beard on his tongue. "Only me."

"Only you."

Sean heard the name Scarlet O'Hara called, then applause.

"Did you win something? Which prize did you win?"

"We. We won tonight, baby. And the prize is bigger than anything they're giving away here."

Confused, Sean batted away an orange balloon floating toward him. "You're happy, right? It's been a good holiday, right?"

"Yeah, baby. I'm happy."

Sean pulled himself up using Rusty's shoulders, and kissed him on his scarlet-red lips. "Happy Halloween, Rusty."

"Happy Halloween, Sean."

Jingle My Bells

CHAPTER ONE

Friday before Christmas. Almost. So close. Almost.

From the back of the choir row, Rusty listened to Sean, along with the tenor and soprano section sing the melody line. *Count, two, three, four...*

He took a breath and hit the bass line along with the other six guys next to him, smiling at the rich, blended harmony.

Christmas music made the holiday season seem more real than any lights dripping from roof eaves or animated Santas crowding store displays.

They'd had the Christmas spirit at their house for a while now, since he and Sean had been practicing their parts at home as well as at choir practice ever since the Sunday after Halloween.

Cliche'd or not, they made beautiful music together.

Music wasn't all that put cheer in their holiday. The plane tickets home for Christmas topped the fa-la-la's by far.

Home for Christmas. Rusty could hardly wait.

An elbow in the ribs reminded him to pay attention as the score got tricky.

While the Unity Church choir was open to anyone, whether he could sing or not, the Christmas Cantata was special. They sold tickets for donations, raising money for the teen youth shelter the church sponsored. So Rusty was putting more than just grins and giggles into this one—when he could keep his mind on where he was instead of where he was going to be.

Home. Home for Christmas.

He bounced on his toes in time to the music, then readied himself for the last measure, the grand finale.

At the music director's pointed cue, he let his voice crescendo, bigger and bigger, letting out all the joy he'd barely been able to contain as the backdrop of a star brighter than a super nova descended behind them. As the bottom tip came to rest just inches above his head, the director made the motion to end.

Their voices halted. The church lights went out. And they were left with the remembrance of song in the glow of that burning star.

Shivers shook him at the beauty of it all. The awe was big enough to keep him still and silent while the congregation filed out in the glowing darkness.

Yeah, he was in the Christmas spirit.

Sean felt the last of the notes fade into the woodwork.

This was good. If everything else in this much dreaded holiday season went to hell, tonight would make up for it.

In this one shining moment, surrounded by darkness cut by a fake star's glow, he felt okay in his own skin. He felt accepted. No pretending to be someone else required.

Home. This was his home. This church. This city.

He craned his neck, looking up at Rusty, barely able to see him in the dimness of the choir loft. Rusty was home.

Sean had never felt so safe. So comfortable, like he really fit.

He made a point of remembering this moment, this feeling. He would pull it out and relive it whenever he needed to.

Needing to was inevitable. Returning to New Orleans, to Rusty's family who treated him like their own even when he wasn't, underscored what he had only by virtue of pity and not by virtue of birthright.

Rusty's family was his extended, unofficially adoptive family, substitute for his sister, his mother and his father, who no longer claimed him as son or brother.

Movement started around Sean. The swish of heavy choir robes brushing past as so many choir members stopped to pat him on the shoulder and tell him 'good job' reminded him of where he was, reminded him of how much he was valued, loved and included as one of theirs.

This could be his family if he could find it within himself to let them in.

He smiled as Mr. Miller gave him a strong hug. Mrs. Miller added her equally warm kiss to his cheek.

Consciously, he visualized letting the warmth seep in to fill the empty place that had been so cold ever since his father had kicked him out.

Someday, he would let himself fully believe the hugs and handshakes, the kisses and kindness from friends. He was working hard on it. Working hard on trusting, not keeping himself so guarded, not hiding behind his shyness. Not hiding behind Rusty.

"Ready?" Rusty put his hand on Sean's shoulder.

Sean nodded, returning Rusty's happy grin with the brightest smile he could muster.

Instead of dropping his hand, Rusty squeezed, giving Sean a steadiness he leaned into. "What's wrong?"

"Just coming down from the nerves."

"It was perfect." Rusty grinned. "Pitch perfect."

The four part harmony they'd done a capella with two other choir members had been making Sean's stomach churn for days, especially the part where Sean sang solo for four measures. But now it was over.

Relief as much as pride had him saying, "It did turn out pretty well, didn't it?"

"More than pretty well. I can't wait to see the video."

"Yeah, me, too." Sean said it but didn't really mean it. He knew he'd been close to flat on at least one note, probably two. Maybe, in the video, no one would know whose mouth those less-than-perfect notes had come out of. He hoped so. It was their gift for Rusty's parents, who deserved more than a faulty performance.

They deserved more than a video, too, but the budget didn't cover much more than necessities.

However, in his pocket was a little over thirty-five dollars, left over from the hundred bucks he and Rusty had given themselves permission to spend for the holidays. Enough for a few more gifts. He never ate in airports anyway.

Hopefully, the church-sponsored arts and craft show set up tonight in the Family Life Center might yield a few more presents if he chose carefully.

He'd bought Rusty's gift a few weeks ago. Made it, actually, at another arts fair. The fair had a booth where a customer could craft his own jewelry, so he'd made Rusty a necklace, with a charm in the shape of a fleur de lis, another one with a heart cracked through the middle, and a round metal disc that he'd stamped with 'you keep me whole' on one side and 'for better or worse, my heart is yours' on the other and strung them all on a leather cord while Rusty was off talking to the guy with the exotic house plants that he'd made friends with at a different fair.

Arts and crafts fairs seemed to be his thing, a thing his father would make derogatory remarks about. According to dear old Dad, artsy-fartsy wasn't a masculine trait.

But that was in a different world, a world well-left behind.

Just because he was going back to New Orleans didn't mean he'd run into his dad. They'd rarely crossed paths when he still lived there and they were both excellent in pretending they hadn't seen the other. It might be the only trait they shared.

Not that his dad was usually passive-aggressive, going out of his way to avoid anyone. The restraining order had probably taught him to be that way with Sean.

Sean was close to suspecting that maybe *he* wasn't naturally passive-aggressive, either. He was starting to suspect that his father had taught him to be that way. It was a common enough survival trait.

His counseling sessions with one of the pastors, freebies thanks to the church, were helping him look at a lot of things in a different way.

If only counseling could help him to not get airsick.

He was *not* looking forward to tomorrow morning's flight.

Rusty chatted with friends while waiting for Sean to finish shopping. When Sean picked up the money clip for the fourth time, dug into his pocket and handed over a couple of bills, Rusty tried to hide his grimace.

"What's wrong?" Mrs. Miller asked.

Rusty shook his head. How could he explain his—disappointment? Sadness? Heartbreak? He couldn't even find the right word inside his head much less say it out loud.

He pretended not to notice the furtive glance Sean shot him as the new purchase made its way into Sean's coat pocket.

Rusty felt the weight of his wallet in his back pocket, taking what comfort he could in knowing he had enough cash to feed both himself and Sean on the trip home tomorrow morning. But that comforting feeling vied with the heavy unease, the sense of dread when thinking about that money clip in Sean's pocket.

Rodney Delahunt didn't deserve a present from his only son. Hell, he didn't deserve his only son.

Why couldn't Sean cut those ties, and all the pain that went with them?

Rusty didn't even try to force a smile as Sean joined him. "Ready?"

Sean had his hands crammed into the pockets of his oversized trenchcoat. "Sure."

Rusty should feel bad about the ill-fitting coat. At the Halloween costume party, when Sean had won third place in his category and a store voucher for a very expensive Burberry overcoat, he'd traded the fourth place winner for two airplane tickets. They'd found used coats at a local vintage store, vintage being a very kind euphemism for well-used. Knowing Sean had done it for him, Rusty should feel regret about Sean's coat, but he was too excited about going home for Christmas to spend emotion on anything other than pure joy.

But the shadows in Sean's eyes had worry creeping in anyway.

Why couldn't Sean let the past go and be happy?

Rusty shrugged into his own Navy-surplus pea coat. "Let's get going then before it gets any later."

After a flurry of hugs from Mr. And Mrs. Miller, he pulled on his gloves and knitted hat, then waited while Sean wound his scarf around his neck and plopped on the natty fedora Rusty had insisted he buy. The hat really suited him. Rusty reached out to adjust Sean's scarf, his heart warming when Sean leaned toward him instead of away, even out in front of people like this.

Progress. Celebrate the baby steps. That's what their counselor said. But patience wasn't one of Rusty's frequently used virtues.

The counselor had also explained why Sean would be feeling anxious about this trip home, but Rusty just didn't get it.

His parents, his brothers and sister and his nephew all loved Sean. Sean didn't need any other family, especially not a father who beat the crap out of him for being gay while his mother stood by, wringing her hands. Why couldn't Sean let go and move on?

A blast of cold air hit him as soon as he opened the Family Life Center door. Instead of putting his hand on Sean's shoulder to guide him through first, Rusty walked through himself. Yeah, it was petty, but he wasn't feeling—damn it, he didn't know what he was feeling. He just knew it wasn't good.

As soon as Sean caught up, he gave Rusty a tight nod.

Sean ducked his head. "Busted, huh?"

"Not my business." Rusty knew the effects of his words and yes, he was spoiling for a fight.

Sean didn't oblige him. "Drop it, okay? Just—not tonight."

The way Sean's eyes looked sad, tired, beaten down, the way his second-hand coat hung on his shoulders, the way his feet dragged in the slushy snow should have made Rusty drop it, like Sean had asked.

But tomorrow morning they were heading into a fight for Sean's happiness, a fight Sean would lose, again and again. A fight that could be avoided if Sean would just walk away from the hurt and pain and, instead, walk into the love and acceptance that was his for the taking.

Rusty tried to make himself walk away from this particular fight. That he couldn't turn his back on it gave him empathy for Sean— empathy was one of his new counseling words—but he couldn't keep himself from trying to save his lover pain. "He's not worth a fraction of a second of your thoughts."

Sean hunched deeper into his collar and dug his hands deeper into his pockets. "He's my father."

"We got gifts for your mother and sister. That was enough."

"And all we're giving your parents is a video of our performance tonight. Should we have gotten them something more?"

Rusty saw Sean's change of subject for what it was, avoidance. Maybe, with the roller coaster moods Rusty was riding, avoidance was better after all.

Deliberately, Rusty turned his thoughts to the exotic houseplant seeds he had carefully wrapped in his luggage for his dad and the signed script of the new off-Broadway version of Cinderella he'd gotten for his mother.

Dad would be ecstatic over the seeds, knowing Rusty had spent care and effort to deliver them safely. Mom wasn't really into theater but she would like the script knowing her son had been part of the play, even if he'd been nothing but manual labor. That's how parents were supposed to be.

"I haven't had a chance to tell you." He kept his head down against the freezing wind. "I got them a little something more, compliments of that exotic plant nursery I worked for this morning for moving his plants after the garden show and from the theater company for tearing down their set last night."

"Good." Sean wiped his watering eyes with the back of his gloved hand. "I'm glad. A video of our cantata is a lame-assed gift."

Rusty straightened his back. "It's not lame-assed."

Sean stopped and turned to look straight at Rusty. A ghost of humor twitched the corner of his mouth. "Says the man whose parents have never missed even a grade school play before."

Pushing away his annoyance at Sean's smart-mouthed remark, Rusty's heart broke at the envy in Sean's voice. "They'll be just as excited to watch your performance as mine." The awesome thing about his parents was that they really would be as enthusiastic over Sean's performance as his. They really meant it when they said they loved Sean like a son. If only Sean could let himself be loved that way.

Hatred for Sean's father boiled inside him. Hatred was a strong word, especially since he was leaving a church service that preached peace on Earth, so he should replace it with something not so violent.

Nope. That's the one that fit.

Sean reached out a hand. "I'm sorry. That was snarky."

Rusty was about to brush away the apology with humor but the strain in Sean's face stopped him. Their counselor had warned him, time and time again, that moving the conversation past the painful parts was doing both him and Sean a disservice.

"Okay. Apology accepted. I shouldn't have gotten pissy about your gift for your—." He couldn't make himself give the man even the token honor of calling him a father. "—for him."

Sean nodded, ducked his head, then looked straight ahead at nothing. "Holidays are hard for me."

Even admitting that something was hard was difficult for Sean. To admit to anything that smacked of weakness had been whipped out of him at an early age.

As he watched Sean's throat contract, Rusty swallowed the thick knot in his own throat.

Rusty reached out his wool-thick arm around Sean's shoulders and pulled him close. "I know they are. We're going to get through them, together."

Sean stepped out of Rusty's embrace. "I'm pulling you down."

The therapy had Sean raw. Rusty knew it. This was the worst possible time to be heading to New Orleans.

But it was always all about Sean. Just this once, Rusty needed it to be about Rusty.

The image of their flight itinerary held with a pair of strong magnets on their fridge overrode the anxiety in Sean's eyes.

"I've got enough happiness inside me about going home for Christmas to prop us both up." He pulled Sean back to him, this time tightening his grip hard enough Sean would have to struggle to pull away. "Have I told you how glad I am you came in third in the contest, and how grateful I am you traded that gift certificate for the plane tickets?"

Sean grinned up at him. It was flat but a valiant try, nonetheless. "About a thousand times."

Rusty ignored the shadows in Sean's eyes, focusing on the sparkles that proved Sean wanted Rusty to be happy.

"Maybe I could do a little something to show you my gratitude?" Rusty lifted his eyebrow, doing his best Groucho Marx leer.

"Maybe you could." Sean blushed, but didn't look away. In fact, he let Rusty keep that tight grip on him the rest of the two blocks home. That kind of prolonged public intimacy was a big win for both of them.

CHAPTER TWO

When Rusty broke away from Sean to dig their apartment key from his pocket, Sean took a moment to look at Rusty. Really look at him.

Caught up in getting from here to there, in getting the details of living done, he didn't do this often enough.

But now, as Rusty bent, glove between his teeth, and poked the key into the keyhole, Sean took a deliberate moment and looked.

Rusty's navy pea coat made his shoulders seem even broader than they were. The ends of his dark curly hair flipped around the edges of his knit cap.

Sean knew, as soon as they were inside, Rusty would yank the cap off his head, stick his hands under the nearest faucet and run his fingers through his hair, trying to unflatten his squashed curls.

In New Orleans, caps in the winter were fashion accessories, not necessities. But Boston wasn't New Orleans. Sean thanked God for that every morning, feeling guilty and selfish as he did so. Rusty missed home so much.

Rusty opened the door and held it for Sean. He was always kind and considerate like that. That Rusty loved him still filled Sean with awe after all these years.

Why? Why did someone like Rusty love someone like him?

Sean brushed past him, shrugging out of his coat as soon as he cleared the door.

The trench coat, at least one size too big, made him feel like a kid playing Inspector Gadget from the cartoons. He threw it toward the couch where it slithered onto the floor. He forced himself not to take those steps over to pick it up. Not part of the plan.

Instead, he turned and shoved his hands under Rusty's coat. His roving hands started working on the buttons on Rusty's white dress shirt. He tugged as he unbuttoned, pulling the tails from Rusty's dress pants.

Rusty shrugged, making his coat fall from his shoulders, giving Sean full access.

Sean leaned in close, his lips tickling Rusty's ear. "You look good tonight."

As he'd hoped, Rusty shivered, leaning closer, wanting more.

Rusty's throat worked as he answered, "Yeah? You, too."

Sean felt the vibration of Rusty's voice deep in the pit of his stomach. He spread his legs to rub against Rusty's thigh.

The needy groan could have come from Rusty's throat or his own. He wasn't sure. Right now, the only thing he was sure of was that he wanted to touch Rusty's skin, run his hand down Rusty's spine, feel the muscles of Rusty's back flex under his palm. Feel him arch into Sean, begging, demanding, for more.

And that's what he got. Rusty's eyes glazed as he let his own coat drop to the floor.

For a split second, Sean thought of tugging Rusty down to the carpet, but they'd both learned that the cheap acrylic left rug burns that could be avoided with fewer than a dozen steps.

Sean half pushed, half dragged Rusty toward the bedroom while Rusty pulled Sean's shirt tail free from his pants. It should have been awkward the way they wrapped around each other, the way they moved with hands and arms and legs all intertwined. Maybe the mechanics of it all was awkward, but the move in the right direction, the feel of fingertips low on his bare belly, made the motions as graceful as a ballet in Sean's mind.

When the edge of the bed hit the back of Sean's calf, he twisted, pushing Rusty down, then falling on top of him.

Bracing on Rusty's chest, he pushed himself to the side to unfasten Rusty's pants, knocking Rusty's hands out of the way when he tried to help.

"I'll do it." Sean had to do it, had to do it all. As his world spun dizzyingly around him, he had to be in control of something. Of someone. Since it couldn't be himself, it would be Rusty instead. The snarl he heard came from his own throat while the whimper came from Rusty's.

But, looking into Rusty's eyes, Sean was certain that wasn't a whimper of distress.

Rusty's dark eyes looked totally black, his pupils blown with passion, at odds with his smile, all toothy-white.

"Want you," Rusty said, manic happiness behind his words. Happier than he'd been since they'd moved to Boston.

Hell yeah, Rusty was happy. He was going home. That place Sean thought was here, but Rusty thought was there. Home.

Sean grabbed Rusty's waistbands, both pants and briefs. "Lift up."

Rusty obeyed, his hands clenched in the comforter to keep from helping.

Sean pulled the pants and briefs free, scraping off Rusty's socks and shoes too, then kicking everything out of the way.

He went for Rusty's shirt next, undoing the last two buttons and dragging his tie free from its knot. He ran his hands along the fur on Rusty's chest, remembering when it was as smooth as his own. God, he loved this man.

But right now, love took a back seat to fucking. He needed to plow into Rusty, to forget all the dread that had begun growing bigger and stronger inside him ever since he'd traded for those damned plane tickets. He wanted to feel good, feel free. Feel ecstasy.

Looking down on Rusty, naked and open for him, fully erect for him, while he stood, completely dressed made him feel powerful. He reached out, running an open palm down Rusty's cock. Rusty squirmed, hands convulsing into the comforter, stomach muscles and ass cheeks flexing at Sean's touch.

He did this to Rusty. He made this wonderful man squirm with need. In this moment Sean believed in himself. He had value. Worth. Power. A right to exist.

"You're so hot," Rusty breathed out, his voice in that lower register that made Sean's cock twitch.

"Roll over." Sean grabbed the lube from the nightstand. A flash of memory intruded, the night Rusty had held out a handful of condoms, thinking Sean had been unfaithful. He slammed the drawer closed. Rusty had wanted him, even then.

He did *not* deserve this man. He was *not* worthy.

Dropping the lube on the bed, he forced his clumsy fingers to unfasten and unzip. As he let his cock come out, he let a moan of relief escape, too. Relief and more from somewhere deep inside him. It felt good. Like he was letting go of something too big to be bound and trapped inside for so long.

Rusty wiggled his butt. "Freeing Willie?"

The laughter in Rusty's tone made Sean smile. He didn't glance at himself in the dresser mirror, though, afraid it wasn't a nice smile.

His tone was gruff when he answered, "Not for long."

Slapping Rusty on his ass cheek, Sean ordered, "Up."

Rusty craned around while climbing onto all fours. "You okay?"

"Great. You?" Sean stared him down until Rusty broke eye contact first.

"Yeah. Great." Just as Sean was about to nudge Rusty's legs apart, Rusty shifted, doing it without urging. "So fuck me already."

No. Sean would decide tonight, not Rusty.

Sean reached between Rusty's legs, cupping balls as familiar to him as his own.

He held them, just held them in his open palm, until Rusty clenched his ass. Impatience? Anticipation? Concern? All those were good.

"Sean?"

"Sh, baby." He ran a palm across Rusty's ass cheek and thigh. The feel of Rusty's coarse dark hair made Sean quiver. "When I'm ready, okay?"

Rusty shuddered in Sean's hand. "Yeah, okay."

The hand holding Rusty's balls tightened, squeezing slowly until he took Rusty outside the comfort zone.

From the looks of Rusty's cock, swinging stiffly, gentle comfort wasn't what Rusty wanted right now, anyway.

Neither did Sean. He didn't want it. Didn't need it. Didn't deser—.

"Damn it, Sean. Do me before you castrate me."

Immediately, Sean loosened his grip. No more thinking. Just giving into the urge to taste and touch. To fill. To feel Rusty surrounding him. Anchoring him. Belonging to him.

He ran his fingers along Rusty's taint while running his tongue along Rusty's crack.

Rusty's arms, so strong and sure, collapsed, making his ass even more open to Sean.

Sean breathed in the scent of the man he loved. Warm, musky, familiar.

Going with instinct, he bit down, marring one perfect ass cheek with his mark.

The inked band of fleur de lis circling Rusty's upper arm mocked him, reminding him who really owned Rusty.

Louisiana. Home.

No thinking.

One-handed, he flicked open the top of the lube tube, smeared the slick across his fingers, then down his cock. Wiped the remainder across Rusty's asshole, plunging his finger in as he did so.

Rusty's body accepted the intrusion easily, without hesitation, as Rusty pushed back onto his finger.

Sean added another, teasing, wiggling, touching that place that made Rusty's eyes roll back in his head.

But Rusty's face was buried in his pillow so Sean couldn't see. No eyes looking into his, trusting, wanting. No mouth grimacing at the strain of waiting, waiting.

Just the tense muscles in Rusty's back flexing.

Sean lined up and entered.

The goodness. The completeness, took his breath away.

Fighting the urge to move, he closed his eyes, savoring the perfectness welling up in him.

Rusty tried to push back, but Sean held him still with a firm hand on each ass cheek.

"Please. Sean, please."

He'd never meant for his baby to beg. Sean moved, knowing how far he could go to stay inside Rusty. Under him, Rusty moved, too, falling into a rhythm they'd learned together all those years ago. Yet the rhythm had changed as they had changed. Now it was more bold. More certain. More....

And then Sean was picking up the pace, maximizing the depth, fucking Rusty with everything in him.

Their grunts clashed, synchronized, discordant, raw.

And it felt so damned—

Tears blinded Sean to the man under him, the man who was taking everything he was giving, the man who was giving back as good as he got. The man who made Sean feel real, feel solid and connected and alive.

So close. So close to letting it all go.

"Now, damn it. Now," he demanded from Rusty, fisting Rusty's cock and tugging.

"Yes," Rusty demanded back as his jizz sprayed the comforter and his ass hole clenched around Sean's cock.

It was too much. Too much to respond to. Too much to let go of. Too much.

And then Sean's body took over, separating from anything and everything that would hold it back.

He orgasmed, his cock pulsing, his stomach muscles contracting, his heart pounding. On and on and on, out of control, his body poured into Rusty everything Sean had, everything he'd held back all these weeks, everything he wished he could have, he wished he could give, everything.

Until there was nothing left of him to hold him up. Nothing left of him to think or to feel. All he could do was be. For right now, just being was nirvana.

As he lay on Rusty, heat poured off him, creating sweat where skin touched skin. Rusty, breathing heavily underneath him, made him draw in his own long breaths as they became tuned to each other. He blew out, knowing it was his air that raised chill bumps along Rusty's back and arms.

Sean lifted his head just enough to lick Rusty's skin. The saltiness of Rusty's sweat comforted him. Rusty was strong. Sean was light. Still, he should roll away and let Rusty take a full breath without being crushed. But not now.

He needed Rusty's warmth. Needed Rusty's solidness, his scent, his taste, his touch. He needed to feel Rusty's life force vibrating through him, through both of them, threading them together.

He needed—

Abruptly, Sean rolled away, not even aware he was doing it until the chill in the air made him shake.

"Sean?" Rusty stretched, slowly coming out of his fuck stupor.

"Bathroom."

Closing the door, locking it—which he'd never done before—, Sean turned on the shower. He waited just long enough to take the edge off the iciness of the water before climbing into the tub. Standing under the spray, he let his shivers take over, bringing him to his knees.

What was happening to him?

God, what was happening to him?

CHAPTER THREE

"Sean?" Once again, Rusty slapped his palm against the bathroom door then plastered his ear back to the unyielding wood, hoping to hear more than water running.

Splashing, groaning, anything.

Nothing.

Something was wrong, scary wrong. He could feel it in the marrow of his bones.

"Sean, answer me." Rusty eyed the door, wondering how much it would cost to replace after he put his foot through it.

The water stopped, the pipes squealing like they always did.

"Are you okay?" *Say 'yes'. Say 'yes'.*

"Yeah, fine."

Sean didn't sound fine. But then, he was muffled by the door.

Damn. Rusty knew Sean wasn't fine. He even knew what would make Sean all better. But he couldn't do it. Couldn't say it. Stuck to the refrigerator door, that piece of paper with their airline ticket bar codes meant—meant more than Sean's distress right now.

Rusty buried his face in his hands. He was being so selfish.

But wasn't it his turn? Wasn't it his turn to get his way? He'd moved all the way from New Orleans to Boston, giving up a career that had just started to take off, for Sean.

And all he wanted to do was fucking go home for Christmas. Was that asking too much?

Fuck the drama. Fuck the counselor warning him that Sean would need some TLC through this critical time. Fuck it all. He was going home. He needed to go home. Needed to feel his momma's hugs. His daddy's, too. Needed to have his belly full of oyster dressing he could only get once a year from his momma's kitchen. Needed his brothers to tackle him in the middle of the living room floor, piling on like a litter of puppies, even though they were all too old for that kind of thing. Needed to feel like the loved and protected little brother again instead of the failure that couldn't find a steady job.

He needed this more than Sean needed—

Shit. All he had to do was say they weren't going. No airplane. No chance to run into Sean's family. No Sean feeling like he was on the outside looking in.

Just safe and sound in their own little world-apart with plenty of invitations to dinner from friends who would do their best to make the Louisiana boys' holidays merry and bright.

He lay his head against the bathroom door. "You're certain you're okay?"

"Can't a guy take a crap in peace around here?"

"Yeah, sure. I'm going back to bed, then. Come snuggle soon, all right?"

He didn't wait for Sean's reply. Instead, he scurried back into bed, craving sweet sleep to keep away all the things he didn't want to think about.

As he pulled back the comforter, he breathed in the scent of sex.

Sean had been wild, demanding, desperate.

Rusty was chicken shit and he couldn't make himself deny it.

For the hundredth time, Sean leaned up and looked at the alarm clock. Three minutes since the last time he'd looked.

After too many torturous hours of trying to lay still while Rusty snored, Sean gave up on sleep, untangled his legs from Rusty's, replaced his shoulders with a pillow so Rusty would have something to hold onto, and slid from beneath the covers.

He skirted past their packed bags into the living room and booted up the laptop they shared.

His sister hadn't sent him an email in over two weeks. But then, a seventeen-year-old girl would have better things to do than to sneak around to write her estranged brother.

Wishing things could be different, he opened up her last email and studied the photos she'd attached, trying to read her mood in her eyes.

All dressed up for the homecoming dance, she looked much older, much more mature, than seventeen. And that boy she was dating—a jock his father approved of—was way too interested in her cleavage for Sean's peace of mind.

He should be there to protect her, to advise her on the ways of boys, to listen to her as she fell in and out of love.

Hell, he couldn't even protect himself.

Forget them, Rusty had said, over and over again. *You don't need them.*

Rusty was right. He didn't need them, just like they didn't need him.

"It's only three thirty." Rusty's voice startled him. "Come back to bed."

"I can't sleep."

That's when he noticed how cold he was. Rusty was always warm. No one else could chase his chills away like his lover. Rusty could warm him from the inside out, finding all those frozen places inside and thawing them.

Ever so casually, he closed the emails so Rusty wouldn't pay attention to what he was looking at. Rusty had this theory that if Sean pretended his family didn't exist, they wouldn't bother him. Even after all these years, Rusty didn't get it.

By the tightening in the right corner of Rusty's mouth, Sean knew Rusty had seen the family pics. But Rusty was really good at pretending, at pushing out the thoughts he didn't want to deal with.

Stretching, Rusty reached his arms up to the ceiling, showing off a hint of treasure trail as his T-shirt raised up. He dropped one hand to his belly, the other to the waistband of his gym shorts, running his thumb under the elastic. "Who said anything about sleeping?"

Maybe Rusty was right. Pushing away reality and pretending was the way to go. Maybe Sean's father was right, too. Maybe Sean wasn't strong enough to resist living with the wrong things in his head. Maybe his counselor only told him what he needed to hear, and not the truth at all.

"I'll rub your back." Rusty gave him a sweet, drowsy smile, the smile that was reserved for him alone. Sean know how to respond to this.

"My back, huh?"

"And then your front."

"And what will I be doing all through this massage?"

"You'll be telling me how much you like my hands on you."

Sean wanted to play along, wanted to wipe away the worry in Rusty's eyes, wanted to pretend everything was okay.

Hell, wasn't it time he found the willpower to do what he wanted?

He reached for the band of his flannel pajama bottoms. "And your mouth on me, too?"

But in the end, Sean couldn't pretend well enough to fake an erection and they both ended up pretending poorly that they weren't frustrated and disappointed.

Finally, Rusty held Sean tight, big spoon to little spoon. Slow and steady, he breathed near Sean's ear, his body's warmth seeping into Sean, giving him enough peace to close his eyes and relax.

When the alarm rang later, Sean woke up, knowing he'd gotten a few hours of deep sleep thanks to Rusty's tender care.

The airport security check went surprisingly fast, considering the holiday weekend. Rusty stowed his backpack overhead while Sean shoved his under the seat in front of him.

They were in a row with only two seats.

"As squashed together as we are, it's a good thing we like each other."

"Um." Sean barely grunted out his reply as he fished out the ends of his seatbelt from under his butt and adjusted the length.

The row across from them had three seats crammed together, but only two of those seats were occupied. Rusty didn't envy those passengers their space. He would rather have a reason to be close to Sean than have the extra room between them. Sean needed him this close.

Rusty settled into his seat next to the window, trying hard not to bounce like a little kid. Home. He was going home.

Next to him, Sean sat clenched up tight. Mouth. Hands. Assuredly butt cheeks. He was pale, a sickly kind of pale. He'd refused food or even water, hoping that would keep him from throwing up. Some day, Rusty would know why Sean reacted like this to flight, but today, he just discreetly rubbed his elbow against Sean's while watching the guys down on the tarmac chunk luggage into the belly of the plane.

Two rows in front of them, a baby started whimpering. The big guy in the musty suit in front of Sean decided to lean his seat back as far as it would go. Another half an inch and Sean would be staring into the guy's bloodshot eyes.

But then, Sean's eyes looked pretty bad, too. Dark circles. Red rimmed. Bleak.

Deliberately, Rusty looked out the window again. No turning back now. Sean might as well make the best of it.

As if Sean knew what he was thinking—of course, he did, Sean always knew what he was thinking—, Sean shifted only his eyes toward

Rusty and sent him a fraction of a forced smile from the corner of his pressed lips.

Rusty smiled in return, holding nothing back. "This is going to be great."

Sean gave a sharp nod, then leaned back into the headrest and closed his eyes. Hand flailing blindly, he reached for Rusty, found him, then threaded his fingers through Rusty's and rested their clasped hands on the armrest between them. This was new. Intimate and comforting touching in public. Rusty squeezed, his heart expanding even bigger than when he thought about walking onto home soil.

From across the row, Rusty felt the stare of the middle-aged woman, her eyes burning into their interlaced fingers like a laser.

Rusty gave her a wink, then leaned over and whispered into Sean's ear, "Love you."

Eyes still closed, Sean whispered back, "Love you, too." Then he cleared his throat and said in full voice, "Love you, too."

Rusty thought his knuckles might disintegrate from the vice grip Sean had on them. Then Sean blew out a breath. Rusty wanted to loosen his hold enough to be comfortable but still be comforting but he dared not, when somewhere deep in Sean's psyche, he might sense rejection.

Damn. Rusty would end up being a counselor himself before this whole therapy thing was over.

As the flight attendant went by, checking seatbelts, the woman reached out and snagged him. Pulling him close, the woman murmured something incomprehensible over the airplane noises but definitely not friendly by the look on her face.

The attendant gave her a frown, wrinkled his brow and looked to the back of the plane. He nodded, pointed and answered, clearly giving her permission to change seats. She made a big deal about digging her luggage from under the seat in front of her, glaring at Rusty and Sean the whole time, before stalking off down the aisle. Rusty craned his head to see where she ended up, in the middle seat between two really large men.

Alrighty then. That's when he noticed Sean staring straight ahead, color high in his cheeks, but he didn't make a move to unlock their hands.

The attendant gave him them an apologetic shrug.

Rusty grinned at him. "Hope she has a good flight."

The attendant grinned back, a glimmer of snark in his smile. "Me, too."

For the first time since they boarded, Sean relaxed his shoulders from around his ears. Rusty could feel the tension lessen in Sean's body, although the death grip on his hand remained.

"Karma."

That's all Sean said, but it was enough. Karma. Their counselors had been working on letting go. Letting the universe take care of making things right. Letting karma happen. For a guy who always thought he had to be in control, that he had to be responsible, this was huge.

"Karma," Rusty echoed back.

Then Sean leaned forward and kissed Rusty on the cheek, out in public, on an airplane.

Rusty was stunned. Ecstatic. Deliriously happy.

This was a good day.

CHAPTER FOUR

Not today. Not today.

Today, he would keep himself together. He would breathe through the adrenaline rush, not fighting it—fighting it had never worked—but accepting it. Breathing through it.

Sean settled back in his seat, concentrating on feeling Rusty's fingers against his, the connection that was more than physical. On keeping his mind away from the way his pulse ramped up along with the jet's engines. On the way the plane moved backward away from the terminal. On the way his stomach churned, threatening to make him puke.

He'd practiced this during one-on-ones with his counselor, practiced it at home alone. Now he would do more than practice. He would do it, damn it.

Strapped down, he couldn't run for the restroom. If he tried, as they waddled out to the runway, he'd be thrown off the plane.

Cold sweat made the back of his neck clammy. His ears roared as his stomach roiled.

"Look at me." Rusty said it low, but firm. "Look at me, now."

Sean shifted his eyes, afraid that if he moved his whole head, he would upset the tenuous hold he had on keeping the bile in his stomach in place.

Rusty's half-smile said concerned, but not worried.

"I'm okay." He sounded pathetic. Whiny. *Be a man.* He was trying. He felt like a failure.

"Sure you're okay. You're doing fine." Rusty put his hand to Sean's cheek. "I'm really proud of you. I know this isn't your favorite thing, but you're doing it-and you're doing it for me. You're the most wonderful man in the world."

He forced out a grimace masquerading as a grateful grin. "Thanks." It's all he could manage as the jet's motors raced, throwing everyone back into their seats. Even as the plane started to hurtle down the runway, Sean was able to take a deep breath like the one Rusty took. Then another one. And another one.

And then the clatter of the wheels folding up broke his rhythm.

Rusty leaned over close, his lips touching Sean's ear. "Last night, when you stripped me, pushed me onto the bed…God, I was so turned on."

Rusty was trying so hard. Sean pretended to be distracted. "Yeah?"

"Yeah. I'm hoping we can do it again."

Sean had been being fairly selfish at the time, going after what he wanted without much thought to Rusty.

"Not at my mom's though, unless nobody's home."

Home. That word again. He hadn't realized his stomach had stopped clenching until it started again.

"You know what I've always wanted to do?"

"What's that, Rusty?"

"Make out in a coat closet during a party."

Sean turned to look Rusty in the eye without thinking about the consequences to his equilibrium. "You're kidding."

Yup, dizzy and disoriented. But maybe as much for Rusty's confessed fantasy as for the movement.

"Maybe we could at the Christmas party tonight?"

Once again, saved by the flight attendant.

"Drink? Pretzels?"

Rusty reached across him to snag a pretzel package like he was starving. "A Coke, please."

"Sure, and you, sir?"

Salty sounded good—which had him thinking of the closet question. Maybe a fast blow job? "The same," he answered the waiting flight attendant. "Thanks."

Popping down his tray gave him zero clearance since the guy in front of him had reclined his chair again once they took off. If he needed to make a fast exit for the restroom this could get awkward.

He passed his pretzels to Rusty, knowing his stomach couldn't handle them. But if he sipped the Coke really slowly, maybe….

What would it hurt? Just a quickie. Rusty did so much to make Sean happy.

But then, Rusty didn't seem to have any inhibitions. Never had. Thankfully, he seemed to enjoy coercing Sean out of his.

Rusty opened both packages of pretzels across the tiny airline napkins then dug in his pocket. He pulled out two familiar pink pills, Benadryl, and dropped it among the pretzels.

"Eat this." Rusty held a pretzel to his mouth. The salt made him need to lick his lips. Instead, he shook his head.

"Eat the damn pretzel so you can take the Benadryl. Then you'll sleep, which you need to do, and I'll wake you when we get there."

Benedryl made him drowsy enough that he couldn't control the queasiness. He shook his head again.

"Please." Damn it. Rusty knew how to work him.

He opened his mouth and Rusty fed him the pretzel.

"Three more."

Resigned, he chewed and swallowed. "I can do it."

He picked up three pretzels, knowing Rusty was counting, forced himself to put them in his mouth and washed them down with sips of Coke.

"Happy?" Sulky wasn't a good look for him, but right now, he didn't care. He just wanted off this damn airplane.

"Not yet." Rusty peeled off the silver backing on the pills' blister pack and handed it over. "Take these."

"So when I puke on you, you're not going to complain, right?"

"Right."

Apparently, the guy in front of him had been listening, because he abruptly shifted his chair up, getting as far away from Sean as the limited space would allow.

If Sean hadn't grabbed for his plastic cup half-full of Coke, he would have worn it the rest of the flight.

Instead, he used it to swallow the pills then plopped up his tray none-too-gently. *Passive-aggressive much, Sean? Yes, much.*

But that didn't really matter right now. What mattered was getting off this plane without losing any more of his dignity.

Rusty took the cup from his hand and set it on his own tray. He dug around in his pocket again. "Want my earbuds?"

"No." He sounded as surly as Rusty's three-year-old nephew, Tommy. *His* three year-old nephew. He'd been there when Tommy was born, just like Rusty had. Tommy had never known him except as part of the family.

Sean rubbed his ring, the one that matched Rusty's. The one Rusty had given him when he'd proposed. February. Valentine's Day. They would be married for real, at least in the states that recognized their marriage. Not Louisiana though.

But Rusty's family had always recognized Sean as part of the family, as the other half of a committed couple.

After a night of broken sleep, many nights of broken sleep to tell the truth, and Benadryl on an empty stomach, the effects hit him fast.

He closed his eyes again, breathing through the feeling of being off balance. As if Rusty knew what he needed, the back of Rusty's hairy hand slid under his palm, giving him something—someone—to anchor to.

Without breaking their hold, Rusty pushed the arm rest up so they were no longer separated. He guided their hands to his thigh, now solidly planted against Sean's.

Rusty leaned over, his breath hot against Sean's neck. "I got you, babe."

Ridiculously, the old Sonny and Cher song started playing in his head, blocking out the noise of the plane's engines, blocking out everything but the feel of Rusty leaning against him, touching, side-by-side.

I got you to hold my hand. I got you to understand.

Before he could catch it, a yawn escaped.

"That's it, baby. Sleep for me."

That's all it took for Sean's grasp on consciousness to let go.

Rusty debated about waking up Sean until the bump and grind of the jet's wheels lowering took away his decision.

Sean bolted upright, fear written on his sleep-marked face.

Rusty threw his arm across Sean's chest like his mother used to do in the car at red lights. It had always comforted Rusty.

Sean reached up and grabbed Rusty's arm like a safety bar, fingers digging into Rusty's forearm, as his eyes darted, taking in the confines of the cabin.

As the flight attendant made his way down the aisle, Rusty said, "Seat up, babe," to distract Sean, to let him know everything was fine, everything was normal.

Sean nodded, taking a ragged, shallow breath, then another. He loosened his grip on Rusty's arm with one hand, reached down and worked the lever to bring his seat up. The other hand rubbed along Rusty's arm, as if he were giving comfort instead of taking it.

That's how it always had been. Sean always felt like he had to give as much as he was given. Noble, it might be, but in a family like Rusty's it was damned awkward, sometimes bordering on rude.

Receive graciously. Rusty had been taught that since he was born.

Sean had been taught to take nothing from no one.

Holiday conflict, much?

Rusty counted backwards in his mind. If he counted from when Sean had moved in at sixteen after being kicked out of his own home, then this was number seven. If he counted from when he and Sean secretly became a couple, then it was nine Christmases together.

Casting a sideways look to see if Sean had his shit together yet, Rusty noted the tight lines bracketing Sean's mouth, the steady, shallow breaths, the clammy, ghostly pale of his face.

"Gonna make it?" He started fishing in the seat pocket in front of him for the air sickness bag as he asked.

Sean gave a shoulder shrug that probably looked nonchalant to someone who didn't know him.

"When we land and the door opens, I'll grab both our bags. You just take off. I'll meet you at the restroom."

The careful stiffness around Sean's eyes softened as he answered with a short, controlled nod.

Rusty would prefer to chatter, to help Sean keep his mind off his stomach. That's what Rusty would have wanted if he had been Sean. But he wasn't Sean. He could never bury himself that deep into his own head like Sean did, like Sean was doing now. He would never have that kind of self-discipline.

If it were him, he would have already been puking from the moment he stepped on the plane until the moment he stepped off again.

Sean was doing this for him.

Like he'd left his home to move to Boston for Sean.

But then, who was keeping score?

Way to cover your guilt, Duchene. Get yourself good and worked up so you won't feel sorry for your lover, so you won't feel responsible for the mental and physical torture he's been going through ever since he traded for the airline tickets.

Sean rubbed his thumb along Rusty's wrist, capturing Rusty's attention.

"You okay?" Sean whispered more than spoken. With worry added to sick and tormented in Sean's blue eyes, Rusty had to turn away.

"Fine." His flat reply wasn't very convincing, he was sure. "Just concerned about you."

Yeah, that just doubled the turbulent storm in Sean's eyes.

"I'm fine, too." The quirk in the corner of Sean's mouth underlied his sarcasm. "Since we're both fine, then why do we both feel like hell?"

The plane finally stopped moving. "Almost there, babe."

"Almost in hell?" Sean lost even the tilt of his lips as he gnawed his bottom lip. Then he squared his shoulders and gave a jerky nod. "This is going to go well. We're going to have fun."

"Yeah, we—" the bell dinged, freeing them from their seatbelts. Finally, the doors opened and Sean popped up from his seat, elbowing his way to the front despite all the glares from the people still seated in front of him.

Rusty watched until Sean cleared the door, ignoring the frown of the first class passengers' flight attendant.

Grabbing Sean's bag from under the seat, he waited politely until the aisle had cleared to grab his from the overhead compartment. As if to make up for Sean's brusqueness, he deliberately let everyone in front of him out first, no matter how long they took to gather their things.

Maybe Sean would be done by the time Rusty met him at the restroom. He hoped so, anyway.

Once inside the terminal, he took a moment to text his dad who was in charge of having him and Sean picked up at the airport.

The answer came back, 'Your mother and I have been here for at least an hour. She's anxious to see you. LOL'

Mom would blame their earliness on Dad, of course.

Home. Where he was loved and valued and cherished. Where he didn't have to be strong all the time. Didn't have to be grown up all the time. Didn't have to be anyone but himself.

The safe, warm glow spreading from his heart to the rest of his body assured him that coming home for Christmas was the best decision he and Sean could have made.

CHAPTER FIVE

Made it. As plane rides went, that one hadn't been his worst. In fact, with Rusty helping him keep it together, it hadn't been that bad at all. Sean hoped Rusty was outside with his backpack. He *needed* his toothbrush.

Peeking his head around the angled wall separating the restroom from the general public, he spotted Rusty staring toward the escalators while bouncing on his toes.

Rusty must have felt Sean watching him because he immediately turned around with a "You okay?"

Sean nodded. "I need my bag. I've got to brush my teeth."

"Mom and Dad are already here, waiting on us in the cell phone parking lot." Rusty held the backpack close, like handing it over would cause a major delay.

"I'll be as fast as I can." Sean hooked his hand in the strap and dragged it off Rusty's shoulder. "I gotta do this."

"Yeah, sure."

"Go on down to baggage claim. I'll catch up with you."

Rusty was turning away before Sean finished his sentence. "See you there."

As Sean brushed his teeth, he stared at himself in the mirror. No half measures. He was going to go with his inclinations. Hold Rusty's hand when he felt like it. Say what was on his mind when asked—or maybe he wouldn't even wait to be asked. Take up as much space as he needed without trying to stay out of the way, without trying to be invisible.

He would bring his Boston self to New Orleans, no apologies for who he was, what he thought, what he liked or didn't like.

Being all that would be even bolder than his Boston self.

He spit into the sink, then sluiced the water around to rinse away the foam.

His real self. That's what he'd bring to the table. Anyone who didn't like it, well, to hell with him—them. He meant them. Sean was certain he wasn't even going to see *him*. Running into anyone in his family was highly unlikely.

He would drop their gifts off on the front porch tomorrow morning, knowing they'd be in church and that would be the closest he'd have to be to them.

The terminal was thick with travelers, but then, what should he expect for the Saturday before Christmas?

Out of habit, he checked the signs to baggage claim which seemed to be against the flow of traffic.

If possible, Rusty would already have their bags drug off the carousel and be waiting for him. At least, he might be waiting. As excited as Rusty was, he might try to carry all their luggage to the car himself to get to see his parents those few moments sooner.

Sean stopped and took a breath. Therapy practice time. What was he feeling?

Anxiety. Why? Maybe the Duchenes wouldn't like the 'new' him, the one who spoke his mind, who didn't apologize for taking up space, the one who had opinions that might not always fit with everyone else's.

But Rusty liked him. Had always liked him. And Rusty knew what he really thought of things. And the Duchenes had known him a long time. They probably knew him—the authentic, no holds barred him, better than he thought they did.

A man carrying a huge duffel bag bumped into him. "Sorry."

"No biggie." It was as much Sean's fault as the man's. Actually, it was all Sean's fault. He'd stopped dead still in the middle of a busy airport, causing the problem.

Therapy time again. Before he beat himself up about it, he thought about it.

He'd stopped dead still. And it was okay. Maybe a little inconvenient but not a major tragedy. He'd needed time to think and it was okay that he'd taken that time and space to think.

Still, he could think and walk at the same time, right? That would stop all the people dodging around him from glaring at him.

What else was he feeling?

He got on the conveyor and tried to scoot around a mother and daughter, but they took up the whole width with their luggage and weren't moving even though the little girl was pulling back on her mother's hand and sniffling. "Don't wanna go to Grandma's."

He gave her a sideways sympathetic grin. If he hadn't clamped his mouth shut this morning when they were boarding, he would have whined the same way to Rusty.

"Grandma's going to be so glad to see you. She's going to have the biggest hug for you," the girl's mother said to soothe her daughter. When that didn't work, she pulled out the big guns. "Grandma's got presents for you."

That did it. The girl stopped pulling backward and started pulling forward. "Then let's get this over with." Her adult expression on her childish face was such a contrast, Sean had to laugh.

Her mother looked at him and laughed, too, despite her stressed-out eyes. "Holidays. Time for family togetherness, huh?"

"Yeah." Sean thought of the Duchenes, waiting for them—waiting for him—in the parking lot. If it had been only him arriving, without Rusty, they would be waiting just as eagerly. He breathed that thought in, getting okay with it. Trying to believe it with his heart while his head knew it was true.

Rusty's dad always felt so stable, so accepting. Sean was at his calmest when Dad Duchene was in the room.

Dad Duchene. That's what Rusty's sister-in-law called him. Since Sean moved in with him, he'd asked not be called Mr. Duchene, inviting Sean to call him by his first name, or anything else Sean was comfortable with. Sean had gone through a lot of effort to not call him anything.

Dad Duchene. Sean rolled that around in his mind as he broke free at the end of the conveyor and took off at a fast clip toward baggage claim.

He arrived just as the light started flashing and the motor started grinding.

Diving for a small hole in the crowd, preparing to pounce on his bag, he saw Rusty across from the second opening in the carousel. It was anyone's guess where the luggage would spit out first.

Rusty gave him a thumbs up, then turned his attention back to the dark mouth that had yet to spew a bag.

By luck, Sean's end delivered up the goods first. He snagged Rusty's bag, then his own and then the mother's behind him, easy to spot as it matched her pink polka dot carry-on while he waited for Rusty to join him.

He had his backpack on and his suitcase handle extended when Rusty joined him.

"Ready yet?" He tapped his foot, acting impatient.

Rusty gave him a playful swat as he positioned his own bag for rolling. "I'm excited, okay?"

"Me, too." Sean said it because it was the right thing to say, like he'd done a million times before. But thinking about how Momma Duchene's hugs always made him feel important, like she really missed him, made him realize that yeah, he *was* excited to see them.

Instead of lagging behind like he usually did, he stayed even with Rusty, even getting ahead of him heading through the sliding door as Rusty keyed in his dad's cell number.

"We're here, Dad," Rusty said over speaker.

"On our way, son."

During their five minute wait, Sean breathed in the scents unique to New Orleans. Unique to the place he'd once wanted to leave so badly, he'd even considered going without Rusty. He wasn't sure if his psyche would have survived either staying or leaving Rusty behind.

But he hadn't had to make that decision.

Rusty had given up everything he cared about for Sean.

Letting go of his baggage, risking it all toppling over onto the sidewalk, he threw his arm around Rusty, pulling him close. "I'm going to be my best for you."

Rusty turned from watching the traffic, giving Sean his total attention. "You're already perfect for me."

"Not always. Not when I hold back. Not when I let my shit get in the way. Then I'm awkward. Distant. I know that makes it hard on you."

He didn't have to search hard to find the truth of that in Rusty's dark eyes.

Raw. Scared. Determined, Sean gave Rusty a trembling smile. He had to swallow twice before he could verbalize his commitment. "I'm going to be me for you. All the time. Not when it's just us, but all the time."

"That would be good, baby." Rusty blinked then swiped at his eyes. "Real good."

CHAPTER SIX

The sincerity, the yearning to be more showed in every muscle, every breath, every shadow in Sean's eyes. The intensity and pain made Rusty want to look away. But how could he, when Sean offered his soul on a platter right on the sidewalk of the New Orleans Airport?

Even if he had the words to reassure Sean, Rusty's throat was too swollen to say them. He'd barely squeezed out his simple acceptance of the gift Sean offered him.

Before he shattered, the honk of a horn saved him, let him step into the real world and out of Sean's.

His father brought the family Tahoe to a stop right beside them. Before the SUV stopped rolling, his mom had the passenger door open. She hurtled herself at Rusty, grabbing him around his neck, pulling him down to cover his cheeks with kisses.

Looking over his mom's shoulder, he watched Sean stoop to grab the handle of his bag, not even expecting the same kind of reception Rusty had just received.

Sean's need for acceptance, for unconditional love, was like a gash in his soul. He'd scarred over it by protecting himself, by hiding the vulnerable parts, the parts his family had attacked with emotional daggers sharper than any physical knife. But he covered it, protecting himself so well in self-sufficiency, nobody knew how much Sean needed. Rusty didn't even know the depth of it.

But then, Rusty's dad was there, wrapping his arms around Sean and pulling him tight.

Over Mom's happy noise, Rusty heard his dad say to Sean, "Good to see you, son. Welcome home. I've missed you."

Rusty had never loved his dad more.

And Sean, instead of respectfully tolerating being hugged like he usually did, surprised everyone by dropping the handle of his bag knowing it would crash and returned the hug just as fiercely, just as strongly as he got.

"Thank you, sir. It feels good to be here." No polite brush-off but an honest admission of how he felt.

While Rusty had never doubted Sean's intentions, he'd been wary of his ability to follow through. But now—

Then his mom was tugging on his dad. "My turn, Sam. I've got to get my hugs in here, since the boys will be swamped by the rest of the family once we get home."

With that, Mom reached up, put one hand on Sean's shoulder and with the other, brushed an imaginary strand of hair from his face. "I made brownies with walnuts just for you, sweetie. I hid them in an ice cooler in Sam's shop."

Before Sean could answer, she kissed his cheek. "I'm so glad you're home."

Emotional overload made Sean's eyes wild as he darted a look toward Rusty.

And--Rusty was back to saving Sean from his own family.

"Looks like security wants us to move, Dad. We better get the bags loaded up."

After chunking their stuff in the back, Rusty climbed into the backseat of the SUV, next to the car seat that took up most of the room. He'd ridden back here plenty of times but today it seemed to be snugger than usual.

"Have trouble getting here?" Dad asked from the driver's seat.

"No, sir. Just an early start. With the holidays, we didn't want to get caught in a traffic delay. But the buses were running fine, so no problems."

His mom cranked around in her seat, concern in her eyes. "It must be confusing to take a bus or a subway everywhere. I worry about you."

Rusty knew she didn't mean anything bad by that, but she made it sound like he wasn't smart enough to get around. "Not to worry, Mom. Sean and I are grown men, but even kids take the bus or subway."

"Rusty had all the connections figured out the first week there." Sean. Always his champion.

Rusty changed the subject by bringing up his traditional chore list. "As soon as we get home, Sean and I will hit the roof and get the lights strung in time for tonight's party."

They'd been doing it since he'd turned fourteen. It had been like a rite of passage, being trusted to climb on the roof without breaking their fool necks, as Rusty's father described it. It was a strange thing to look forward to, but he always had counted down the days until the annual Duchene Ugly Sweater Christmas Party.

That's where he'd asked Sean to go steady, all those years ago. That kiss, and the groping that had accompanied it behind the attic gable, was seared into his heart.

"No need, son. I got a couple of the new yard boys to take care of it this year. The weather was good and they needed a few extra bucks. No sense in your coming home and being put to work."

"Oh." He felt Sean look at him from across the car seat but he didn't look back. It wasn't like he needed sympathy or anything. Feeling sad about not being able to climb on the roof was pretty silly, after all. "I wouldn't have minded. Really."

He couldn't avoid his dad's eyes in the rear view mirror, though. "We'll save it for you next year, okay?"

"Okay, sure. Unless it works better for you to hire someone." Yeah, he felt like a dork.

"Did you decorate your place?" His mom, always trying to save the day. Sean said he was just like that. Always knowing what to say to smooth things over.

He didn't feel like talking right now, though.

Sean leaned up to make better eye contact with his mom. "We have a big window in our bedroom that faces the street. We put lights around it this year. And Rusty brought in a couple of branches from the cedar trees he trimmed when he delivered them for a garden store. We tied them together and put them in a big vase. Then we strung popcorn and put them on the branches. It turned out really fun."

The fun part had been throwing popcorn in the air and trying to catch it. When the pieces kept falling down Rusty's shirt, Sean had volunteered to retrieve them, sans hands, mouth only, in keeping with the game. Apparently, Sean had thought the popcorn had fallen into Rusty's jeans and underwear, too. Afterward, they had declared it a new family tradition.

Sean gave him a long wink and he couldn't help but giggle.

His mom gave him a happy smile. "Stringing popcorn, Dad. Sounds like something we need to try."

"If that's a euphemism for something else, Helen, I'm all for it. Now that the house is empty…."

Now that the house is empty…. The cocky way his dad said that struck Rusty that his dad might have been saying things like that a lot lately.

Of course, the house had been empty when he and Sean had lived away for two years while Sean finished college, but they'd often popped in and out, especially when they were looking for a home-cooked meal.

Rusty had never attempted to cook that much, had never seen the need to, until the move. Now, with Sean working, he was in charge of the kitchen unless he was doing one of his odd jobs, or hanging out at the theater.

"Hey, Mom, while I'm here, I need your oyster dressing recipe. And how much sage do you put in your chicken and sausage gumbo?"

"I don't know, son. I don't measure." She leaned back in her seat. "I'm glad one of my children is interested in cooking. Amanda was saying the other day that with her going back to work and Ben coming in early with the light fading so fast, she talked to him about starting supper, but—well, it was a big argument, right there over Sunday dinner, with your grandmother taking Ben's side like she always does, then forgetting who she was mad at and insisting Ben join her right then in the kitchen and she would show him how to make a roux. Made him wear an apron and everything. You know how she is. Burnt one of my best pans but he finally learned just to make her stop showing him. Amanda was laughing her butt off by the time he learned. We all were."

Rusty remembered Sunday dinners like that. They'd all go to church then meet at Mom's. There was no predicting what would happen, but with the bunch of them, something always would. And it always ended up funny, at least by the third or fourth retelling.

As if his mom was following his train of thought, she said, "I'm glad you've found a church you like. I was telling Grandma the other day about all the activities you're involved in."

He wondered if she'd mentioned Sean's therapy. While it wasn't a secret, it wasn't really for general discussion.

His dad pinned him with that rear view mirror look again even though he spoke to Sean.

"We know, we have you to thank for keeping Rusty active in church, Sean. If it were up to Rusty, he'd just sleep in."

Rusty couldn't deny it. Sean had always been the spiritual one. It was one of the many traits Rusty loved about him. Sean made him reach and stretch and grow in so many ways when his natural inclination was to be laid-back and complacent.

"We really like it at Unity. We have a potluck there every Sunday after services. Rusty made your banana pudding last Sunday and everyone fought to get a bite," Sean answered, as always diverting any criticism for Rusty, no matter blatant or subtly it was delivered. Another thing on the 'Why I love Sean' list.

Just like his dad's chiding was a line item on his 'What I don't miss about being home' list.

"Amanda's going back to work?"

"For your father. She's doing some of the work you were doing and studying for her landscape horticulturist license, too."

Again, Rusty got the look in the rear view mirror from his father. "She says she wants to make sure there's more than one of us with a license. I always said your brother married up. She's a smart girl."

That Rusty never got his license sat heavily between them. Working under his dad's landscape horticulturist license, he hadn't needed any other qualifications other than family reputation.

Rusty searched for a diversion. "Why doesn't she want to work in Mom's florist shop?"

Amanda had her florists' license but hadn't used it since Tommie was born.

His mom answered. "She says she doesn't want to be stuck inside a small building all day. She'd rather do outside work."

Rusty understood that. He'd never wanted to do inside work, either. If he had to wear a suit and tie and work in an office all day, like Sean did, he'd go crazy in six months.

But then, he was going slowly crazy being unemployed, too. At least he was finding odd jobs here and there.

"Tommie is so social that he loves going to the little preschool in his neighborhood and playing with the other children. Amanda's pretty social, too. She wasn't cut out to stay at home all day."

"Amanda going back to work isn't something you want to bring up around your brother. Ben is not pleased."

"Why?"

Rusty's mom frowned, her mouth going tight. "Because he's spoiled. Amanda has been doing all the housework and now he needs to do his share."

Again, the mirror gaze from Dad. "Son, maybe you should consider getting your license. I'm sure it would help with your job search."

It was a discussion they'd had ad nauseum. Not one he wanted to have right now—or any other time. He'd sworn Sean to secrecy about taking—and failing—the test twice already. He and tests did *not* get along. It was only because Sean had helped him that he'd passed high school with a very modest grade point average.

"Massachusetts doesn't require licenses, Dad." How had Rusty only remembered the joys of home and not the headaches?

His dad gave him that cheerfully condescending, 'I'm your father and I know best, smile. "When you come back to Louisiana, it would be good to have that license in hand."

Who said anything about coming back to Louisiana? Sure, it had been in his head, but not as a real thought. *Not a discussion he wanted to have right now.*

Mom kept him from having to respond by saying, "Just think about it, honey. I'm sure Amanda could use a study partner, even long distance. And it sounds like you have plenty of time to study right now."

She sounded like she was trying to convince Tommie to eat his vegetables instead of trying to convince her grown son to live his life her way.

Despite the bulky car seat between them, Sean's foot hooked out to rub Rusty's ankle. "Rusty is staying plenty busy. We're doing fine."

Sean was always on his side. He never felt dumb or inadequate or foolish like the baby brother that would never grow up when Sean was there for him.

As if everyone ran out of things to say at once, they stopped talking the last few miles to the house.

CHAPTER SEVEN

Through the foggy steam left by the shower, Rusty looked at Sean, then at himself in the clouded bathroom mirror.

"How many times have we shared this mirror? How many times have we snuck around and showered together when my parents weren't home?"

Sean gave him a puzzled grin with something feral underneath it. "We didn't sneak around today. We didn't make an announcement that we would be sharing a shower or anything, but we didn't sneak."

"No, we didn't. We never will again."

The angry challenge went away, leaving Sean's eyes clear. He picked up Rusty's hand and kissed the ring on his finger. The ring that meant commitment, and legal marriage in just a few short months. "Mine."

Rusty turned Sean's hand over and kissed the matching ring. "Yours."

"When I moved in, did you ever think we'd end up like this?"

"I wasn't thinking much about anything but keeping you safe."

"Me, neither." Sean rubbed his hand along Rusty's bristly cheek. "You did. Your parents, your brothers and sister, all kept me safe. From my dad and from the thoughts in my head." Sean drew a heart in the mirror fog, adding his plus Rusty's initials equals home. "Family. Before your folks took me in, I never knew it could be this good."

When Sean moved in during his sophomore year in high school, his parents had put Sean in his own room by himself but they'd still shared this bathroom—just discreetly.

But then came college—at least for Sean. Rusty had gone right to work after high school graduation. The student loans Sean had racked up to afford a ratty off-campus apartment with Rusty were worth it to have a place of their own, even if their place was only twenty minutes from here.

Those few months moving back home temporarily while Sean job-hunted had been a financial godsend. This place had still felt like home then. But now?

"You okay?" Sean pushed a piece of hair into place before his gel set. Concern made his eyes squint.

Beside him, Rusty shaved for the second time that day. The towel hanging low on Sean's hips tempted him. Just one pull.

When they still lived here, in this house with his parents, Rusty might have done it. Might have given the towel a yank and then dared Sean to make a sound as he blew his baby. But they didn't live here any more. That they were just visiting was evident in every inch of this house, starting with the pull-out futon in his mom's craft room that used to be his bedroom.

Shit! They'd never wrapped themselves up in towels after a shower before. Never felt the need to cover up. Sean was shy, but not in front of Rusty. And modesty wasn't a word that had ever really applied to Rusty. But now…. In this house….

It was just so damned different.

"I'm fine." Rusty had been so insistent that Sean come back to this place he dreaded. How could Rusty admit this wasn't the perfect homecoming he'd thought it would be? "And you?"

"Better than I thought I would be. You know how you build stuff up in your head and reality doesn't match it?

"Yeah, I know."

"Your mom said she'd make another batch of cookies tomorrow and we can decorate them."

"Not the same." Could he sound any more churlish? Still, he'd always been the one to write every family member's name on a gingerbread boy or girl. That his sister had done it this year, and called it a chore, had made his stomach hurt. And she hadn't even done anything but write their names. No fancy hairdos or happy smiles. Just their names across their bodies.

Sean eyed Rusty's towel. "I could kiss it and make it better?"

A pounding on the door made Rusty jump.

"Rusty? Sean?" His sister had that edge in her voice that made him want to cover his ears. "You've got hosting duties, remember. Guests will be here in less than ten minutes."

At home, he never had a big sister rush him out of the bathroom. Sean started sucking on Rusty's nipple, making promises with his tongue that went right to Rusty's dick.

"And guys?" Why wouldn't she go away? "Mom laid out two sweaters on your bed just in case you need them."

"Come see my ugly sweater, Uncle Rusty." That was Tommie, effectively putting a stop to Sean's mouth work.

Sean gave him an apologetic shrug. "Can't do it with an audience, babe."

"Me, neither." Rusty rubbed his nipple, pebbled hard and aching. Between his legs, his wilting cock throbbed with disappointment.

Following his mom's orders delivered by proxy, he yelled through the door, "Clear out, sis, so we can get to our bedroom."

Sewing room, turned guest room. Not their bedroom at all.

"Eight minutes." He heard his sister pick up Tommie, tickling him and making him giggle all the way down the hallway.

"Coast is clear." Having to sprint while holding his towel pissed him off.

"I'll come back for our stuff after I dress." Sean's reminder that they had to live out of shaving kits and travel bags made it worse.

What was wrong with him?

Determined not to think on it any more, Rusty opened the door, peeped his head around to make sure no one lurked in the hallway, then rushed toward his bedroo—the sewing room.

Sean was right behind him, bumping into him once the door was firmly closed. With a giggle, Sean dropped his towel. "Guess what you're getting after the party?"

Yup, Sean was semi-hard and getting harder.

"Screw ten minutes." Rusty dropped his own towel, snagged Sean around the waist and pulled him close. Dropping to his knees, Rusty said to Sean's cock, "Mine."

And then the damned doorbell rang.

Absently, Sean pushed aside the Christmas T-shirts on the bed and dug through his luggage for his black jeans. They were in New Orleans with temps above seventy degrees and the central air conditioner running. Sweater was more of a pretense. Anything Christmas-y always worked for the contest.

Next to him, Rusty groused as he wriggled his underwear up his still-damp legs. "We're grown men. We can buy our own ugly Christmas sweaters."

Sean thought about defending Rusty's mom—*Mom Duchene*. He'd been practicing it in his head. Maybe he'd try it out tonight—but decided to let Rusty grumble himself out instead.

Rusty shook out the second-hand Christmas sweatshirt he'd bought when they had gone shopping for their coats. It had been marked one dollar, but he'd gotten it for a quarter because of the torn lace. A skinny girl elf in red and a matching boy elf in green kissed under the mistletoe. The girl had worn a bit of lace skirt, but it was falling off, so he'd unraveled the three stitches holding it on and voila', two boy elves kissing.

"Are you sure? The t-shirts are—"

"Safe?" Rusty pulled his sweatshirt over his head. "I'm making a statement."

At the time, they'd both decided to make a statement. Now, Sean wasn't so sure.

"We don't really want to make your mom and dad uncomfortable, do we?"

Rusty looked at him like he'd just shot candy canes from his butt. He pointed to his shirt. "My mom's gonna love this."

Then he pointed to Sean's pride and joy. "And you're going to fucking win."

The bravado in Rusty's voice meant something. That he wanted to cause trouble? That he was making a point, like he said? Sean wasn't sure what. It just didn't feel very warm and fuzzy.

Sean layered his sweater vest over a short sleeved white T-shirt. Patchwork knitting of red and green covered the background while two neon pink-and-lime green plaid hippos in pink and green netting tutus did pirouettes. It was hideous.

Rusty was right. For the first time ever, Sean had a shot of winning the ugliest Christmas Sweater prize.

For the first time ever, they weren't wearing the much more conservative T-shirts Mom Duchene always bought for them when they would have rather not participated at all.

"Okay, babe. This is your Christmas homecoming." Sean fumbled with the sweater vest's buttons. Fastening them felt awkward since the holes and buttons were reversed. It wasn't until they'd picked out and paid for both sweaters, and Rusty had gotten his awesome price break, that the sales clerk had pointed out the sweaters came from the women's section of the store. It seemed women had much more ugly sweater choices than men. *Oh, well. No big deal. Nothing to get hung up on. Might as well grin about it.*

Which made it a big deal, according to his therapist. Attitude adjustments were prized milestones.

Hey, he'd dressed in drag for Halloween—and won a prize. Now, he could wear anything and be okay inside his own skin.

So maybe his change in mindset was a big deal.

Rusty pulled on red and green Christmas socks, intending to forgo shoes inside like he always did. "What are you grinning at, baby?"

"I think I might have a good time, tonight."

"Well, duh. You get to be bartender. Best job in the house. Everyone always loves the guy who pours the drinks. At least we don't have my grandmothers' job. They're both in charge of the kiddie section."

"Which they like as much as you like your assignment as Mr. Congeniality." The job was perfect for Rusty. He'd talk to a post if it would stand still long enough. And tonight, all he needed to do was circulate, making sure no guest was stuck in the corner staring into his glass.

Sean had been there, done that too many times not to appreciate someone like Rusty drawing him into a conversation.

"You look good." He wanted to lean into Rusty, stick his hands in Rusty's back pockets, pull them pelvis-to-pelvis and see whose bulge was bigger, like they'd done since they were fourteen.

It was comforting as well as sexy as hell.

But his poor penis had already been teased enough in the last half-hour. Tonight, blue balls belonged on Christmas trees, not on his body.

Rusty eyed Sean, his focus on the sweater vest. "Those hippos are something else."

"So are your elves."

"Me." Rusty pointed to the red elf then the green one. "And you. Now to find the mistletoe."

Against his better judgment, Sean leaned in, inviting the kiss. "I'm good at pretending."

Rusty leaned in, too. Just as he started to nibble—

"Boys, the guests are arriving." Mr.—Dad Duchene called through the door. "I've got your bathroom stuff here to put away."

"Ugh." Rusty threw himself face down onto the futon.

Sean took a step back, opening the door in the same movement. Taking the shaving kit and travel bag, he swallowed down the teasing taste of Rusty's toothpaste kisses and said, "Thanks."

Dad Duchene looked over Sean's sweater, then down at his own T-shirt covered with Elvises dressed as elves. "Not gonna win this year, am I?"

"Sam?" Mom Duchene's voice wafted up the stairways.

"We're on our way, Helen." He took a few steps down the hallway then turned back towards the open door. "Come on, boys. I'm not going down there without you."

Out of nowhere, Sean turned shy and panicky. He and Rusty were being so blatant with their sweaters and their rings and their touching and these were the Duchene's business associates as well as family and friends. Maybe their Christmas sweaters weren't such a good idea.

The futon creaked behind Sean and Rusty was right there, holding him back and whispering in his ear. "I'm going down on you the minute the last guest leaves."

From Rusty, sex talk always chased away fear. "I don't do empty promises."

"You'll never hear one from me."

Sean grinned, knowing no matter what else the evening had in store for him, no matter how late the party lasted, he'd get his blow job tonight.

Rusty always kept his word. That comforting thought could get Sean through anything.

CHAPTER EIGHT

Rusty took a sip of his rum and Coke, certain that Sean had watered it down. Which was why Sean was bartender instead of Rusty. Rusty never watered down drinks. Or paid attention to who was drinking how much. Or alerted his brother who was in charge of car keys and taxi rides.

Sean did all those things, gracefully, discreetly and vigilantly.

Now two hours into the party, Sean was using all his skills to keep the drinks flowing smoothly without flowing over the legal limits.

Rusty did what he did best. He talked.

He'd chatted up everyone in the room at last twice. Everyone except Levi Graham and his sister who had just now shown up.

Damn, Levi was fine. Muscled and tanned from physical labor instead of a gym membership, he filled out a pair of jeans just right. He'd forgone the Christmas sweater contest for a hunter green Henley that went really well with his blondish hair. Not as blond as Sean's. Sean called it honey blond. He was more Sean's type than Rusty's, but he was still worth a second-or third—look.

Yeah, they'd discussed Levi before. Speculated. There was something about him—something that made Sean think Levi was gay, or maybe bi. Rusty went back and forth on it. Yes, then no. Then maybe.

Not that it mattered. But then, both he and Sean agreed there was nothing wrong with looking as long as they didn't touch.

A glance toward Sean proved that he sure as hell was looking. Sean looked toward Rusty, grinned and raised his glass. Rusty raised his back, took a sip, then meandered in Levi's direction, noting that Levi's dad reached him first.

Graham Construction did a lot of work with Duchene Gardens and Landscaping. Levi was a thorough and reasonable general contractor and Rusty had always worked well with him.

Mr. Graham was okay to work with, too, but not someone Rusty would seek out if he wasn't playing host tonight.

As Rusty neared, he overheard Mr. Graham's tone before his words, "...run late to your own funeral."

He stopped short to wait until the parental admonishments ended before greeting Levi and his sister Nikki.

"It's a party, Dad. Not a scheduled business meeting," Nikki said. Then, "Oh, there's Sean, Rusty Duchene's boyfriend. I didn't know they were coming in from Boston."

"Boyfriend." Mr. Graham frowned and shook his head. "They've certainly made that clear tonight. Rusty's running around in a shirt that has two boy elves kissing on it. Look at that boy, Sean, wearing girl clothes. What's he trying to prove?"

"Apparently, he's trying to prove he's got the ugliest Christmas sweater, Dad. At least, that's what that huge ribbon he's wearing says." Nikki looked over her dad's button down dress shirt. "Looks like you didn't get the memo."

"No son of mine—" he glanced over at Levi and shook his head. "I don't know what Sam Duchene was thinking to let that boy move in here. Then to act like he's okay with all this blatant homosexual togetherness thing. There are impressionable children here."

Nikki elbowed her brother. "Levi, say something."

Levi glanced up, his eyes going past Rusty, then going back again momentarily before he looked away. "Dad, we're guests in the Graham's home. This isn't really the time or the place...."

Mr. Graham took a long sip of the drink Sean had poured for him. Rusty hoped he choked on it.

A friend of his mother's gently touched his elbow. Rusty couldn't remember her name and he didn't know how much she'd overheard, but he was sure it had been enough to put that sympathetic smile on her face. "He's from an older generation. They just aren't up on things."

Rusty stared down into his drink, catching hold of his temper.

Up on things? There was so much he could say, so much he wanted to say to her, and most especially to Mr. Graham. But he held his words back. The Grahams where business associates. If Rusty went off on every one of Duchene Gardens' business associates that had the same small-mindedness as Mr. Graham, then his father would be out of business.

Mr. and Mrs. Miller were at least a decade older than Mr. Graham, but certainly able to accept everyone as worthy of basic human rights. He glanced around, wondering who else was whispering behind his back.

He would have never overheard a conversation like the Grahams at the party he and Sean had attended after their cantata.

"Please, don't tell Mom. She'll come unglued on them."

"Don't I know it!" She pat his elbow again. "For what its worth, I think your little boyfriend is adorable."

"My fiance' is also a damn fine engineer." He finished off his drink before saying anything he would regret later. Seeing Levi standing by himself now, he gave the well-intentioned woman a tight smile. "Excuse me."

Levi saw him coming. He squared his feet as if to brace himself.

"Hey, Levi, want a drink?"

"Hell, yes."

Levi followed him back to the table Sean was using as a bar.

"Hey baby, give me another one. This time, full strength, okay? I'm not driving anywhere."

The look Sean gave him said no. Sean poured him straight Coke and handed it over. "Full strength, just like you requested. Don't want to put your promise in jeopardy."

They locked eyes for half a second until he conceded. "Fine."

Levi stepped up, taking Sean's intense attention off Rusty, for which Rusty was grateful.

"I *am* driving and it's been a long day. So I'll have one just like his, please. If I have a drop of alcohol, I'll be sound asleep under your Christmas tree after the first sip." He smiled, showing dimples. Making Rusty jealous when Sean smiled back.

"Hey. I want one of those," Rusty said.

Sean squinted at him, gesturing to the drink in his hand. "You got one."

"No. One of those smiles."

Sean looked into Rusty's eyes, his own softening. "I'll do better than that. Come here."

Sean leaned across the table and Rusty leaned toward him.

The kiss Sean planted on his lips was light and easy, tasting of grapefruit juice and vodka. So Sean had been indulging a bit, too.

"All better?"

"Much better, baby."

As focused as Rusty was on Sean, a small part of him fractured off, trying to judge Levi's reaction. Was he just like his old man?

Nah. Rusty had been around Levi often enough to know better. He and Sean had eaten lunch with him a couple of times and he'd always been okay. More than okay.

Curious? Maybe even envious?

Rusty sipped his Coke, thinking Sean was right. Thinking through too much rum made his head spin off in odd directions.

"So how's Boston?" Levi asked.

"Nice," Sean answered. His enthusiasm showed in his voice. "I love it there."

"I've always wanted to visit."

"You should. Come up and stay with us. You'll have to sleep on the couch, but it's not too uncomfortable."

Rusty wiped his mouth to cover his surprise.

Sean had never done that before. Never opened up their home to someone else. Home was sanctuary to Sean.

"Come up any time," he added to Sean's invitation.

"Email me. We'll make arrangements." Levi dug into his wallet, pulled out a business card and wrote an email address on the back of it. Then he handed it to Sean, correctly thinking Sean would keep up with it better than Rusty would.

"What's the working climate up there?"

Was Levi thinking of moving? "Gotta tell you, man. It sucks for landscaping, at least this time of year. It's definitely seasonal."

Levi frowned. "Probably the same for construction, too, huh?"

"I could check."

Levi shook his head. "No, thanks. Just wondering."

To keep the conversation from turning into a big black hole, Rusty asked, "How are things around here?"

"Busy. I really miss you, Rusty. You can read the minds of clients and give them what they see in their heads, only better."

"My sister-in-law, Amanda, will be doing my old job after the first of the year. I think you'll like working with her."

"I look forward to it." He clinked his ice around in his drink then pointed to Rusty's ring. "One of your brothers told me you and Sean are officially engaged. Congratulations."

"Thanks. Wedding's in February."

"Be sure to send me an invitation."

"Will do." Was he trying to prove he wasn't like his father? Or was he sincerely interested? It seemed to Rusty that Levi might really care.

With another lift of his cup, Levi headed toward the food where his sister stood loading up her plate.

Sean cleared his throat. "You're studying him pretty closely. What do you think?"

Rusty toasted the departed Levi. "I think, if he's gay, with that father of his, God help him."

Sean frowned, poured more vodka into his glass and held it high. "God help him."

Thinking of homophobic fathers and gay sons, Sean braced himself for that gut-punched feeling to hit him. But his palms didn't start sweating. His breathing didn't become desperate and labored. His head didn't spend, making him feel dizzy. All he got was a bit of weakening in the knees. He leaned against the wall behind him to take care of that.

Not having to pretend to be all right was a nice feeling. Truly being all right was an even better feeling.

"Rusty, do you think Levi's safe?"

Rusty crossed to Sean's side of the table and put his arm around Sean's shoulder, making *him* feel safe. Although, this time, he didn't need it so much. He wanted Rusty's touch—but he didn't *need* it to keep from falling apart.

"He's fine." Rusty tracked Mr. Graham through the crowd. "I don't think his dad's violent, and Levi's a pretty buff guy, too. But his dad has some deep-seated prejudices."

"Who's that son? Someone giving you problems?" Dad Duchene—and didn't that feel good, calling him Dad in his head—grabbed the plastic bottle of Sprite to top off his glass.

"Do you really want to know, Dad? You gotta work with him." Rusty reached for the rum bottle. Sean pulled the bottle back from him, shoving his own cup of Dr. Pepper into Rusty's hand instead.

Dad Duchene gave Sean a big smile before frowning at Rusty. "Since when has lack of knowledge been a good thing, son?"

"Mr. Graham." Rusty handed Sean's D.P back to him and grabbed a cup of Sprite instead. "I overheard him say some things like being gay is a bad influence on young children. Like we recruit or something?"

"Did he say anything about you directly, son?" Dad Duchene wasn't a big man, but the look in his eyes would make anyone back down if directed at them.

"No, Dad." Rusty shook his head, but Sean could tell when Rusty skirted around the truth.

"You okay, Sean?"

"Yeah, Dad. I'm fine." He'd said it. He'd called Mr. Duchene *Dad*. He felt damned good. Whole. Full of love.

The way Dad Duchene blinked with his eyes welling up, it meant something to him, too. His voice was thick when he said, "That's good, son. Real good."

Rusty capped off the love fest by raising his cup. "To family."

Sean raised his cup, the plastic making a snicking sound against Rusty's. "To family."

Dad Duchene raised his glass, too, his knuckles brushing both Sean's and Rusty's

For the first time in his life, Sean felt like a welcome and essential piece of a bigger puzzle. "To *our* family."

CHAPTER NINE

Sean woke and stretched, smiling at the soreness that was *not* caused by sleeping on the thin futon mattress. When Rusty delivered on a promise, he didn't hold back.

And then there was Sean's reciprocal thank you gift.

So far, none of the nebulous, dreaded bad stuff he'd anticipated had happened.

Which was an abrupt reminder of what he planned to do this morning.

He raised up and grabbed his phone laying on the suitcase that was acting as a nightstand next to the futon.

Absently, automatically, Rusty stirred, reaching out and finding Sean's butt with his hand. "It's okay. I'm here."

The pat on his ass, followed by a slow, sleepy run up his back went a long way to giving Sean the ability to take a deep breath and think through his concern.

He would drive by his parent's house while they were at church and drop off the gifts on the porch. No hassle. No confrontation. Just a simple drive-by.

It had worked that way ever since he'd moved out. There was no reason to think this year would be any different. Still, thinking about climbing those porch stairs made him too antsy to lay still any longer.

Noise downstairs was a good excuse to get up. He leaned over and murmured to Rusty, "Going to help with breakfast."

Rusty's sleepy, warm, musky smell made Sean want to snuggle in instead. But Sean was already starting to bounce his foot against the futon frame. Any more wriggling would wake up Rusty, not a good thing after all the rum Rusty had drunk last night.

He slipped on sleep shorts, did his bathroom business, including hopelessly trying to smooth down his hair, and made his way toward the light.

Mom Duchene looked up with a smile. "Morning, precious."

It's what she said to all her kids every morning.

"Morning, Mom." It's what they said back.

And what had her whirling around slinging her arms around Sean.

"Thank you," she whispered. "You've just given me the best Christmas present I've ever had."

Sean found himself patting her back as she hugged him tight.

Why had he held himself back from this for so many years?

Because you had to heal, is what his therapist would have said. *You have to grow into being okay with yourself to be okay with anyone else.*

Rusty, Sean had offered as an argument. *I can accept love from Rusty.*

Because you're okay with who you are around Rusty. You've given yourself permission to be loved by him, right?

Right. And now he was okay around Rusty's parents, too.

God, it felt so good.

"Waffles well done?" Dad Duchene's question made him jump.

Sean didn't know how long he would have stood there, soaking up the love, if Dad Duchene hadn't come in, sniffing the burning waffles.

Reluctantly, he let go of Mom Duchene and turned to the waffles.

"Sorry. Didn't mean to interrupt." Dad Duchene ruffled the spikes of hair standing up on Sean's head.

In the past, Sean had to make himself stand still to keep from affronting the man who wanted to make him a part of the family. This morning, he leaned into the touch.

And then he was wrapped in another hug, this time from Dad Duchene. "I'm so glad you're here."

"Me, too." And he meant it. Now he understood Rusty's homesickness, truly understood it. This time, it wasn't an academic understanding like it had been before, but a heartfelt one. This is what Rusty had left behind *for him.*

Dad Duchene released him to pour a cup of coffee. "So, tell me about Boston. Tell me about snow."

"Snow." Sean smiled as he poured a cup of hot water then searched in the cabinet for the tea bags Mom Duchene kept there for the two of them. "It's cold."

"Hard to drive on?"

They both scraped chairs back in unison as they took seats at the kitchen table already set with plates, forks, knives and syrup.

"I take public transportation most of the time."

Mom Duchene met them both at the table with a platter of waffles and her own cup of tea. "Forget the snow. Tell me about the drag queen competition."

That's when Rusty stumbled in. "I've got pictures. I can be bribed with waffles and aspirin."

He looked good, all stubbly and relaxed, with the slightest hint of a headache reflecting in the squint around his eyes.

Sean knew Rusty was teasing, that he would be happy to show his own pics, but wouldn't dare show super-sensitive Sean's.

So when Sean said, "Go ahead. Mine too," then pushed his chair back to get the aspirin, he was ready for Rusty's lifted eyebrow.

Yes, Sean was feeling courageous today.

Of course, Rusty had his phone in his hand, so the pics were right there to be shown.

And that's as far as Sean could take it. Knowing they would be ooohing and aaahing over what a pretty girl he made pushed the boundaries of his comfort level too hard.

"While you look at them, I'm going to get dressed."

Mom Duchene frowned. "Sean, we don't need to see them if you don't want us to."

"It's okay. I've got an errand to run and I need to get ready for it."

The exchanged looks told him everyone at the table knew what his errand was.

Again last night, Rusty begged him to to let it go. But Sean couldn't. His family might have disowned him, but he couldn't let them go, no matter how hard he'd tried.

The neighborhood was Sunday morning quiet as Rusty drove past Sean's old house for the second time. He didn't like this. Didn't like it at all. "Looks like it's clear."

"Okay. Slow down, then." Sean strangled the bright and cheerful holiday sack with the three wrapped presents inside.

Rusty wished Sean didn't insist on this. If they'd stayed in Boston, they could have avoided this whole thing.

With the restraining order Rusty insisted Sean keep against his father, Rusty was always worried they would be accused of something shameful like trying to trick his father into violating the order.

Rusty pulled up to the curb and held his breath while Sean jumped out, walked quickly to the porch, climbed the steps and dropped the sack next to the door.

Rusty kept one hand on the door handle and the other on the phone. The last time Sean had seen his father, Rusty had had to make the call that had police and paramedics storming this house. But Rusty was older now and bigger. The man wouldn't have a chance to put his son in the hospital this time.

Rusty could swear he saw a shadow cross the window and the curtain move. But Sean was back, buckling his seat belt and smiling.

And smiling? In the past, he'd been hiding tears.

Sean reached over, grabbed Rusty's arm and shook him, laughing. "It didn't hurt so much this time."

Rusty smiled back as he eased away from the curb. "Yeah? It's different this year?" Obviously, but he wanted to hear it.

"Yeah, different." Sean's foot bounced against the floorboard. In fact, his whole body bounced. "I practiced it in my head like I'd done in therapy. I practiced what it would feel like to go up their stairs and think about all the things I had instead of all the things I didn't. I practiced thinking of you, sitting hear waiting for me. And I kept reminding myself that I wasn't alone. You were here for me. You loved me and your love is worth everything."

Rusty turned into an empty parking lot, too shaky and distracted to keep driving. "That's what you've been practicing in your head?"

"Yeah." Sean bounced enough to make the seatbelt tighten across his chest. He unbuckled and shoved it off his shoulder. "And it worked!"

Rusty unbuckled his own seat belt and turned sideways in his seat. "So that's why you've been dropping off the presents all this time? To get over your fear—" wrong word to use around Sean. He knew it the second he said it. That Sean settled down and his smile faded was further proof Rusty didn't need.

"No. I give the presents to—" Sean leaned back into the car seat, and blew out a breath. "To remind them I still exist? To tell them I'm still a part of them, that I still lo—"

He looked out the window, his hands twisting on themselves. "Still love them—at least my mom and my sister."

Rusty waited, knowing there was more. Patience was the one thing he was learning in their joint therapy sessions. Patience and letting Sean hurt instead of trying to divert him. It was damned hard.

"I think I was always hoping for—I don't know. For them to open the door and say it was all a mistake. That they loved me, too. And missed me. And we would make everything all right. But that's not going to happen." Sean turned to Rusty, one hand going to Rusty's arm, the other to Rusty's hand resting on the steering wheel. His grip was that of a man hanging by an unraveling rope. "And that's okay. Because I'm not alone. I have you. And I have your family, too. They love me, don't they?—Don't answer that. I know they do. Your parents love me. And your brothers and sister and sister-in-law and Tommie, too."

Tears fell so hard, Rusty couldn't see Sean all that well. But he heard, he felt what Sean was saying loud and clear. "Yeah, they do."

"Me, too. I love them, too." Sean wiped his face with the hem of his T-shirt. "Can we go home now?"

Home. The picture in Rusty's mind was of their apartment in Boston. Right now, at this crucial moment, he wanted Sean all to himself. Wanted to be touched, to be held, to be filled by Sean. He needed to know that Sean was still the man who loved him more than anyone else in the whole world. That he wasn't losing Sean to his family.

That Sean still needed him.

"Sean? Could we go somewhere private first? And talk?" Yeah, he realized *him* wanting to talk was a first in their relationship.

"Okay?" Sean kind of crumpled in on himself. Rusty felt like the world's biggest schmuck.

How could he be so proud of Sean, so happy for him that his baby could finally accept the good people in his life, yet be so worried about himself.

He was a selfish jerk.

As he pulled into their favorite parking lot fronting the Ponchartrain, he turned to Sean and said, "This shouldn't be about me."

Sean was rocking, hugging himself.

Rusty was grinding his teeth, hating himself. He just blurted it out. "Now that you don't need me any more, will you still love me?"

Sean stopped rocking. He wiped his eyes and nose with his sleeve then glared at Rusty. "What do you mean, not need you any more?"

"You've got it figured out. You've got a world of people who love you. My parents are only a part of that."

Very quietly, Sean asked, "And you're not a part of that anymore?"

There was a hint of something sharp and strong and lethal in his question. And it cut pretty damned deep.

"What the fuck? Are you asking if I love you? You know I do." Sean's hands clenched, then unclenched, back and forth. Rusty was mesmerized by the muscles flexing Sean's wrists.

"Then why are we having this conversation?"

"Because I'm an idiot. A selfish moron. This is your moment. This isn't supposed to be about me."

"My moment?"

"You know, like in books or in the movies when everything clicks into place."

"So now, an awesome musical score plays in the background and I get this sexy half-shadow, half-spotlight lighting on my face?" Thank God that came with a giggle.

Rusty took a breath, a deep one but he couldn't force an answering grin. "Yeah, like that."

"It's always been about me, your emo boyfriend. Maybe it's your turn."

"Nobody ever said—"

"Yes, they did. I'm not deaf *or* stupid." Sean reached for Rusty's hand. "But I am grateful. You've stuck with me through some bad shit, a lot of it in my head. And Rusty?"

"Yeah?"

"I've got a lot of shit still in my head. I'm trying to make it better—for me, but for you, too." He gripped his fingers around Rusty's fist. "But if you ever leave me—I don't think I would do so well."

"I'm not leaving you. Ever." Rusty's stomach soured as the thought of their friend from high school who died in a car crash last year. He'd gotten his girlfriend pregnant, promised he'd be there forever if she would marry him, and then couldn't keep that promise. "Not if I can help it."

Sean nodded, accepting Rusty's truth.

"And you aren't leaving me, either." Without wanting to, Rusty thought of the decision Sean had struggled to make when he moved to Boston. The decision Rusty had struggled with, too. Those worries seemed so long ago. So inconsequential. "Say it, Sean."

"I'm not leaving you, ever." The ring on Sean's finger cut into Rusty's hand. "Not if I can help it."

Sean readjusted his grip, threading his fingers through Rusty's hand. "I'm alive because of you," he whispered.

Rusty sucked in a breath. He could name a half-dozen times that he'd suspected, but he hadn't really wanted to know. Not really.

"You're not leaving me," he repeated. He looked away, unable to bear seeing his darkest fear in Sean's eyes.

"No. I'm not." Sean leaned over and kissed him, just a brush of his lips on Rusty's cheek. "I haven't been in that place since your parents took me in."

Sean put his hand on Rusty's chin and turned him to look into his eyes. "I'm okay. And I'm getting more okay all the time. How we are is going to change. That's what happens in relationships, especially when we work on them as hard as you and I have been working on ours. But ours is going to keep getting stronger just like I'm getting stronger. We both want that, right?"

Rusty nodded, but had to add, "You're the strongest man I know."

"The strength I've learned to have is because I know you've always got my back. I know when I'm tired, you carry me. When I'm spinning, you anchor me. When I go beyond my comfort zone, you're there to hold me and keep me safe. I want to give to you, Rusty. I want to bring something to us, too."

Rusty framed Sean's face with both his hands. "You do, baby. You do."

"Yeah? What?"

"You bring me joy in that crooked, shy smile of yours. And in the way you go after life, you're always reaching for more. I get complacent. Lazy, even. But you—you're all energy and exploring the world and seeing what's out there. Keeping up with you, having your back, makes me step out of my comfort zone and grow. My world is so much bigger and richer and fuller because of you. I'm a much better man because of you."

The intensity in Sean's eyes made him swallow hard. Such deep, raw emotion. This was the uncomfortable he was talking about. "And Sean?"

"Yeah, baby?"

"Your cock fills my ass better than any—" He let the sentence drift. Timing was everything.

At Sean's lifted brow, he continued. "Better than anyone else's that I can imagine."

As he had hoped—as he had known it would, his remark dialed back the emo in Sean's eyes. Yes, they balanced well.

Sean's hand dropped to Rusty's crotch. "You just keep that imagination in your pants and we'll do just fine."

"I promise. Forever."

Sean squeezed enough to really let Rusty feel it and make him want to squirm. He didn't, out of obstinacy, but he really wanted to.

"Me, too. Forever." Sea punctuated his promise with a kiss that turned into a tonsil probe which suited Rusty just fine.

CHAPTER TEN

As soon as Sean pulled open the door, the scent of ginger and cinnamon rushed out at him.

"Rusty? Sean? Is that you?" Mom Duchene stuck her head out of the kitchen doorway and yelled into the front room.

"Yes, ma'am. It's us," Sean answered, like he'd done a thousand times before. This time, it felt damned good. So welcoming. So accepting. Like never before.

Perception was everything.

Rusty pulled the door tight behind him. "Nothing like high school memories to make you feel like a kid again, huh?"

His father didn't bother to look up from his newspaper to add, "You're still a kid. Wait until you're my age."

Sean had never understood what that meant, exactly, but it sounded ominous.

"Everything go okay?" Momma Duchene came into the front room, wiping her hands on a kitchen towel.

Everything. That included a hell of a lot this morning. "Yes, ma'am. Everything went fine."

Rusty's hand on Sean's back had him leaning back into it, savoring the connection.

"No trouble?"

No doubt she noticed the red-rimmed eyes on both of them. She wiped her hands again while studying them, as if her focused attention would make them confess. While it had worked on Rusty, it had never worked so well on Sean. Now, Rusty seemed to have become immune to those maternal superpowers, too, because he looped his arm around Sean's shoulder and neck, pulling him in close for a kiss on his ear and answered, "Everything's fine, Mom. Really."

Dad Duchene looked up from his paper, inspected Sean and Rusty then went back to reading, while addressing his wife, "They said they're fine, Helen. They're grown men, now. If they want to say they're fine, they can do that without us trying to badger the truth out of them."

Rusty let go of Sean to reach out and ruffle his dad's hair. "Thanks, Dad."

"Umm-hmm." Dad Duchene shook his paper to turn the page. "If you really want to thank me, you'll climb up on the roof and figure out which bulb is burnt out and keeping the whole line in front of that top gable from blinking."

"Sure, Dad. We can do that." Rusty smiled so big anyone would have thought he'd just found Santa's lost bag of toys or something. Yes, *that* kind of toys.

"And when you're done, I've made more gingerbread cookies that need decorating."

Anyone with half a brain would have been suspicious. Sean prided himself on having a whole, mostly functioning brain. But the sly looks exchanged between Mom and Dad Duchene sealed the deal.

Rusty had such great parents. Apparently, he wasn't using his whole brain, though, because the entire time they were screwing and unscrewing Christmas bulbs into their sockets, he complained. Happily complained, about the shoddy job the hired guys must have done, about how they hadn't even bothered to clean out the gutters while they were up there, and about how they'd draped the lights on top of the gable eaves instead of under them. The one thing Rusty didn't complain about was Sean's kisses as they lay hidden between the valley formed by the roof's two peaks.

Sean made sure Rusty had nothing to complain about there.

Finally, they found the barely screwed in light, the one closest to the roof's edge that would have only required a ladder to reach. By then, they'd spent a good solid two hours scrambling across the elevations and recreating old times.

Who said two guys couldn't be romantic? That certainly didn't apply to Rusty when he asked Sean to go steady again, and to marry him again, and to love him forever again, while they lay between the roof peaks trading memories and kisses.

Mom Duchene insisted they eat lunch, a big bowl of seafood gumbo that couldn't be found for love or money in Boston. Rusty wrote down the recipe as his mom dictated from memory and Sean kept his fingers crossed that this one would become one of Rusty's culinary successes.

Then the gingerbread decorating commenced. And yes, Rusty had just as much fun getting creative with the icing as he had in years past.

As Sean put the last of the green Medusa hair on his gingerbread girl and Rusty finished off his hula skirt on his cookie, Dad Duchene came into the kitchen, again with the sly eye contact with Mom Duchene.

"I was wondering, boys, if you could do a little work for Duchene Landscaping tomorrow. I could slide you a little something under the table for your trouble."

"We'll be glad to, but you don't need to pay us."

Rusty kicked Sean under the table. "If he can pay those idiots to string lights the wrong way on the house, he can pay us for good, honest labor."

Dad Duchene put a hand on Rusty's shoulder. "Spoken like a man who has worked for his father before."

Rusty grinned up at his father. "What do you need us to do, Dad?"

"I've got a list of addresses that need to be checked to make sure the holiday yard ornaments are still where they're supposed to be. No humping reindeer, or Santas tackling elves, that kind of thing. And the florist department needs help with deliveries. You can take the floral van. Then when you're done, feel free to take it to visit friends, or whatever."

Just like old times. Sean and Rusty had gone on too many dates driving that huge old florist van wrapped in the shop's logo of a too-cute little boy holding out a wilted flower to a delighted old lady. Everyone in town knew that van. Everyone in town reported every mile over the speed limit or every unsuitable parking place that van had ever been a part of.

Sean hadn't realized until now how secure that had always made him feel.

CHAPTER ELEVEN

"Same, but different." Rusty sat in the stillness of midnight Mass as everyone around him took a moment to reflect. With the lights low and candles making flickering shadows on the cathedral walls, the church had a spooky feel, not in a scary kind of way but in a mystic kind of way.

Beside him, Sean had his eyes closed and head bowed with his hands folded quietly in his lap. He looked spectral, otherworldly. Beautiful.

The last few days had been filled. The whole family had met to listen to the choir at the St. Louis Cathedral on Sunday night. Monday had been spent uncoupling reindeer—his dad had been speaking from experience, obviously—, delivering flowers and staying to chat with the folks whose children had sent the floral apologies in lieu of coming in to visit—which might be he and Sean some day—, and visiting with friends. The ribbing about driving the florist truck hadn't changed at all, even though his friends had.

Some were married with babies. Some had babies and weren't married any more. A friend from his high school soccer team who he would have sworn was straight had shacked up with two other guys in their duplex in Marigny and apparently had orgies every night. At least, that's what soccer-boy tried to convince them of.

Since their normal Plum Street shop was closed for the winter, they'd driven all the way out to Metarie for SnoBalls, served in a Chinese take-out box nestled in a leak proof plastic sack. He'd gotten fuzzy navel crowned with strawberry. Sean had gone for Chocolate Decadence with ice cream in the center and coated with condensed milk and even more chocolate syrup on top.

Then today, on Christmas Eve, a day early, the whole family had gathered today and opened presents then had their traditional

Christmas Dinner because he and Sean had to fly out first thing in the morning. In just a few short hours, he'd be stuck on a plane with an airsick Sean all Christmas Day. The things you did for family.

Yeah, he hadn't forgotten. He was the one that had wanted this so badly.

He fingered the necklace Sean had made him and teared up again. Just like his dad, they'd all teased when he'd opened it. His dad had cried while they all watched the video of his and Sean's Christmas cantata, so he hadn't been the only one to wipe his eyes that day.

And Mom, who never cried, had been caught wiping her eyes when she walked in on Sean packing up their dirty clothes right before church.

Now, sitting in St Andrews' Episcopal, the church they'd attended ever since his Mom had started searching for a gay-friendly spiritual home when Rusty had turned ten and they'd all stopped suspecting and started knowing, Rusty felt like time had turned back and was moving forward at the same time.

Same but different.

Organ music began quietly, then rose in volume, the last hymn of the service.

In just a few minutes, they'd head to the house, have a cup of decaf tea, pack away their church clothes and spend one last night on that torturous futon-thing.

And tomorrow night, he'd sleep in his own bed.

On that very cheerful note, he took a deep breath to blast out the chorus of his favorite Christmas hymn, feeling real joy in his world.

As they made their way outside, Rusty saw her first. There was no mistaking who she was. She might be eight years younger, but Sean's sister looked just like him.

Sean rushed past Rusty and whoever else was in his way. "MaryAnne?"

She was crying, mascara dripping down her face. She launched herself at him and he held her as she clung to him.

"You're okay, Sean?" She pushed away enough to look at him. She was only a few inches shorter then him. When had that happened?

"I'm fine."

Through her tears, she said, "I've missed you so much."

He looked her over, searching. "Are *you* okay? He didn't hurt you, did he?"

"I'm okay. I'm fine. As long as I color in the lines, everything's sitcom perfect." Putting her hands on his shoulders, she separated them but only arm's length. "You look good, Sean. My big brother, all grown up."

"You, too." He amended that. "Not quite grown up but almost."

"Eighteen next year."

"I know." He studied her, pleased she was wearing the vintage Boston Spaceship cover T-shirt he'd given her for Christmas. Especially pleased to see she was standing straight and tall, looking confident. He had hoped, had prayed, that his dad would be a good parent for MaryAnne. She dug a tissue out of her bag to wipe her mascara. All she did was smear it around, so he took the tissue and cleaned her up, "Just like I used to, remember?"

"You were always looking out for me."

"I tried. But life was easier for you after I left wasn't it?"

Even though she looked down fast, he still caught the answer in her eyes.

He raised her chin. "It's okay. I'm glad it was."

Knowing Rusty was right behind him. Feeling Rusty there, right where Sean needed him, he reached back and pulled Rusty even with him. "Mine has turned out okay, too."

"This is from Mom." She handed him an envelope. "She's in the car. Will you come over and say hello?" Tears welled in her eyes again. She took the tissue from Sean and dabbed. "She said she'd understand if you didn't want to, though."

He fumbled for Rusty's hand. When Rusty interlaced fingers with him, Sean knew he could do anything. "Sure. I'll say hello."

His mom sat in the passenger seat of the car with the window rolled down as if she were trying to catch any sound that would alert her to what was happening around her.

Sean could tell the second she spotted him. With unfocused eyes, she stared at him, stricken, then looked away until he was even with the car window.

"Mom?"

"Are you okay?"

"That seems to be the question of the holiday. I must look like shit."

That made her head pop up. Now, she looked at him, really looked at him. "No, son. No."

Her hand fluttered at him before she pulled it back into the car, into her lap, where she clutched a handful of tissues like his sister's. On her wrist was the bracelet he'd made her, the one that said Mom and had a girl charm in one link and two boy charms in the other.

He and Rusty were a pair. He wanted to make sure she knew that, though he'd expected her to at least take off one of the boy charms if she chose to wear it. Maybe she hadn't had time to and had just slipped it on for his benefit.

"You look good, son."

Because looking good is what matters to us gay guys at times like these. He kept it inside his head, but barely. Sarcasm wouldn't help any of them.

"How are you, Mrs. Delahunt?"

She ignored Rusty's question, but said instead, "Thank your mother for me, please, for letting me know I could find Sean here tonight."

At Rusty's shocked expression, she clarified. "I saw her at the grocery store last week. She said Sean would be home and then mentioned something about services at St. Andrews, so I hoped," she turned to Sean, "you would be here."

"We've been here since Saturday. We fly out tomorrow morning."

"Do you still have trouble flying?"

Sean ignored her question. Exposing weaknesses wasn't something he was comfortable doing around *her*. There was nothing wrong, and everything right with setting boundaries.

"Mom?" MaryAnne said into the silence. "Don't you want to give Sean a hug?"

The look in his mother's eyes was one he'd never seen before. Sorrow. Wistfulness. Pain.

"If he'll let me," she answered MaryAnne, looking down again.

The steeple bells started playing 'Silent Night.'

Sean nodded, feeling as if he were making a momentous decision. Maybe he was, but he couldn't think about that right now. Right now, he just had to keep breathing.

Rusty tightened his hold on Sean's hand and put his other hand on Sean's shoulder. That's when he realized he'd backed into Rusty, leaning into his warmth and strength.

Sean's mom clicked the door handle, then slowly, as if the door weighed more than the cathedral's heavy wooden doors, she pushed and climbed out of the car.

Except for a few lines around her eyes and a limpness to her hair and maybe a slight sag to her shoulders, she looked almost the same as she had the last time he'd seen her, seven years ago.

He'd had glimpses, as he drove around the block of his old house, as he'd seen her in the checkout line at the grocery store before they both ducked down different aisles, on candid photos MaryAnne posted on social media sites. But to stand this close to her, to really see her, had been over seven years ago.

With shaking hands, she reached out.

Rusty let go and Sean stepped forward. His stomach twisted so hard he thought he might puke. Looking over her shoulder instead of into her eyes, he let her put her arms around him. Behind her, his sister watched, mascara flowing freely again.

Feeling awkward, feeling needy and hating it, he loosely wrapped his arms around her back.

With a sigh, she leaned into him. If she would just say it. Just say she was sorry.

After two deep breaths, she pulled back. He could feel her gathering herself to step away even before she made a move.

"Merry Christmas, son."

Not once had she looked at or spoken to Rusty. Not once.

Sean nodded. With too much to say to speak, he said nothing.

And that's when he realized, he was like her. They didn't say the things that needed to be said because it hurt too much.

But he was strong enough now. And Rusty had his back.

"Mom, I was sad for a long time."

She jumped as if he had startled her by speaking. He understood that. He had startled himself, too.

She nodded, letting him know she'd heard him.

"And hurt. Beyond the physical."

Tears ran down her face as she twisted her hands—just like he was doing.

He reached back and Rusty's hand was there for him. Absently, he wished she had someone there for her, too.

"But I'm much better now. Getting better all the time."

Another nod.

"Rusty has been a big part of that."

For the first time he could remember, she looked up, past him to Rusty. Looked Rusty in the face and nodded, acknowledging him.

Then, as if her legs were about to give away, she dropped into the car seat and patted the door, as if to signal she was ready to leave.

"I love you, son."

Sean wasn't sure he'd heard it. Maybe he'd only wanted to hear it.

"You, too, Mom."

Gently, MaryAnne closed the door then threw herself at him.

He caught her as Rusty put a steady hand on his back.

As she finished her hug, she asked, "Got that envelope?"

He looked down at his hand, surprised he'd forgotten about it.

"Yeah." He waved it at the window. "Thanks for the gift, Mom."

His mother stared straight ahead, but said, firmly, "It's not a gift. It's a trust fund from my parents, your grandparents, for your college education. You should have had it a long time ago."

Sean's hand shook on the envelope. He would work through these feelings later. Right now, he needed to keep breathing.

MaryAnne put a hand on his shoulder. "She filed divorce papers Friday. Dad doesn't know it yet. He'll find out Monday. Or figure it out when he wakes up. We're moving out tonight. We'll be at a friend's camphouse for a while. I may not have internet access very often, but I'll keep you updated. This is a good thing."

"Yes," his mom said, stronger than she'd spoken at any time tonight. "Yes, it is. And son, I'm going to heal, just like you have. You've shown me I can."

That's when he noticed the car was packed full with boxes and clothes.

And that's when the church bells broke into a happy rendition of 'We Wish You a Merry Christmas and a Happy New Year.'

And somehow, Sean thought it would be.

CHAPTER TWELVE

Rusty stood at the door to their apartment. Thank God, they were finally here.

Between the late night, no breakfast and the Benadryl Rusty had stuffed down Sean's throat, they'd made it through the plane ride with only the puking at the end after they landed.

He jostled a sleepy Sean who was leaning drowsily on him as he searched his pocket for his keys.

"Hey, you," he said as he balanced Sean between his shoulder and the wall.

Sean blinked heavy eyes. "Hey you, back."

Rusty stuck his key into the lock, pushed open the door and shoved their bags through with his foot so he didn't have to let go of Sean.

Sean pushed himself off the wall. "Did you have a good time?"

Rusty's emotions flashed through a hundred gyrations. Overall, "Good things happened."

Sean squeezed his hand. "Yeah, they did."

"You know what I want to do?"

"What's that?"

"Strip you, then strip me. Then, we're going to walk naked around our apartment while I fix you something with a lot of caffeine in it."

"Yeah?"

"Yeah. Just because we can. Because we're home."

Sean blinked, trying to clear the sleep from his eyes as he stumbled through the door behind Rusty, closing it firmly behind them. "Then what?"

"Take a long, hot, warm, soapy Christmas shower with you. No sister to pound on the door. No guests waiting downstairs. Just you and me, naked as the day we were born."

"That sounds wonderful." Sean jiggled the knob to make sure they were safely locked in. "And then?"

"Then, we're going to fall onto our big soft, sturdy bed."

"And then?"

"And then I'm going to make your Christmas very, very merry."

Coat unbuttoned and thrown across the couch, Sean started on his shirt buttons. "God rest ye merry gentlemen?"

"Who said anything about rest. Baby, I'm gonna jingle your bells." Dropping to his knees, Rusty started on Sean's jeans zipper. Looking up, he said, "And Sean?"

"Hmmm?" The look in his eyes said the Benadryl was burning off fast.

"Visiting is good, but it's even better to be home."

Home.

Rusty meant that with every nuance of the word. "This is my home."

"Our home, baby. Our home."

For Better Or Worse

CHAPTER ONE

Sean wrote it again, this time without the flourishes. *Sean Duchene.*

Just three days away, Sean Delahunt would be no more. No. He would be *more.*

Taking on Rusty's name, dropping Delahunt forever and becoming Sean Duchene, seemed big, as big as their impending wedding. Maybe even bigger.

He wrote it again. *Sean Duchene.* This time he emphasized the **S** and the **D** like he'd never done before. Made them take up space on the paper. Just like Rusty made him feel like he had the right to take up space in the world.

With each stroke of the pen, he concentrated on letting go of himself and letting Rusty in. On opening himself up—for possible pain. But, it also opened him for a deeper joy, a warmer and safer world than he'd ever lived in.

Knowing it and letting it happen were two different things.

The kitchen table wobbled with the force of his pen. But then, it wobbled with the slightest of provocation.

Now that his student loans were taken care of, they had talked of shopping for new furniture. But the secondhand furniture he and Rusty had scavenged along with the hand-me-downs they'd trucked from Rusty's parents' house in New Orleans to their own place in Boston's South End made the place feel like a well-lived-in home instead of a tiny, uber-expensive apartment.

He and Rusty both loved where they lived, surrounded by friends.

From the bedroom, Rusty's voice carried a note of worry. "But you'll be here in time, right?"

Crap. Rusty's whole family was on the road, traveling up from New Orleans for the wedding. Calling it The Grand Wedding Adventure, his mom, dad, grandparents, siblings, nephew and Sean's sister were all caravaning from New Orleans to Boston in two huge rented vans. Hotel arrangements for that many were out of everyone's budget so he and Rusty had spread them out among friends so they all had a place to stay.

Had something gone wrong?

When Rusty let out a happy whoop, Sean took a relieved breath.

Hearing Rusty say, "No, Dad. With Mom in charge, I'm not worried at all. Sounds like she's got a plan," made Sean relax his grinding jaw which left behind a tension headache.

Rusty's outgoing laugh had always overshadowed Sean's tentative smile. He had both hated and been grateful for the shield of Rusty's big, happy personality.

Sean traced the engraving on the front of the Thank You note for the wedding gift that he was supposed to be writing.

Theater tickets. Rusty and he had great friends. He was still proud of himself that he'd reached out first, making his way into the social circle during those months Rusty had been back in New Orleans.

This was so different than it had been during grade school and high school when Rusty had paved the way for both of them. He hadn't been liked because he was with Rusty, but because his new friends liked him for himself this time.

Living in Boston, just the two of them, Sean had never been happier in his whole life than he was now. And Rusty was finally happy about being here, too, or at least he was getting that way.

What would Rusty say when Sean told him this might all go away? What would he say when Sean confessed how bad he'd fucked up?

No matter what, Rusty would still marry him. That's the kind of guy Rusty was.

That certainty was the only thing that kept him from puking when his worries made his gut burn.

But should he ask it of Rusty? Rusty had been through so much for Sean, had sacrificed so much for him.

God, he hated feeling so grateful—and so damned vulnerable.

A noise from the bedroom had him curling around the notebook he'd used to document all their wedding plans as if keeping the paper safe would keep their future safe.

He looked down at his scribblings and smirked with embarrassment then tore out the page he'd written his married name on, like he'd torn out all the others he'd practiced on.

He felt like a high school kid—in fact he'd done this same thing during high school, keeping it secret like he was doing now.

That's what he did with all the big things in his life. Kept them secret. Kept them safe. Kept himself safe—from ridicule. From criticism. And sometimes, from physical harm.

He flexed his sore muscles under the guise of stretching. Even though he'd been working out, his swimmer's body would probably never bulk up. But he had Rusty to keep him safe.

Somehow, that didn't make him feel any better. Relying on someone, even the man he loved more than anyone else in the whole world, made him feel weak, like a leach who couldn't take care of himself.

It didn't help that Rusty had said the same thing about leaving behind a solid career to follow Sean, yet he'd done it. He'd trusted Sean to keep them financially safe. And now....

Fuck. He'd made such a mess of everything.

"Whatcha doing?" Rusty's voice over Sean's shoulder had him jumping.

The man he'd loved since Sean knew what love was lay a hand on his shoulder.

Sean consciously made himself relax into that hand. He picked up the balled up paper and smoothed it out so Rusty could see it. Trying to make himself sound nonchalant, he answered, "Just practicing."

Reverently, Rusty traced the looping script. Then he leaned down and wrapped Sean's shoulders in a hug, his breath warm on Sean's neck.

"Do you know how much I love you?" His voice was thick with emotion.

Rusty never held back. Never kept any part of himself from Sean. The desire, the need to give himself to Rusty like Rusty gave to him was so big it hurt.

So much for keeping himself safe from pain. And, in this case, from guilt.

Rusty had never asked for or expected more than Sean could give.

He breathed in the scent of Rusty and did the best he could. "Yeah, I do. I know you love me."

The hard squeeze Rusty gave him told him that Rusty understood. Claiming love, feeling worthy of being loved—he was trying. Trying so hard.

Swallowing, Sean shoved the Thank You note over to the empty chair beside him. "Love me enough to write these out?"

Rusty faked a hard shudder. "How about I love you enough that I cleaned the bathroom all by myself, instead?"

After last night's shaving cream wars that bathroom had been pretty nasty.

Sean shifted, thinking of the manscaping he'd given Rusty. The play was new for them, inspired by a gay romance book he'd been reading while Rusty studied. It seemed, the closer their wedding day came, the hornier and more adventurous Rusty became. Sean wasn't complaining. Although he was a little worried that this was more about reassurance than anticipation of their public forever vows.

"Fair enough." He pulled the note card back in front of him then let his eyes drift down. "How are you feeling?"

"Code word for, have you recovered enough from last night?" Rusty grinned. "I'm fine. A little breezy." Then he frowned, but his eyes still twinkled. "Just remember your promise when it starts to prickle."

"Trust me. I won't forget. I promise to keep an eye out for stubble. Wouldn't want you uncomfortable."

Rusty shifted, adjusting himself. "You didn't seem to mind whether I was comfortable or not last night."

"You didn't either. I'm just glad the neighbors are out of town."

Rusty seemed to consider, rubbing his hand down to his crotch. "They aren't coming back until tonight. Isn't reciprocation part of a marriage?"

Sean was pushing back his chair and grabbing for Rusty's hand before Rusty finished his sentence. His tongue felt thick and clumsy as he said, "I'm pretty sure, yeah."

Rusty leaned in close and said deep and low, "And you're more flexible than I am."

After all these years, Sean still lost his breath when Rusty whispered like that in his ear.

"Yeah." Sean didn't know what he was agreeing to, but it didn't really matter. With Rusty, he'd agree to anything, anywhere. Take a risk and let go.

"Yeah," he said again, feeling all his worries get fuzzy around the edges. A different kind of tension took hold of him as Rusty tugged at the hem of his shirt.

Rusty lay back, more asleep than awake, as Sean ran fingers over bare skin that had never been bare before. Even in his fuck-dumb state, Sean's touch sent tingles through him, making him jerk involuntarily every few seconds.

That Sean hadn't rolled over and gone to sleep, taking advantage of nature's sedative, meant he needed to talk. Rare as that happened, Rusty had learned a long time ago he needed to pay attention.

He roused himself enough to say, "That's gonna itch like a bitch in a day or two." It came out more as a thick-tongued mumble instead of real speech.

"I thought you said we could keep it this way. I thought you liked it." Apparently Sean had no trouble interpreting what Rusty had grumbled. After all, Sean had had years of practice.

Rusty thought about Sean's reply. Thought about what led up to the shaving experiment, what followed it, and felt himself begin to wake under the brush of Sean's knuckle.

"Yeah. We could. I did." He breathed out, pleased that he now sounded more like a human than a dog gargling oatmeal.

Just as he was getting into Sean stroking him there, Sean dropped his hand and lay still, staring at the ceiling and breathing.

It was coming. Whatever he wanted to talk about was trying to surface. Rusty just had to be patient and not twitch. It was a true test of will power.

Part of Rusty wanted to roll over and make Sean forget what brewed inside him. Remind him they should take advantage of their youth while they still had it. Recovery would take longer the older a man got, his dad always said.

That idea died when Sean sat up and neatly replaced the pillows along the headboard. If his need for order wasn't hint enough, Sean then straightened the sheets, giving a clear sign that this would be a pretty intense conversation. But it would happen in Sean's own time. Patience. Rusty willed himself to relax and think. Whatever worried Sean, Rusty needed to have the right words to allay Sean's fears.

Rusty let his mind drift to the man who always had the answers.

Not for the first time, Rusty wondered how his dad did it. Talked so normally, without hesitation about guy stuff like sex to his gay son just like he did to his straight sons.

It's not like they had a lot of gay family members Dad could have practiced on. Although Mom had mentioned that she thought maybe her older brother might have leaned toward gay but the sixties hadn't been a good time to come out. Her brother had been killed in the Viet Nam war, so they'd never know.

When Rusty was almost twelve and had found the words for why he was different, he'd asked his dad if he or Mom had regretted that their late-in-life surprise kid was gay. His dad had teared up and held him so tight he could hardly breathe, said Rusty was God's gift to them and he was perfect just the way he was made to be. His dad had said he couldn't have asked for a better Rusty than the one he got.

That feeling of security, of being okay, of being whole, had carried him through so much shit, even through his teen years which weren't as fun as his brothers' or sister's had been.

Thank God, and his dad. That wholeness had also helped him carry Sean through more pain than any one man should ever have to survive.

Now, if he could figure out how to make Sean okay....

On cue, Sean said into the darkness, "Rusty?"

"Yeah, babe?"

"I made a big mistake."

"Yeah?" Rusty circled his big toe along Sean's ankle and waited.

"Yeah." Sean shifted, moving his leg away then back again, ending up with his thigh almost, but not quite, touching Rusty's. "I'm screwing up at work."

Rusty closed the gap, hip to hip, and shoved his arm under Sean's shoulders pulling him closer. Holding was so much easier than words, especially when Sean's words frightened him.

They lived on Sean's salary. Rusty's odd jobs only made enough to take care of weekend partying expenses and the occasional trip to the grocery store. Having worked for his dad in the family business, Rusty had no idea how big corporations worked. Had no advice to give. Didn't even know how to reassure Sean.

What would happen if....

"Do you think you're gonna get fired?"

Sean shrugged against Rusty's arm. "My manager and the department director both keep coming to me, asking me about the specs I've been verifying, asking about labor hours I've been estimating. I spent all afternoon today in accounting while the senior accountant drilled me about where my numbers came from and how they fit into the overall budget."

"Drilled you? Like he thought you were stealing or something?"

In the dark, Sean's head rubbed against Rusty's shoulder. "More like he thought I was an idiot."

"Did you understand everything he asked about? Did you know the answers to his questions?"

"Yeah, I did. But the guy kinda smirked and then he said, 'I heard you're getting married. And changing your name, too. Why are you doing that?'"

"How did he know that?"

"I turned in the paperwork last week. Since the next pay period, we'll be married, I guess it made it's way to payroll."

Rusty fished around until he found Sean's hand, then threaded his fingers through Sean's, pressing against Sean's ring.

"What did you say?"

"That my reasons were personal."

The firmness in Sean's voice was in direct contrast to the doubt Rusty had been hearing.

"Did he say anything more?"

"No. He seemed to back off after that."

"You must have given him the stare."

"The stare?"

"That look you have that says 'if you cross this line you're going to regret it.'"

"I don't have a stare."

"Yeah, you do." Rusty rubbed his big toe up and down Sean's calf, so proud that this man was his, heart, soul and body. "You've only turned it on me twice. Both times, I was glad when you finally blinked."

"I don't know what you're talking about." Sean captured Rusty's fingers that had been circling, peaking Sean's nipple without a lot of thought on Rusty's part. "Are you trying to distract me?"

More like comfort myself. Rusty kept that thought to himself as he tried to decide whether he would ask the big question looming over them or literally bury his head under the covers.

No way in hell would Sean ever want to move back to New Orleans. Jobless, homeless—under those conditions, Rusty wasn't sure he did, either. What choice would they have? Rusty would have a job there, could take care of them there.

But Sean hated being taken care of. And now that Rusty had had a taste of it himself, he totally understood why. Self-confidence. Pride. Without it, how could any man be okay with himself?

God, this silence was heavy. He should say something. But what?

As he had hoped, Sean took that decision away when Sean turned on his side to look into Rusty's eyes. "Tomorrow, I'm being sent to the job site of another engineer's project. Her project is further along than mine. I'll be there for one of her inspections. I don't know if this means my project is being taken from me and I'll be assisting her, or—. I just don't know what it means."

Rusty ran his hand down Sean's shoulder to his fingertips then rested it on Sean's hip, needing the contact. He was at a loss to help.

If he'd screwed up working for his dad, they'd discussed it over supper if it was a little mistake, privately in the truck if it was a big one. But he'd always known he was never in danger of losing his job.

As usual, he stalled long enough that he didn't have to say anything. Sean's deep sigh was the clue he was about to talk more, for which Rusty was grateful because he had nothing.

"I'll be diving tomorrow for the inspection."

Rusty tried to keep his voice calm. "What? It's cold out there."

"I've got the right equipment, plus, I've trained for it when I got my rescue certification."

"That was a long time ago."

"Not that long ago."

"But you haven't done it since then, have you?"

"It will be okay. I won't be diving alone. Bob Frazier, the recruiter who hired me, and the R&D department's vice president are going down with me."

"Are they good divers?"

"I don't know about the VP. But Bob and I talked diving at the interview and when we ran into each other at the dive shop. He seems to know what he's talking about. I've seen his dive card and he's a certified rescue diver like I am."

"What about the project engineer? Why doesn't she do it instead?"

The petting hand Sean rubbed on Rusty's stomach didn't settle Rusty at all.

"I don't know. I didn't ask. I'm not really in a position to protest, you know?" The excitement in Sean's voice totally overruled the way he was trying to downplay this dive. That protest about maybe being fired sounded like a tacked on excuse. Instead of placating Rusty, Sean's flimsy rationalization made him mad.

Rusty raised up on one elbow. "You want to do this, don't you?"

"Yeah." Sean sat, that non-negotiable look making itself known in the way he crossed his arms and held his jaw. "Hell, yeah. If I'm going to get fired, at least I'll have an awesome experience to take away with me."

"I hate it when you dive." He hated it when he sounded sulky, too, but nothing short of Rusty's best emotional manipulation would stop Sean when he made up his mind.

Rusty took a deep breath. This situation wasn't life or death—no matter how scary diving seemed to him—and didn't warrant deliberately twisting Sean's emotions until he gave in.

"You'll be careful?"

"Of course."

"And call me as soon as you're done?"

"I'll text you as soon as I can. But I'll be working, so I can't promise when."

Sean was meticulous in being honest and truthful. Sometimes, Rusty wished he wasn't. Like now. He wished Sean had kept the dive to himself until it was over.

No, he didn't really wish that. Honest and truthful. It was a vow they made to each other a long time ago. Whenever one of them broke it, life was not good for too long afterward. Experience had taught them both that forgiveness was harder and more painful than keeping their promises to start with.

"I don't like this, but—well, you do know what you're doing. So I hope you have a good time with it." His tone wasn't as supportive as he'd tried for, but it was the best he could do.

It must have been good enough because Sean leaned into him, whispering "Thanks," just before he covered Rusty's mouth, deep-kissing him until Rusty couldn't think of anything but Sean's mouth stealing his breath away. Sean's hands lighting up his skin. Sean. His world.

There was no time. No worries. Only now and Sean.

After Sean got finished with him, Rusty was mellowed enough to think of nothing but cuddling in and letting sleep happen.

CHAPTER TWO

Rusty took another look at his phone. Afternoon and still no text from Sean yet. He hadn't thought to ask what time Sean thought he might be making his dive.

But the text from his oldest brother made him grind his teeth even harder.

His maternal grandmother's mutt, Cindy-poo, or Poo as they all called the stinky, yappy, little frayed mop head, had caused them to take a break every time they came across a highway rest stop.

'We're getting further behind schedule, but don't worry. Dad says he'll chunk that damned dog out the window if he has to, to get us there before he misses anything.'

They had already stopped hours early yesterday at a dog-friendly motel that smelled like day old shrimp instead of pushing on.

With a sour stomach Rusty clicked on the job description for mail room clerk. No experience required. It was on the bus route so he added it to his growing list.

He'd never wanted an inside job. Never wanted to dress for work, put up with office politics. Never wanted....

He took the last swallow of the beer he'd opened right after lunch when he'd made his decision.

If Sean was going to get fired, maybe Rusty could make enough with a day job to stretch the budget until Sean found another one. He hoped to find one that didn't interfere with his part-time theater work, but if it did, *c'est la vie.* At least that was the attitude he would try to have.

Grabbing another beer from the fridge, he downed a quarter of the bottle in one big gulp, trying to drown out the desperation he felt as he read through the ads, trying to drown out the despair he and Sean had both lived through when Sean had job-hunted after graduation, trying to drown out his very strong desire to pick up the phone and ask his dad for the job that was his for the taking back in New Orleans.

Because Boston was home now. Sean was happy here. *He* was happy here.

They had great friends who knew them as the men they were, not as they boys they used to be.

Other couples coped with job losses. It was part of life. They could handle it. They could handle anything together.

Clichéd words. Brave words. If only he could make them true words.

But the doubts had him clenching his fists to keep from hurling their laptop across the room.

Thankfully, his phone started playing the baby cry ringtone that meant his upstairs neighbor was calling.

"Hey, Jody, what's up?"

"I know you're busy with wedding plans and all, but can you babysit? Just for an hour or so? Carter will be home as soon as his class is out."

Rusty glanced at his watch. Carter wouldn't be done with classes for at least an hour and a half and then there was the commute. But watching over four-year-old Elizabeth would be a nice distraction.

"Sure. Your place or mine?" He said it with a leer, needing the light flirtation he knew Jody would give him.

"Mine, sweetheart. And wear something comfortable."

"Comfortable?"

"Yeah." Jody used his best sexy drawl. "And washable."

"Washable, huh?" Rusty grabbed his keys from the bowl on the kitchen table and headed for the door.

"Uh-huh. Think glitter and glue. Oh, and you might have to wear a tiara."

The teasing loosened the knot in Rusty's chest. Or maybe it was the aftereffects of the beers. "Whatever it takes."

Rusty heard a squeal in the background then a squeaky little voice said into the phone, "Rusty, Jody said you were coming to play with me."

"I'm on my way, beautiful." Phone in hand, not breaking the connection, he ran the flight of stairs taking him to Jody and Carter's floor. The exercise felt good, reminding him he should do more of it. But Boston winters....

"Daddy says brilliant is better than beautiful."

"As usual, Daddy's right, Lizard Breath," he huffed.

Little girl giggling filled his ear. "Not Lizard Breath."

"Baby breath?" He knocked on Jody's door.

Jody opened the door and Elizabeth rushed through to wrap herself around his legs. "Big girl breath."

Jody held the door wide "More like Dr. Pepper breath."

"You fed her sugar? Thanks, man." Rusty grimaced at Jody as he caught up Elizabeth in his arms. He made chomping sounds on her neck. "Does that make you sweet, like candy?"

She held up her glittery hands. "And sparkly like a fairy princess."

Jody shrugged. "She'll crash soon."

As Elizabeth snuggled into Rusty's neck, the innocent smell of her baby shampoo made him smile. He and Sean hadn't talked about it, but he hoped, now that they were officially getting married, maybe....

Hell, what was he thinking? He didn't even know how they would feed each other right now, much less a child.

Elizabeth kicked, leaning back so Rusty had to tighten his grip.

Eyeball to eyeball, she pat his face to make sure he was paying attention. "Wanna see the picture I'm making for you and Sean?"

Over his shoulder, Jody waved a silent goodbye, sneaking out to avoid Elizabeth's separation meltdown.

"Sure." He held onto her, taking her into their spacious kitchen until he heard the front door click then set her down in her booster chair. Quickly, he asked about the sparkling, glue-covered mess she had been working on to distract her.

If only he could be distracted from his problems so easily.

Sean tried to cover his anxiety as Bob Frazier explained that the vice-president had come down with a sinus infection so he couldn't dive.

"So, it's just you and me, kid." Bob gave him an apologetic smile. "I'm a great dive buddy, but I won't be any help at all with the inspection. If it's a resume' you need evaluated or company benefits you need explained, I'm your man. But I don't know anything about welding joints."

"I've got that part covered." Sean didn't have to fake confidence in that area. His dive buddies in New Orleans had been mostly off-shore oil field welders who taught diving on the side and had let Sean tag alone for free as long as he helped with the students. He'd seen more than one example and heard more than one rant about shoddy work.

"We don't expect any trouble. We've subcontracted with this firm for a while now. Signing off is just a formality. But we like to check all the boxes, you know?"

Mindless box checking was the major complaint his buddies had about engineers who overlooked crucial inspection points. Still, Sean nodded, not feeling right about giving a safety lecture to a man who'd worked for the company a lot longer than he had.

"Ready?"

"Ready." Sean pulled his mask into place and flipped in before the frigid air temperature turned his lips blue.

The water was much, much colder than in the Gulf, but he'd known that going in and carefully watched his time as well as paid attention to his body temperature.

The foreman of the welding crew made the inspection challenging. He tried to keep Sean's attention on the port side of the ship so long that Sean would have to make a hasty inspection of the rear and aft side to keep within his diving limits. But Sean waved him off, took his photos, and moved on to the next weld, not letting the foreman take the lead.

Before he was done with the inspection, he'd reached his personal temp limit and did have to do a hasty job to finish up, but he'd seen enough to know that what he'd missed didn't matter overall.

Once again on land, he was first to hit the work trailer's changing area and peel off his dive suit while Bob and the foreman chatted about the dive and the project in general. Freezing, he poured himself a cup of hot water and mixed in a packet of chocolate, doing his best not to shiver in front of the welding crew who worked in these conditions all winter long and seemed immune to the temperature.

While waiting on the others to change, Sean fiddled with his camera, rotating through his shots to find the ones he wanted while he waited for the right moment to talk to Bob.

Once the foreman and his men were distracted with pouring their coffee, Sean motioned Bob back into the scant privacy of the changing area.

Conscious of the open door, he softly said, "I can't sign off. Those welds aren't right."

Neutrally, Bob asked, "You've got the photos to back that up?"

"Yes, I do." He set down his mug to scroll across the camera display, showing Bob the two dozen cold cracking welds he'd found.

Bob stuffed his hands in his pockets, glanced at the foreman waiting for them inside the office portion of the poorly heated work trailer and frowned. "I don't know what I'm looking at."

"I do."

If he was going to lose his job, it wasn't because he did the wrong thing here.

He wanted--*he craved*--Rusty. Rusty would know the perfect tone and words to get his point across and leave no hard feelings. But Sean was coming up blank in the diplomacy department.

Bob studied him for a few moments, while Sean forced himself not to squirm.

Finally, Bob blinked. "This is all yours, Sean. I'm behind you all the way."

Sean met Bob's eyes, trying to read if Bob really had his back or not. "Dragging this out isn't going to make it any easier."

Bob slapped his shoulder. "You're the engineer. It's your call."

It didn't matter what Bob thought. Sean had a responsibility here. He squared his shoulders and nodded. "Let's do this."

The foreman looked up as Sean approached. Maybe Sean was projecting, but he could swear he saw a sneer in the guy's expression before the man shoved the sign-off sheet across the desk toward him. "Cold business if you're not used to it, especially for a little guy like you. I imagine you're ready to get this over with and go home."

Behind him, a welder poured a cup of coffee and stirred in powdered cream. He stopped stirring, looked straight at Sean and grinned, the kind of grin that had taught Sean to watch his back and to not get caught by himself in the restrooms during high school. "I hope your wife has a warm supper waiting on you tonight."

Another welder joined him, same grin on his face. "How do you know he's got a wife?"

The first guy took the bait like they'd done this routine before. "He's wearing a ring, ain't he?"

Back to the second guy. "Ring don't mean he's married to a girl, though, does it?"

Without looking back, attention drilled on Sean, the foreman thumped his pen on the paper. "He could be married to a damned goat for all I care, as long as he signs this paper."

Sean set his chocolate down on the desk, no longer feeling cold. In fact, he felt nothing. "I'm not signing it."

The pen stopped thumping. "What do you mean?"

"There's a problem with a lot of those welds."

"Problem?"

"Yeah. Problem. They're cold cracking." Sean held out his camera display.

The second guy raised his eyebrow. "Learned that term in school, did you?"

Ignoring him, Sean spoke directly to the foreman. "I'll hand over my results to the project manager and she'll follow up with where we go from here."

The first guy came over, coffee mug between his two hands, and crowded next to Sean, presumably to see the display. But he didn't even glance down.

"How long you been welding, boy?" He stood close enough that Sean smelled the coffee on his breath when he spoke.

Bob stepped up, literally bumping into Sean's back. "He knows what he's talking about. We've already emailed the photos in."

That last part was a lie, but Sean just nodded.

Bob might be trying to help, but all he'd done was box Sean in between the desk, the wall and the other guy. Claustrophobic didn't begin to describe how Sean felt.

The last time he'd had such a hard time catching his breath was when his father....

This was chicken shit. He hadn't been that scared sixteen-year-old in a long time.

Sean tucked his camera in his coat pocket. "We're done here."

Despite the way the guy with the coffee blocked him, Sean moved toward the door, leading with his elbow. That he jostled the man hard enough to make him spill his coffee wasn't an action Sean regretted in the least.

The guy took a step back, giving Sean enough room to squeeze between him and the desk. Behind him, he heard shuffling as Bob created more room to make his own escape.

Neither he nor Bob spoke until they were back in Bob's company car. Even then, Bob took his time cranking up the car and putting on his seatbelt before he said, "Remind me to never make you mad."

"Huh?" Sean was pushing the tab of his own seatbelt into the catch, willing his hands to quit shaking. Whether from anger or fear was anyone's guess. He certainly couldn't have told them.

"The look on your face--. Perfectly, intimidatingly confident." Bob held his hands in front of the warming air vents, studying his fingers instead of looking over at Sean. "Calm and cool, like you stood up to bullies every day of your life."

Sean tightened his mouth, not about to admit how true that had been for a while. But Rusty had saved him from all that. Rusty and the whole Duchene family. They had shown him what being safe felt like.

Sean shrugged. "It's all part of the job, huh?"

Bob twisted in his seat to look Sean firmly in the eye. "No. No, it isn't. Not working for this company, it's not." He rubbed his hand over his face, looking bleak. "This answers why Melissa wanted to be pulled from this project, though. It would have helped knowing what we were going into. She should have—but that's a discussion her manager will have with her. I'll put in the paperwork to officially file a complaint about the foreman and those two welders of his. Before I send it, I'd like you to read over it to catch anything I might miss."

"Yeah, sure."

"Those idiots. Didn't they know what their behavior would mean to their jobs?"

Sean bit at his bottom lip until he realized what he was doing. "Actually, they were pretty clever. Taken word-for-word, they didn't really say anything threatening or offensive."

"Well, take my word for it. I was offended and feeling pretty damned threatened, too." Bob slammed the steering wheel. "Damn it, this shouldn't happen in today's workplace."

The PFLAG card Sean had seen fall from Bob's wallet when he'd seen Bob's dive card clued him in that this might be more personal than professional. He felt compelled to comfort Bob, assure him that everything was all right. But he had nothing. The silence grew heavier and heavier, passing into grossly uncomfortable.

Not able to think, just needing to break the oppressive mood, Sean blurted what was topmost on his mind. "If it had been just me without you here as a witness, if I had filed a report on what had been said, would Oceanic take any action? Maybe mark me down as a whiner or a troublemaker?"

There you go, Sean. Challenge the company's ethics. If you aren't already on the short list out the door, this will put you there.

Bob blinked, as if pulled from his dark thoughts but the frown he gave Sean wasn't much better.

"I'm ashamed to say that I'm not sure." Bob rubbed his hands along the steering wheel, flexing his fingers. "Our HR department head is, well, old-fashioned." He barked out a bitter laugh. "Old-fashioned. That's putting it too kindly."

Sean stared directly ahead out the windshield, too aware of the tension radiating from Bob, too uneasy to do anything but try to be invisible.

Beside him, Bob took a deep breath and slowly let it out.

The atmosphere dropped several levels of intensity allowing Sean to take his own deep breath.

"Well." Bob settled into his seat and gave Sean a tight smile. "I let that run away with me, didn't I?"

Sean was never good in emotional situations like this one.

Maybe he *was* the emo-king of the world, but he usually did it quietly, except around Rusty. God, he wished Rusty was here right now. Better yet, he wished he was anywhere but here with Rusty's arms around him, kissing that tender spot half way between Rusty's neck and ear, taking comfort in the scent so unique to his man.

Even the thought of Rusty helped Sean find his balance.

He forced out an answering grin to Bob's clenched smile. "I don't think either of us expected this inspection to go the way it did."

"But you handled it perfectly. Professionally and with integrity."

"Thanks."

With a nod of recognition, Bob put the car in gear and pulled out of the parking lot. The rest of the trip quietly blurred like the scenery outside Sean's passenger window. Thankfully, Bob didn't feel the need to make conversation even as he and Sean took the elevator to their separate office floors.

Once at his desk, Sean download the photos from his camera to his PC, saved a copy on his private partition on the company's server and added them to his thumb drive for good measure. Then he booted down, locked up and headed home along with the old timers who rarely felt the need to stay late and impress.

Sean had done all the impressing he could stand for one day. He took a moment to text Rusty, 'The dive went fine. I'll be home early tonight.' He'd been putting in some extra time at the end of the day, making sure he was on top of things. But tonight, screw it. He needed Rusty.

What he really needed was to screw Rusty. Too aware he was surrounded by coworkers, Sean bit back his punch-drunk grin.

The woman next to him exited the elevator, throwing out a politely indifferent, "Have a nice evening."

"Thanks. I intend to." Thinking about letting down his guard, sinking into the couch, snuggling against Rusty, breathing in the scent of his man while mindlessly watching TV gave him the energy to keep from dragging his feet as he made his way home.

Compulsively, Rusty swiveled his attention from the clock, his empty text message queue and the macaroni and cheese he stirred for Elizabeth.

Where was Carter? Rusty didn't mind babysitting, but today, of all days, he'd received an emergency call from The Cabaret. Someone had tried to move some sets and had tipped them over and broken them. Could he come and fix them before tonight's show?

He'd said yes, of course. Not only had the owners offered to pay well, they were personal friends.

But now, Carter was running late.

And Rusty wanted to be home and have a nice supper fixed to coax Sean to give him the real scoop on his day.

And then there was his family, too many miles away when he wanted them right here, right now.

His sister had texted. They were stopping for the night. They would be a whole day late.

There was nothing he could do to make Carter show up any sooner. Nor could he make his family arrive on time.

Aaaaagh!

Elizabeth came up and gave his calves a hug, making him stand still when he would rather keep shifting his weight to keep himself from taking off at a full out run to nowhere.

"What's wrong, Rusty?"

He plastered on a plastic smile and fake tone. "Nothing to worry about, Lizard Breath. Just grownup stuff."

God, he wished he wasn't a grownup right now.

"When I'm a grownup, everyone will do what I tell them to so I don't get mad at them."

He regarded the thirty pound, midnight-haired cherub with the big gray eyes who was unapologetically standing on his foot. "I believe you will, Lizard Breath. I believe you will."

The rattle of a key in the door dialed his anxiety level down a half a click.

"Honey, I'm home." Carter sounded happy. At least someone on Rusty's intimate circle was. Happy wasn't always easy for Carter so this was an added bonus.

Rusty called from the kitchen, "I'm not your honey, but I'm glad you're here."

Carter joined him. He and Rusty were about the same height and size, but Carter always felt bigger.

Now, as Carter looked over his shoulder, the man felt looming.

Jody might like it, but it made Rusty feel damned uncomfortable.

"Daddy!" Elizabeth transfered her body from Rusty's legs to Carter's.

With an exaggerated groan, probably to cover up his real groan, Carter bent and lifted Elizabeth. "How's my best girl?"

"I'm brilliant, Daddy. And beautiful, too."

"That's my girl."

A deep longing hit him hard.

Now, with Sean's job in jeopardy, was not the time to bring up kids—which meant Rusty would probably blurt it out the second Sean came in the door.

Involuntarily, Rusty found himself glancing at the clock. "Now that you're home—"

"Where's Jody?" Carter interrupted.

"Didn't say. Just asked if I could babysit until you got here."

"Daddy, you're squeezing me." Elizabeth patted Carter's jaw that suddenly looked made of granite.

"Sorry, sugar beet." He stooped to put her down.

Just what Rusty needed to add to his fraying nerves, his best friends' relationship problems escalating.

Why couldn't everyone just play nice?

Looking at the door, Rusty put his escape plan into action. "I gotta go. See you tomorrow?"

"When's your family coming in?"

"Not until Friday. They've had some delays."

"Shit happens." Carter grimaced down at Elizabeth who was grinning up at him, silently repeating what he'd said. "Not a word for you, young lady."

She changed from imp to old soul in a blink. "I know, Daddy. I'm only allowed to say 'stuff happens.'"

Rusty nodded in agreement forcing another smile. If he kept doing this, his face would eventually start to morph into total pain, he was sure. "Yeah, stuff happens."

Carter put his hand on Rusty's shoulder, a gesture that meant more because Carter wasn't the touchy-feeling type. "One breath at a time."

Again, like a bobble head, Rusty nodded. He heard it all the time in Sean's therapy sessions. He really couldn't handle platitudes today.

"Yeah, thanks." Maybe being courteous would make up for being less than sincere.

By the cynical twist of Carter's lips, Rusty knew he hadn't pulled it off. But Carter gave the polite response. "No, man. Thank *you* for watching the rug rat for me—for us."

"Any time." Another canned response. God, he hated this plastic cycle. But he couldn't seem to pull himself out of it. Instead, he turned and headed for the door, closing all that meaninglessness behind.

A glance at his watch showed he would barely have time to feed his hard-working man much less interrogate him.

Aaagh!

"Breakfast for supper, the ultimate quick comfort food." Rusty had been trying to make light conversation ever since he'd burst through the door, yelling that his parents were running late because of Cindy-poo, he was running late because of Carter and would Sean please go with him tonight to The Cabaret.

Sean had wanted to go nowhere but to bed after the day he'd had but one long look at Rusty showed him that Rusty looked like he needed the comforting as much as Sean did.

"Uh-huh." Sean's stomach churned from the scrambled eggs and toast Rusty watched him put into his mouth and chew.

Rusty took a glance at his watch. "We're making good time ourselves. We've got a few minute before we need to leave."

"It's a nice night to walk over as long as we bundle up."

"All these layers of clothes. I don't know if I'll ever get used to winters in Boston."

Maybe you won't have to. Sean couldn't say it out loud without choking. Instead, he picked up his glass of milk but didn't drink from it. The milk would probably sour on his stomach before the night was out.

Rusty swiped his plate clean with his own piece of toast. "Well?"

"Well?" Sean echoed back, knowing he wouldn't get away with it, but stalling nonetheless. Pre-counseling, Rusty never pushed. He missed those days.

No. No, he didn't. Despite all the pain he'd had to dredge up, he was a better man for Rusty because of it.

He took a breath then finished his thought—*a better man for himself, too.*

Someday, being okay about himself would come easier. He promised himself that.

The corner of Rusty's mouth tightened. "You're all uptight. The corner of your eyes are squinty, like you've got a headache. Tell me."

Sean sighed, not bothering to hide it from Rusty. Even if this way was uncomfortable, it was better.

"I wouldn't sign off on the job this morning. The contractor gave me some push back."

By the way Rusty's neck muscles strained, Sean could tell his defender was ready to go kick some ass. Instead, Rusty clenched his glass of milk, took a controlled sip, then asked. "What kind of push back?"

"Just some attitude. Nothing happened." And that was the simple truth. The same truth that the contractor would tell upper management should Sean file a complaint. Not that he intended to file a complaint.

He'd put up with crap all his life. Now was not the time to start acting like a whiny baby. He had his dignity, after all.

Had Bob let it drop? After a good night's sleep, probably. What else was there to do?

As soon as Sean choked down enough eggs to spread the rest across his plate and pass Rusty's inspection, he put down his fork. "You've run into plenty of contractors with attitude before. You know it's not a big deal."

"I know it can be." Rusty stared at Sean, burning a hole into him until Sean returned his eye contact. "I was required to report any kind of shit like that to my dad."

"Yeah, but that's because he's your dad." A twinge of remorse at his snark twisted Sean's stomach even more. This conversation was going past uncomfortable into a place Sean didn't want it to go. His backhanded gig about nepotism was neither nice, nor true.

Before he could apologize, Rusty countered with, "*Every* employee was required to let upper management know about problems on the job, especially slights, both personal and professional."

Rusty took a breath and reached across their small table to put his hand over Sean's. "Sean? Do you know why you should report this?"

No. He didn't want to hear this. Sean fought the inclination to pull away, to slam out the door, to get away from the intensity in Rusty's eyes. His need to not hurt Rusty with his rejection won out so he steeled himself for whatever Rusty was about to say.

Rusty squeezed Sean's hand until Sean squeezed back. "Tell me."

"Because you're worthy of respect." The way Rusty's voice was so tender and gentle made Sean's throat swell.

No.

He blinked, hating that his emotions were so close to the surface now. Before the move to Boston and the new job, before all the changes he and Rusty had been through in the last months, he'd been able to swallow down his feelings. He'd been so good at it, he'd done it without noticing the mental action. Without noticing the internal pain.

But now, he felt like—like a turtle without its shell. Exposed, soft and vulnerable.

Not at all how a man was supposed to feel.

Before his meal came back up again, he lean forward and raised Rusty's hand to his lips, kissed it to soften the disconnect, then ran for the bathroom.

Avoiding looking at himself in the mirror, he rid himself of the taste of comfort food gone wrong by carefully brushing his teeth followed by a swig of mouthwash.

What was supposed to be an early evening was now going to be a long night.

"We've gotta go. You're going to be late." Trying to brush past Rusty without being a total jerk, he headed for the coat closet.

Rusty intercepted him, but only held out the overlarge trenchcoat Sean detested so he could jab his arms into the sleeves.

"Thanks." With intent that was over and above their normal habit, he lifted his chin for their traditional kiss.

"Love you." Rusty showed his love with the rattle and then the weight of the energy bar he pushed into Sean's pocket.

A strength Sean desperately needed began to creep up his spine.

"Love you, too."

He could do this. He could face the world, with whatever came his way. He could do it because Rusty had his back.

CHAPTER THREE

Tired, worried, Sean watched his office clock and willed that little hand to move faster toward four. Work had passed by in a blur. He'd been worthless sitting behind his desk, re-reading emails he'd already replied to, checking figures he's just added.

Last night, while Rusty hammered and painted and Lotta Boute' sang 'It's Got To Be Me' a thousand times, cracking on the same note each time, Sean had been stuck with plenty of time to think.

The eve before his wedding reception, he should have been thinking about his upcoming vows—not that he wasn't. But his upcoming unemployment kept worming it's way over the top of everything else.

Looking back since he started with Oceanic, he'd worked hard. Not only that, he was good at his job. Case in point, refusing to sign off on substandard work.

Not bragging—but then, as Rusty's second brother always said, 'It's not bragging if it's true', the other two new engineers in his department wouldn't have recognized the cold cracking welds problem. They had just started dive lessons when they got the job.

He would fight for this job. Not just for financial security but also for himself.

And maybe, just maybe, everything was fine. Maybe, he was imagining the scrutiny from the department heads and the whispers and covert looks from everyone else in the department.

Three thirty. For the second time that week, he ws leaving before everyone else, testing the company policy that salaried professionals made their own hours. He'd certainly put in enough extra time in the last months to make up for this. And his future husband was home, freaking because the family caravan hadn't arrived yet with only three and a half hours until their wedding rehearsal.

Shaking off his guilt and worry for leaving early, he started backing up and shutting down for the weekend.

Just as he slipped on his coat, his company phone rang, showing Bob Frasier's number.

Crap. Sean couldn't think of any good reasons why Bob would be calling now.

"Delahunt," he answered, taking pride and comfort that Monday morning, he'd be answering as Sean Duchene, a married man—at least that's how he would answer as long as he still worked here.

"Sean, it's Bob. Could you come upstairs for a moment? Meet me in the Director's board room."

Instinctively, Sean glanced at his watch. What was he going to say? No, he didn't have time to make the meeting?

He gave a fleeting thought to gathering his few personal things in a box so he could grab them in one fell swoop on the way out the door.

Instead, he swallowed and answered, "Sure. I'll be right up."

With each floor he rose above, his determination became stronger to fight for his job—fight for himself.

Approaching the frosted glass windows of the conference room, he saw Bob seated with both the Director and VP of engineering along with another woman and a man Sean didn't know, Sean felt an unexpected strength flow through him. He wasn't sure why, but he wasn't questioning it, not now anyway.

He pushed open the door, met each person eye-to-eye but fell short of forcing a smile.

Bob stood, nodded with no sign of a smile, and said quietly, "Please pull the door tight."

Half past four o'clock. Where was Sean? He was going to try to get off early.

This was the night of their rehearsal, damn it. Couldn't he leave an hour or two early for once like all the other engineers did all the time on Fridays?

For the thousandth time in an hour, Rusty looked up from his study guide to check for texts or missed calls.

Nothing more since the phone conversation he'd had thirty minutes ago from his sister-in-law to say they would be there within the hour which prompted him to start his barrage of texts to the friends on standby for his family's arrival.

There had been much laughing and giggling in the background. Apparently, they were all having a wonderful time.

And he was trying to make himself concentrate on passing the test for his Louisiana landscape horticulturist license. Third time was the charm, right?

Rusty gave up on studying, clicking off the online practice tests with a stab of his middle finger.

He was only doing this for his dad, to make him shut up about it. And—he had to admit—because his sister-in-law was about to get her license and there was that competitive thing that happened to him on occasion. Especially when she would be taking his place in the family business as the new up-and-coming designer.

Not that he would need, or even be able to use his license here in Boston. He couldn't even get a steady freaking nursery delivery job. Although, he'd been promised first shot when Spring arrived—if Spring ever arrived. Who knew Boston would be so freaking cold for so long?

A text binged. Not Sean. Just Jody from upstairs.

'Bring 'em on.' Jody and Carter were letting Rusty's brother, sister-in-law and nephew stay with them. Rusty was a bit worried about how Elizabeth—Queen Elizabeth when she was in a mood—would react to his three-year-old nephew, Tommy, also an only child and used to being the center of the large and extended Duchene family's world.

Like Rusty had been as the youngest in the family.

He texted back, 'Thanks. As soon as they get here.'

It had been a while since homesickness had hit Rusty so hard. He took a moment to concentrate on all the great things about Boston, especially living in the South End, and there were plenty of them. Those first few weeks after the move, at Sean's counselor's advice, he'd made a list and memorized it. He'd have to admit Sean's counselor had helped him as much as he'd helped Sean, when Rusty had stubbornly thought he was just fine as he was.

Rusty looked over the spreadsheet Sean had made that showed who was staying where. Two more check ins, which would happen at the rehearsal dinner, tonight. They'd farmed out all the relatives with friends throughout their building, not only trying to keep everyone together, but to help cut expenses.

He glanced at the clock again. Where the hell was Sean?

Needing to do something, anything, he drug out the vacuum cleaner to run over their forever-shedding, ugly carpet.

Rusty was fully aware of how his whole family had sacrificed to be able to afford this trip and was so sincerely grateful to all the new friends they'd made since they'd been here. Had it only been about six months?

For Sean, it had been almost nine months. Most of the friends they'd made in the building were Sean's friends first and had accepted Rusty into their circle because they liked Sean. Until Sean took the job with Oceanic, the job that tore Rusty away from his family, making friends and easing Sean into those friendships had always been Rusty's role in their relationship. The changes they'd been through....

He rammed the vacuum into their 'vintage' coffee table, making the glued-on leg list and toppling all their magazines to the floor.

Damn it! He kicked the leg back into place.

Maybe they could start saving a little something each paycheck for a furniture fund. Or maybe he'd finally find a full-time job. *Or maybe it would snow in New Orleans on Christmas Day.*

His dad always said that. He used to say 'Or maybe when the Saints win the Superbowl' but then they had and his dad had been happy to not say that anymore.

He stole another glance at the clock. They'd be here soon. Not soon enough, but soon.

God, he felt lonely right now.

Dropping to his knees, he gathered the magazines, his nerves making his hands shake. Tomorrow, he would be a married man.

He'd thought of it as a formality, a ceremony that was a big deal for Sean, but—. Well, *he'd* been committed from their first make-out session.

Where the fuck was Sean?

Rusty took a deep breath. This loneliness was temporary and he would survive it for a few hours. It was nothing compared to what he'd suffered through for the both of them.

Those months he and Sean had been apart while Sean trained in his new job and passed his probationary period had been the worst of his life even while they had been great for Sean.

It hadn't helped that while Sean had been making those friends, Rusty had been living back in his mother's house, feeling totally unnecessary, totally left out of Sean's world.

Not something to think about today, the day before their wedding.

And Rusty really was glad that Sean had fit in so well.

Rusty looked at the time again. Where was Sean? Rusty needed him.

Sean was totally comfortable here like he'd never been in New Orleans. They were both surrounded by good friends and acquaintances. Grown-up friends, not like the guys he'd known since kindergarten.

Rusty's South End friends had never known him when he failed second grade. Or when he'd gotten spooked at the Haunted House when he was ten and peed himself. Or the time he'd stuck his head in the cotton candy machine when he was twelve. Or when he was learning to drive and took out three mailboxes before his dad could reach over and guide the car back onto the pavement.

Reaching under the couch for his new Heirloom Roses magazine, Rusty's hand swept across their missing tube of watermelon-flavored lube. Wouldn't that have been awkward for Sean's sister to find? It was awkward enough that she was staying with them the night before their wedding but she'd joined the carpool at the last minute and they'd run out of friends with couches to surf. Plus, Sean had been worried that a seventeen-year-old girl might not be comfortable staying with a couple of guys she didn't know, whether those guys were gay or not.

Rusty loved being surrounded by so many great guys.

His South End friends knew him as a man. A man who worked hard, laughed often, kept his word, and most importantly, loved his soulmate with all his heart. Rusty was proud of that image.

Of course, some of his theater friends—thinking of Jody—would protest being called grown-up, preferring to be in league with Peter Pan forever.

Not only did the theater district provided him with enough set building and tear down work to make him feel like he wasn't a total bum but it had opened up a world Rusty hadn't known existed.

He'd never understood how Sean could be so passionate about scuba, why he would spend every spare minute diving if he could. But now Rusty understood, because he had fallen head over heels for theater. He loved working behind the scenes. Plus, he got to see a ton of shows, usually with complimentary tickets. He was even thinking of taking an acting class that a friend of his was teaching as soon as he passed his blasted landscapers test. Maybe, someday, he would try out for a bit part.

It had taken him a while, but now, he loved Boston and all it had to offer.

Not that New Orleans didn't have theater, but it didn't have a whole theater district.

His phone beeped again. Another text. His family was about ten minutes away.

He grinned. *Let the chaos begin.*

Before Sean even opened the door to the apartment, he could tell the family had arrived.

None of the Duchenes had ever been accused of being quiet or shy.

So much for spilling his news as soon as possible. What he had to say was between him and his future husband, not for extended family discussion, no matter how much he loved them.

Wavering between feeling anxious or relieved about the reprieve, he attempted to do what his counselor always advised. He took a deep breath and just let it roll through him—whatever it may be. *Damned, uncontrollable emotions.*

From the hallway, he heard Rusty boom over the mob, telling his older sister, "I promise, Jolie, if you toast us with something embarrassing, I'll—"

Whatever Rusty would do was drowned out by dog barking and three-year-old boy squealing.

Once upon a time, all that energy intimidated Sean. Now, it welcomed him.

That was a good feeling.

He pushed open the door and the volume doubled.

"Sean!" The sound rushed at him milliseconds before the whole Duchene family did.

Caught up in hugs, Sean breathed into them. There was a time when touching was taboo, something males did *not* engage in. But that was in that other place, that other family he used to have. This family had always given Sean a warmth that breached those inhibitions his parents had set to make him into a man.

Going back to New Orleans wouldn't be so bad. In fact, it could be a very good thing for him as well as for Rusty.

And God knew, he missed real King Cake during Mardi Gras season.

Over the top of Mom Duchene's shoulders, he saw his sister sitting on the end of their couch, folded in on herself. MaryAnne had spent three days in the company of this energetically enthusiastic family and the strain showed on her face.

He understood. How long had it taken him to learn that not all fathers and mothers were people to guard against? That it was okay to be affectionate, okay to actually like your family just as you liked your friends?

From the conversation he'd had last Monday in his counseling session, he was still learning. At least he was now safely surrounded by good people.

MaryAnne had no one else but him.

He accepted all the hugs until the end when Grandmere' Duchene tried to shove Cindy-poo up for a kiss.

Separating that lapping tongue from his cheek with a well-placed forearm, and ignoring Rusty's grinning face as his almost-husband looked on, Sean took a step toward MaryAnne.

Without looking, he knew Rusty was riding herd, giving him space to talk to the only blood relative who would even speak to Sean.

As he sat next to her, keeping two hands-breadths between them, he said quietly, "Hey, sis."

"Hey." She gave him a hesitant smile.

"Long trip?"

"Yeah." MaryAnne's shoulders relaxed a fraction as she muttered, "Damned dog."

"Yeah," he agreed.

MaryAnne studied her hands clasped in her lap. "I'm sorry about Mom not coming."

It was Sean's turn to hunch his shoulders. "You don't need to be sorry, sis. Her behavior isn't your fault."

"Still—" MaryAnne leaned forward as if she couldn't hold herself up any longer.

Sean rushed to close the distance between them, holding her tight.

Into his neck, she whispered, "Why? We were doing fine. Between her job at the fabric store and my babysitting job, we were doing okay. Then she said it was her duty to go back to him. To try again. I can't do it."

He opened his eyes to see Dad Duchene watching the two of them. Not even married yet, and he was going test the family bonds. But for his sister, he'd ask for anything.

"Let me see if I can work something out."

MaryAnne took a deep breath then put her hands between them to push away. "You don't need my problems, especially not on your wedding weekend."

Wedding. That meant more than just committing to Rusty. He was accepting all that Rusty loved, and that included parents, brothers, grandparents, aunts and uncles—everyone. Because they were all more than willing to include him.

Feeling worthy—that was hard. But accepting and being accepted was what Rusty wanted. Hell, it was what *he* wanted. Longed for. Craved with every spark of life in him.

"We're family. Your problems are my problems." He wiped at a tear, smearing it across her cheek. "And you know what?"

"What?"

He looked around at the people crowding his apartment. "They're my family, too. So we have a lot of help here."

Rusty could always tell when Sean looked for him, always knew when Sean needed him. Even in grade school. Those instincts didn't fail Sean now as Rusty broke away from his brothers' conversation and knelt down beside him.

"What's up?"

Sean leaned into Rusty, knowing Rusty would brace himself and hold them both up. "Got some things to discuss privately with you."

"Okay." Rusty's smile was so understanding. So secure. How could simple eye contact make Sean feel so loved?

In the middle of all the voices, all the noise, Sean was surrounded by peace.

"Okay," he echoed Rusty, taking the first full breath he'd been able to draw in weeks. He leaned even harder on Rusty, letting his almost-husband take all his weight. "Okay."

Rusty only vaguely felt the ache in his knees as he wrapped his arm around Sean's waist and held on tight.

That the apartment was full of family, that Sean's sister sat across from them, nerves sending up spikes all around her, had no bearing on the bubble of peace surrounding them right now.

If Rusty ruled the world, he would have stayed there forever, feeling the solidness of Sean against him. Knowing Sean trusted him, felt safe with him, made Rusty feel proud. More than that, it made him feel complete.

Forget the discouraging job hunt. Forget the loss of family within shouting distance. Forget everything but the rightness he felt when Sean let go and trusted him.

In a moment of clarity, Rusty understood.

As if he'd suddenly become a bigger man, he understood that Sean was made for the world. Sean's brilliance was made to make the world a better place.

While Rusty was made to make Sean's world a better place.

This, taking Sean's weight, holding him, giving him security, was Rusty's place in the world, a place he took joy in.

And that joy made the world a good place.

"Hey, husband," Rusty whispered. "I love you."

Sean feathered his lips across Rusty's ear. "You, too."

Annoying chirping rudely interrupted their interlude enough to burst the bubble.

Rusty blinked, as if he'd been asleep, or in a trance or something. Not uncommon when Sean touched him.

Still, he held onto Sean until his love made a move to separate them.

Sean pulled his phone from his pocket. "We've only got an hour and a half to change and get to our wedding rehearsal."

"Our wedding rehearsal. I like the sound of that." Rusty wasn't sure Sean even heard him.

Their shared moment was definitely over as Sean went into Major General mode.

Spreadsheet in hand, he grouped family members and sent them off to apartment numbers, pointing and gesturing and texting advance warnings to the friends who offered room on their couches and spare bed for the weekend.

Sean leveled his gaze on Rusty. "Do you need to shower?"

Rusty had the strongest urge to sniff under his pits. Seeing the serious expression on Sean's face, he gave in and did it. "Uh, no. I'm good."

Sean's little grin at the corner of his mouth was worth any amount of silliness.

"Good." Sean glanced at his spreadhsheet, looked around to make sure the right people were scurrying in the right direction, then asked his sister, "And you?"

"Yes. I promise to make it quick."

"Bathroom's yours. I'll get in as soon as you get out." He hadn't even completed his sentence when he whirled around in the general direction of the grandmothers. "Need helping getting Cindy's leash on her?"

Before Sean could move away to help capture Cindy-poo, Rusty grabbed his hand.

"I know we haven't had a chance to discuss anything yet, but I just want you to know, I've got job applications out all over the city. I'm not qualified for anything big, but I'm thinking that even a little bit of steady income will help if—."

Sean's shoulders tensed. "We need to talk." Only half the relatives had made their way out the door. "As soon as everyone leaves."

Crap. That didn't sound good.

"Boys," his grandmother interrupted, "Cindy must go potty before we take her into a strange place. Otherwise, she'll might be startled and-" his grandmother lowered her voice to a stage whisper, "—make a mess."

He should stay and give Sean the opportunity to tell him the bad news. But not now. Bad news could wait until after the wedding, right?

"I'll take her." Rusty clipped the sparkling pink leash to Cindy-poo's diamonelle collar and headed for the door, carefully avoiding Sean and his need to talk.

CHAPTER FOUR

Rusty balanced his plastic plate of chicken spaghetti and paper cup of tea as he made his way to a round table set up in the Family Center. This rehearsal dinner, big enough to host his whole family and all the friends who were opening up their homes, was a gift from his parents who had supplied the food and the church who had supplied the labor to prepare it, just like their wedding reception tomorrow afternoon would be, too.

Rusty felt well loved.

The rehearsal had gone well enough, although Rusty was glad the sisters were standing in for him and Sean. Practicing that walk across the front of the chapel, standing in front of the altar and facing Sean—it was too big to do more than once.

Rusty hadn't understand why the bride should have a stand-in. Something about she should only have one trip down the aisle, Mom had vaguely explained when she had insisted both he and Sean follow the tradition. But now, he understood the symbolism behind it. While they wouldn't be walking down an aisle, although their minister had said he'd seen it done once or twice recently, they had both opted to make the shorter trek from opposite wings off the sanctuary.

Ignoring the empty chairs at the empty table where Sean sat, Rusty squeezed into the last place between Tommie and Elizabeth. Child chatter would be perfect to help him settle his nerves—just in case Sean wanted to have that talk soon.

And he did have nerves.

Totally unexpected. All along, Rusty had thought this wedding was just a formality for him. Sure, he knew it had a deeper meaning for Sean, making it official that Sean not only became his husband, but also brother and uncle and son.

Rusty didn't get why Sean had such trouble feeling that way, but he didn't have to understand to accept it.

But then, he'd seen his sister and Sean's standing at the altar representing them. At the minister's instructions, the sisters had held hands and looked into each other's eyes just like he and Sean would do tomorrow.

Reciting those vows—

God—Rusty wasn't into spirituality, not like Sean, but *God, please bless our marriage.*

A shudder shook Rusty hard enough that he sloshed tea over the side of his paper cup.

"Uncle Rusty spilled," Tommie tattled to his dad.

Rusty's brother gave him a wink. "He's allowed a spill or two on the evening before his wedding."

Starving, he shoveled in a big bite of spaghetti. Sean probably wouldn't eat a bite until this was all over with while Rusty would be making up for it, keeping his mouth full while his stomach swore it was empty.

Across the table from him, his mom was doing the same thing. Stress eating ran in the family.

He paused between bites long enough to notice his dad sitting with Sean, just the two of them deep into conversation.

Better them than him, right?

Damn. He was supposed to be more mature than that.

What was it about family that made him regress? He hadn't avoided the hard stuff since he left New Orleans for Boston. Since Sean started therapy—since *he* started therapy, too, he guessed.

He'd never thought of it that way. He was going for Sean. But he'd learned a thing or two, too-like how to think things through and make a plan to change his reactions if he didn't like the old way of doing things.

As if his dad could sense Rusty staring into his back, Dad pushed away his chair and headed in his direction.

Yup, Dad was coming for him.

Dad dropped a heavy hand on his shoulder. "Son, can I talk to you for a minute?"

Grown men didn't run from the the hard stuff. "Sure, Dad."

Pushing away from his half-full plate, Rusty followed his dad into a quiet corner behind a fake ficus. "What's up?"

"I didn't want to leave this on the table with the other gifts, in case it got lost." His dad pulled an envelope out of his pocket. "A gift from everyone at work. Maybe use it for a nice night out on the town or something."

"Thanks, Dad. Sean will write a note, I'm sure, but still, tell everyone thanks from us." Rusty took the envelope, folded it carefully and stuffed it in his back pocket. "But that's not why you wanted to speak to me in private, is it?"

Dad never had a problem saying what he wanted to say. But this time, he looked down at this feet, then up into Rusty's eyes. "Sean and I were talking about New Orleans, about how you've made friends here but how he knows you miss being home. I just want you to know that there is always a home and a job for you with us."

Rusty wasn't sure if he should be relieved or miffed. He took a breath, realizing he was both. But most of all, he was sure of himself when he said, "Thanks, Dad. I appreciate the safety net. But Sean and I are okay. And no matter what happens, we'll still be okay."

It wasn't the words. They were just common words, after all. It was the way he felt when he said them, the surety, the way he looked his dad in the eye, man-to-man. The way his dad's eyes flickered with surprise, then welled with pride.

He would always be his father's son but today, he was no longer the baby in the family. His baby days where behind him.

Rusty could tell his dad understood more than the words they'd exchanged but the change in their relationship, too. It was there in his body language, the way his dad stood, a little separate as if he no longer waited for Rusty to fall so he would be ready to catch him.

"Good man." Dad clapped him on the shoulder, then, as if he couldn't resist, pulled Rusty into a tight hug. "Good man," he said again.

"Because I was taught by the best." Rusty rubbed his tears into his dad's collar. Looking over Dad's shoulder, Rusty saw Sean laughing with Mr. and Mrs. Miller. Rusty clung to this pillar of strength, this man who had taught him to be strong, or at least to be strong enough.

"Thanks, Dad, for everything. From the both of us."

"It has been my honor and my pleasure."

"I'll pass it on."

"That's the greatest tribute a father can have, son. I have a fine legacy in you."

Then Dad was wiping tears on Rusty's shirt collar.

Sean climbed into bed snuggling into Rusty's backside, too fully aware of his sister sleeping on their couch, separated by a thin layer of sheetrock and plyboard to feel comfortable.

Rusty rolled over onto his back, sliding his arm under Sean's shoulders. It was a lump Sean had learned to relax into many years ago. Tonight, it did the trick.

He breathed out and stared at the shadows across the ceiling, turning them into shapes. "Nice rehearsal, huh?"

"Uh huh." Rusty scooted closer, fingertips resting on his stomach.

Sean wanted those fingertips to rest on *his* stomach, then move up to his nipple, then maybe drift along his collarbone before tracing a line down his non-existent treasure trail. Sex was a great distracter, after all.

He reached over and caught Rusty's hand, lacing their fingers together.

"I appreciate what you did—the job hunting. The applications. I took a look at your email. Mail clerk. Cafeteria worker. All inside jobs. That kind of work would drive you nuts."

Rusty shrugged against his shoulder. "It doesn't matter. I only need to do it until you find another job—if you lose the one you've got."

One of the shadows turned into a cat, arched and ready to pounce. "What do you think about going back to New Orleans?"

Rusty turned on his side, so that his breath wisped across Sean's cheek. "When I first got here, that's all I wanted to do. I missed my parents and my friends. I missed the work." He shifted, his ice cold feet finding Sean's shin. "I still miss the work. But I love you more."

"So you would go back if you could?"

"Truthfully, if you had asked me that this morning, I would have told you no."

"Really?" Sean pushed one leg between Rusty's calves, needing the anchoring only Rusty could give him—even when Rusty made his reality twist.

Rusty never lied, especially never to him.

The news Sean had to share made him squirm.

Rusty untangled their hands to lay a heavy arm across Sean's chest.

It helped.

Sean took a moment, still couldn't make sense of Rusty's words, then asked. "Why?"

"Why would I have told you I didn't want to go back to New Orleans?"

"Yeah, that why."

"Because I was afraid. This time we've spent in Boston, relying on no one but ourselves to make our decisions, leaning on each other—"

"Me, leaning on you, mostly."

Rusty rolled closer to brush his lips against Sean's cheek. "No. I was leaning, too. Leaning on you to make the money stretch, to manage the bills, to make me feel safe here."

"To make you feel safe? I didn't know you were ever worried about that."

"Of course, I was. I'd never lived anywhere but in our little patch of New Orleans before. Never moved further than the college campus. I know you were really young when you did all that moving around, but you'd done it. You knew about making yourself comfortable in a place that was different—really different. You knew how to accept and roll with those differences, like using public transportation and dressing for cold weather and hearing accents that are hard to understand, and being patient when people are fascinated because you talk different too. And you're strong enough to be okay about all that instead of intimidated by it."

"I didn't know—never knew—all that bothered you."

"Don't you see, Sean? That's the point. With you, all that stuff didn't bother me. It was a grand adventure. A challenge. Fun." Rusty leaned up on his elbow, halfway caging Sean. "But without you, I would have been lost. This whole Boston experience would have been scary, not fun at all. But you kept me safe."

"That's a first."

"No, it's not." Rusty let his weight down onto Sean's chest. "Did you know that being brave for you is what makes me brave?"

"Yeah?" Sean took that in. He could see that. Understand it. Accept it. "Okay."

Sean wiggled against Rusty, trying to remind himself that his sister was in the next room. But Rusty's reaction was making him not care about that at all.

"You know why else I would have been afraid to move back to New Orleans?"

"Why else?" *Concentrate, Sean. This is important.*

Rusty shifted, aligning his bulge with Sean's. *Not helping.*

"I was afraid of losing myself back into who I used to be. Being home at Christmas, I felt like a kid again. And not in a good way. Being around my parents, fitting into the kid brother role, letting Mom and

Dad tell us where to go and when to be there while we slept under their roof—. But I'm not a kid. I'm a man. Your man."

Sean pushed up his hips. "No question about that."

Rusty lifted up, separating them, even though Sean pushed as high as he could to keep contact. "I had questions."

Sean dropped his hips. "But now you have answers?"

"Yeah. I talked to my dad tonight. He offered me a job and a place to stay for the both of us. Just like old times."

"And...?" *Crap.* Sean thought of the wedding gift he'd printed off the internet this afternoon right before he left the office. *This could go so wrong.*

"And I told him, in a very nice, man-to-man way, that we could take care of ourselves."

"So you don't want to work for you dad?"

"That's not the point, Sean." Rusty rolled off him. Sean immediately missed the body warmth. The weight.

He rolled onto Rusty, looking down into his eyes. Tension made his body stiff against Rusty's, and not in the place he wanted stiffness. "The point?"

"We talked as a grown son to his father, like my brothers do. Not like a kid to his daddy. I didn't think I could do that. I didn't think I could ever get to that place of not being a child to him." Rusty plunged up, giving Sean the contact he craved. "But I did."

"Your voice is so damned sexy when it goes low like that."

"Like this?" Rusty's exaggerated rumble made Sean's pulse pound all the way through him—especially, yeah. There.

Rusty put his hand between them, rubbing the extended length of Sean's cock. "Wanna do me?"

"Yeah. I wanna do you." Sean reached for restraint. What he was about to say definitely put a damper on anyone getting done.

"But first...."

Rusty shoved them both up with his hips then reached down to push the waistband of his sleep pants down. "No *first*, baby. Later, okay?"

"Gotta get this over with." Sean rolled off, wishing things could stay the same, wondering if he was about to make them better or worse.

"Shit." Rusty flung his arm over his eyes. "What?"

"I got called into the VPs office today."

Rusty sat up, his hands going to his erection as if to protect it. "Yeah?"

"Yeah." Sean blew out a breath. "I got a promotion."

"What?" Rusty gaped like a fish out of water. "You put me through all this angst because you got a promotion?"

"It comes with a move."

"Where?"

"New Orleans." Sean's heart beat hard enough to make his head pound—and not the kind of head Rusty was fondling.

Moments passed as Sean counted his pulse, one, two, three, four....

"Okay."

"I could turn it down—I think. I guess I could, if you really don't want to move."

"No. I mean I want to. If you want to? I know you love it here. I know how you feel about New Orleans."

"You know how you feel about being a grown up? About not letting your folks affect who you are, how you feel?"

"Yeah."

"I think I can do that, too." Sean swallowed. "If you'll help me."

"That's what we do, babe." Rusty let go of his cock with one hand and wrapped it around Sean's like he needed a handle to hold on to. "We help each other."

Instinctively, Sean pushed up, needing the friction. Then he made himself be still. "I know you love the theater district here. I know you'll miss it, and all your friends."

"With that big promotion of yours, I imagine we can afford plane tickets every now and then, huh?"

"We'll definitely put them in the budget. But in the meantime. I got you a wedding present." Despite Rusty's hold on Sean's cock, Sean reached for the nightstand drawer—and almost came when all his nerve endings snapped and crackled.

Breathing fast, he pulled the folded printout from the drawer, remembered to turn on the light, then gasped at the passion on Rusty's face.

God, he wanted this fuck.

Clumsily, he held the paper out to Rusty but Rusty wouldn't let go of either of their cocks. "What's it say?"

Damn. Stringing words together was getting harder and harder. "They're season tickets. To Le Petit Theater du Vieux Carre."

Rusty moved his fingers, squeezing, then releasing.

"That must be a hell of a raise."

"Uh huh." At one time, Sean knew how much more he'd be making, but right now, numbers took a higher brain function than he was capable of.

The paper fluttered to the floor as he fished around in the drawer for the lube. "Spread 'em, big boy."

"God, yes." Rusty grabbed a pillow, shoved it under his hips and opened wide.

As Sean slicked up his fingers, he had one last rational thought and shoved a pillow over Rusty's head. "Gotta make this a quiet one."

"I'll try."

Maybe Rusty did try but he failed miserably. And that was okay.

As Sean drifted to sleep, Rusty mumbled in his ear, "Let's keep this to ourselves tomorrow, okay?"

"Okay, but why?"

"Don't want to take away from the wedding."

"Really?"

"Yeah, really. You know how I thought the wedding wouldn't change things between us?"

"Yeah."

"Well, it does. It makes it better."

Sean slobbered a kiss onto Rusty's chest. If tears mingled with that kiss, that was okay, too.

CHAPTER FIVE

Sean breathed out as Dad Duchene firmly brushed off the back of his charcoal gray suit. The action was more soothing than functional. Dad Duchene knew him well enough to know it was the closest to a back and shoulder rub Sean could be comfortable with right now.

Not for the first time this morning, Sean wished it was Rusty touching him, taking his nerves down to a level that kept his eye from twitching.

It wasn't the wedding. It was the crowd.

Knowing Rusty's family, his brothers, sister-in-law, nephew, sister, and grandparents filled the first two rows of the sanctuary like a protective barrier thawed some of the chill that had settled onto his clammy skin.

Sean shouldn't think of all their friends and his co-workers as wishing anything but the best for his and Rusty's impending marriage. But he couldn't help but remember all the times he's been terrified that someone would attack him, physically and emotionally, for being who he was.

Standing in front of the hundred or so people, proudly showing everyone he was a gay man who loved another man, heart and soul—he couldn't keep from imagining someone, under the cowardly safety of anonymity, would yell out 'Faggot' or throw something at him or....

The hard grip of Dad Duchene's fingers on his shoulders, the gentle shake, the soft way Dad called his voice, brought Sean back from memories he'd tried so hard to get past.

"It's okay, son. I've got you."

Sean took another breath, trying to pull calm from that place in his heart where Rusty lived. With Rusty, all that hadn't mattered, because they were together. And together, they made their own world.

He should step back, break contact, prove he could stand on his own two feet like a man. But Dad Duchene didn't let go at Sean's subtle shifting of weight. Instead, Dad Duchene pulled Sean closer, wrapped his arms around Sean, regardless of the wrinkles he would put in his maroon and white pin-striped dress shirt and held Sean tight.

"I'm so proud of you, Sean. Of the boy you were, of the man you've become. I love you the same as I love the sons my wife has given birth to." His voice thickened. "If I could create a partner for my son, you would surpass everything I could wish for him. I am so proud to become your father in the eyes of the world and in the eyes of God."

Sean relaxed against the man who had held his sons and Sean so securely in those hard-working arms. He buried his wet eyes in Dad Duchene's neck as Dad Duchene rubbed circles into the tense space between his shoulder blades.

He wanted to say something big and significant. Something to let Dad Duchene know how he felt. He wanted to emphasize how grateful he was that the Duchenes had always let Rusty be himself and extended that same acceptance to Sean. How they had supported Rusty's love for Sean instead of trying to keep them apart. How they had rescued Sean from the hospital and given him a place to live, food and shelter and safety in their own home. How they had cheered at high school graduation when he'd graduated with honors, just as they'd cheered for Rusty who had barely managed to graduate at all, letting both of them know they had done well.

He wanted to thank Dad Duchene for the hours he'd spent with Sean helping him fill out financial aid requests and, when that wasn't enough to send him to college, had reached into the family savings and made up the difference. And all this time, they had never asked for anything in return.

Instead, his sniffling whimpers turned into sobs, emotion spilling over that was too big to keep inside any longer.

The whole time he shook and cried, Dad Duchene held him, murmuring to let it out. Sean was okay. They were okay. Everything was okay.

And for the first time in Sean's memory, probably in his whole life, he believed that he was okay. And at this moment, this single moment in time, his world was okay, too.

As he wound down, feeling limp, feeling empty and weightless and free of all the dark sorrow that had been crammed into his soul, he found the strength to stand on his own, knowing he would never be alone again.

Not only did he have Rusty, he had every person who loved Rusty, every person who loved *him*, for himself and on Rusty's behalf.

As he leaned back, Dad Duchene wiped a tear from his cheek, his callused hand emphasizing the strength he would always lovingly give to Sean.

A love Sean had learned to accept because Rusty loved him, accepted him, showed him how natural sharing and caring could be. Without Rusty, he would be—

—he would be dead, cold and vacant. Whether in fact or in spirit, he couldn't be sure. He just knew that Rusty had shown him that life was worth living.

He swallowed trying to find the words. But what could he say that would cover it?

Thank you was so inadequate.

Again, just like so many times in the past, Dad Duchene rescued him.

"I know, son." He pulled Sean tight again, then held him apart to look into Sean's eyes, no darting away, just total acceptance. "I know."

And Sean no longer felt like the charity case he'd always been. No longer felt in debt. Held tightly in Dad Duchene's safe grip, Sean felt loved.

All because Rusty loved him first.

Rusty had won the Bride's Room in the coin toss. It had been funny last night at the rehearsal when their minister had pulled out a quarter and demanded 'heads or tails'.

But the white and gold gilt painted wood on the spindly vanity dresser and matching chairs and love seat upholstered in pale rose velvet in Unity's Bride's Room made Rusty feel huge, hulking and clumsy.

Adjusting his maroon tie against his navy shirt, Rusty shifted from foot to foot, staring into the full-length mirror but not seeing himself, looking beyond his reflection. Behind him, his mom was a vague blur as she put her hands on his shoulder.

"Deep breath, son." He followed orders and felt the light-headedness drop into his knees. *Breathe through it.* How often had he whispered those same words to Sean, calming him from a nightmare or a panic attack.

"I need to sit down."

He dropped onto a chair that looked too dainty to hold him, adjusting his dark navy dress pants to ease their fit so they didn't wrinkle.

Soon. Soon he would be adjusting himself for a different reason. Instead of easing his discomfort, his skittering thoughts only dialed his nerves up to a ten.

His mom gave him a half-smile. "Unbutton your coat, too. Why don't you take it off. Cool off a little."

No one should have trouble staying cool during February in Boston. Still, he could feel the sweat gather under his armpits despite his triple layer of deodorant.

"Your brother was nervous, too. You'll be fine. It's going to be over soon."   She'd accompanied him into the room this morning, announcing she was going to take care of her responsibilities as Mother of the Groom and Daddy was going with Sean into the other dressing room to do his duty as Father to the other Groom.

"No. This is forever. It's never going to be over." That didn't sound as enthusiastic as he he had hoped it would—as he felt it should.

She gave him the same smile she'd given him when he'd brought Sean home the night Sean had been released from the hospital. That smile said it all. *I love you. I'll take care of you. Everything is going to be all right.*

Shaking, he'd fallen into her arms, letting her hold him up. She hadn't even staggered under his greater weight.

Needing to feel that security right now, he stood. Knowing what her youngest son needed, she opened her arms, braced her feet and squeezed tight, tighter and tighter until he could finally take a deep breath, knowing she would hold him together if he started to fall apart.

Knowing his father as doing the same for Sean, should he need it, made him feel a warmth deep inside that had nothing to do with nerves. "I love you, Mom. I'm so blessed to have such a great family."

"You're blessed to have Sean, too, hon."

"Yeah, I know. I'm going to take care of him, Mom."

Rusty vowed that as strongly as he was about to vow his never-ending love.

Sean pulled back, embarrassment trying to poison his inner warmth.

The shoulder of Dad Duchene's once pristine shirt was damp and smudged.

Sean wrapped his arms around himself, hating the restriction of the suit coat. "I've messed you up."

Dad Duchene frowned, looked down where Sean pointed, then smiled, his eyes twinkling. "Wouldn't be a wedding otherwise."

"Sir?"

"Rusty's brother—your brother now, too—did the same thing." He braced his hands on Sean's arms, his grip strong and reassuring. "That's what suit jackets are for. No one will even suspect."

Imaging Rusty's big, blustery brother blubbering all over his father's shirt took some mental discipline. Thankfully, that controlled focus helped him get his emotions tamped back down into their little box.

"Let's get this jacket off you so you can wash up." Dad Duchene ran his thumb under Sean's eye and held it up. Black eyeliner coated it.

The heat in his face made his cheeks burn. He tried to hide it under cover of taking of his coat.

But there was no hiding from Dad Duchene.

"Love you, son," he said, reminding Sean that there was no need to hide anything from his family.

Son. His throat thickened but he said the words he'd wanted to say all his life. "Love you, too, Dad."

And that quick, he was held in the warmest, tightest, safest embrace he could have asked for.

A knock on the door followed by Jolie's voice gave them a ten minute warning.

Sean pushed away, knowing that strength of family would be there whenever he needed it and stumbled into the restroom.

Eight minutes later, cutting the time too close, he checked himself in the mirror, resigned he could do nothing for his red-rimmed eyes. Maybe nobody would notice. He'd done his eyes the way Rusty liked them, the way he usually reserved for late nights in the clubs, trying to cover the vestiges of his tears. Well, maybe a little more conservatively, but not by much.

But this was him, damn it. And he deserved to be who he was, especially on his wedding day.

The violin began to play. Air on a G String by Bach. Rusty had laughed more than once, suggesting he and Sean each wear a thong to commemorate the music.

He'd done it.

It would be like Sean to do it, too. The secrets his solemn-seeming baby kept from the world and revealed only to him…. Most of Sean's secrets weren't the fun kind, but every now and then….

The honor Sean did him of trusting with those secrets often filled him with worry that he wasn't strong enough to man up to the responsibility, but always filled him with awe that Sean believed in Rusty's strength.

At his mom's cue, Rusty filed out of the wings heading toward the center of the sanctuary, knowing his mom had his back. And knowing Sean would be coming from the opposite side, meeting him in the middle.

Meeting him in the middle. They'd lived together long enough to know there was no middle. There was no fifty-fifty. It was Sean all the time, one hundred percent.

Just like he knew Sean was there for him, no matter what, whenever Rusty needed him.

And yeah, maybe that was an unrealistic fairytale, but wasn't that what weddings were made of?

A thrill went down his spine and he looked up.

Sean emerged from the wing, rounding the corner, his eyes searching, finding, latching onto Rusty's eyes. And he smiled.

Not just any smile, but the one the Rusty rarely saw in private and never saw in public. The one that let his emotions show through.

And right now, as he smiled back, he saw fear skitter past, then away. In it's place was relief, then happiness, then joy.

And as he Sean came closer, he saw desire.

And felt it in his own soul.

God, he loved this man.

He especially loved the way Sean walked when wearing a thong. Maybe it would be the red one.

The sudden urge to adjust his own black silk butt floss made him clench his hands as well as his cheeks.

A prod in his back from his mom reminded him that he should be walking.

He made his foot move, take a step, then another under the guiding press of his mom's hand against his back.

The last two strides needed no encouragement as he rushed the march, overstepping his mark and ending up on Sean's side instead of in the middle.

Sean put out his hands and Rusty took them, palm to palm, then fingers interlaced into fingers. Gently, subtly, Sean pushed him back to center.

The hugeness of what he was about to do, about to pledge, about to share, struck him so hard he couldn't draw breath.

And Sean knew, in that way he had. Sean's fingers tightened on his. The bare place where his ring should be ached for the feel of that circle of metal, that promise that he was finally fulfilling.

He had thought this wedding, this marriage, was only going to be for form's sake.

Instead, as the minister droned on to words Rusty should be listening to intently, he examined the feelings that were flooding him, drowning out everything but the clench of Sean's fingers squeezing his own. Without that touch he would....

He would shrivel up and die.

And now, he was pledging, before his family, before a God he treated so cavalierly but Sean treated so reverently, before new friends who knew him only as Sean's partner and not his mother's son, to be a man who took care of his husband in sickness and in health. A man who gave his all, who rose about petty differences—and big issues, too—to put Sean first in his world. Every day, every breath, was for Sean.

A part of him protested. What about staying true to himself? Being his own person? Keeping his own identity strong?

Feeling Sean stare at him, he looked up, realizing he'd been staring at their joined hands.

Sean's red-rimmed eyes bore into him. Scared. Hopeful. Pleading.

And certainty hit him over the head. How could he have been so foolish to even think—. Sean would never ask him to be anyone other than who he was.

Just like he'd never want Sean to be anyone else for him, either.

The minister cleared his throat, apparently not for the first time as his mom patted him on the back.

"Exchange rings," the minister whispered, but his microphone still picked it up.

Clumsily, Rusty reached back and took Sean's ring from his mother, then grabbed Sean's long, slender finger and rammed the ring back where it belonged.

At Sean's wince, he almost mouthed, 'sorry' but Sean did the same to him, so he left it at that.

"Do you, Russell William Duchene, take Sean Bentley Delahunt to be your lawful wedded husband?"

They had practiced simple, 'I do's' but that didn't begin to cover it.

Rusty knew his smile was watery, but he said, loud and clear so everyone in the church could hear him, "With all my heart, mind, body and soul."

Nodding with approval, the minister turned to Sean. "Do you Sean Bentley Delahunt take Russell William Duchene to be your lawful wedded husband?"

Sean took in a gasping breath, visibly swallowed, then looked into Rusty's eyes, a smile coming from their depths. "I do. With all my heart, mind, body and soul. I do."

"By the power vested in me by God and the state of Massachusetts, I pronounce you married. What God has put together, let no person put asunder." He put his hands on both their shoulders, turning them to the crowd.

Spontaneously, their friends and family began to clap, then to cheer as his arm snaked around Sean's waist, pulling him closer, needing to feel him.

They hadn't talked about it, hadn't practiced it last night at rehearsal, hadn't really avoided it, but—

Sean pulled him close and kissed him, long and hard, in front of everyone.

And that made all the wedding plans, all the nerves, and all the expense leading up to this moment worth it.

In front of everyone and God, Sean claimed Rusty with his kiss.

Rusty leaned into Sean, let himself be claimed, and let the tears flow.

The enormity of what they'd just done made Sean's world spin.

Leaning on a column in Unity's Family Center, he pushed around the pastry filled with cheese, shoving it into the untasted sugar cookie that sparkled with pink sprinkles.

He'd barely been able to swallow the bite of wedding cake Rusty held to his lips. If not for Rusty's hand rubbing circles on his back, he would have choked.

Thankfully, Rusty was showing appreciation for the spread his friends and family had put together by trying some of everything, complimenting the cook effusively, then going back for seconds.

"How are you holding up." Sean's counselor asked, under cover of the chatting going on around them.

"Fine."

The eyebrow arch made Sean cringe.

"Let's try that again."

"I'm a little freaked out."

"Okay. Why?"

"Rusty never cries. Not because he's holding back, but because he's not got all the sadness inside him like—like me."

"So you think he's sad?"

Sean looked over at Rusty, laughing as he took a bite from the soggy cookie his three-year-old nephew held out to him. He looked so good, so grown-up, in his suit and tie. Such a rarity. With nice dinners out before the plays, Sean would try to change that in the future.

Even as he watched, Rusty shed the suit coat, handing it off to Mrs. Miller. "Not right now. But at the service, when we kissed, he cried."

"I saw a lot of people crying. Were they sad?"

"I'm not stupid," Sean bit out, irritated with—he wasn't sure who he was irritated with. He was just so damned edgy. Shouldn't he be having a good time, like Rusty?

His counselor lifted that eyebrow again. "No, you're not stupid. Why were they crying? Why was Rusty crying?"

"Because they were happy?"

"And people cry because—"

Sean quoted from the many times he'd heard in his sessions, "Emotions cause a chemical overload in the in the body and tears are one of the ways to relieve that overload."

"There you go. It wouldn't hurt if you wanted to shed a tear or two."

"Been there, ruined the shirt." Sean cleared his throat. "Dad Duchene took it well. He said Rusty's brother had cried on his shoulder, too. It was tradition."

"You've married into a very physically emotional family."

"Yeah, I have."

"Pretty different from the one you grew up in, huh?"

"Night and day."

"These guys seem to really love you. Do you think they'd ever hurt you on purpose?"

That question caught Sean off guard. They'd talked about trust, talked about intentional harm, talked and talked and talked. But that had all been words. All hypothesis. Sean took a long, intense look around at his family, by law as well as by heart. He knew they loved him. But his mother loved him too, and had let him be hurt. In fact, she'd often added to it, agreeing with his father to save herself from grief.

"No. Not a single one of the Duchenes would ever intentionally hurt me." He couldn't hold it back even as he struggled to.

He stopped struggling. And he smiled, letting all the happiness inside him show on his face, certain that those closest to him wouldn't see his happiness as a sign that he had let down his guard and become vulnerable and easy to attack.

At sixteen, he'd left that home, the father who had beaten him into the hospital and the mother who had stood by wringing her hands but doing nothing else, and a sister who was threatened to receive her own share of violence if she tried to help all because he was gay. And now, almost a decade later, he had a family, a father, mother, sister, brothers, sister-in-law, nephew, and grandparents that loved him. And most of all, he had a husband who truly did adore the ground he walked on.

That husband came up to him and put his arm over Sean's shoulder. "When you smile like that, you light me up inside brighter than the glare off the Ponchartrain at noon."

Then Rusty hugged him, pulling him so tight, Sean could swear he heard Rusty's heart beat. Or maybe it was his own since he was certain those two hearts were doing the romantic thing and beating as one.

"Dance with me?" The growl in Rusty's voice made Sean worry about his pants front. Damned g-string.

They'd never danced in public before. He loved to dance with Rusty in clubs where most everyone there was gay, and it was dark and the lights were flashing and Sean had been at least a little bit drunk, but never like this.

But this was his wedding day. And he was going to dance with his husband.

"Yes."

As Rusty gave a high pitched whistle, which apparently was his signal to the DJ, Sean let his own coat slide off, not caring who caught it—because everyone here wished him well and whoever ended up with it would take care of it for him. More than the weight of his suit coat dropped from his shoulders.

Sean melted into Rusty, his chin on Rusty's shoulder, leaving just enough room between them to shuffle their feet. They'd perfected this after years of practice. Nothing fancy. Just moving to the beat, moving with each other, not really thinking about avoiding each other's feet. They knew where each step would take them.

Camera flashes made spots in his vision. Whispers of how beautiful they looked together soothed his ears. And Rusty's arms wrapped him in warmth.

It was the perfect moment. The perfect beginning to a life that would *not* be perfect.

But Sean would spend every second of every day being okay with life just the the way it was because Rusty was in it with him.

EPILOGUE

Finally, after weeks of reading ads and looking, followed by too many days of packing, driving and unpacking, Sean could lay in his own bed next to his own husband and stare at the New Orleans' moonlight coming through his own duplex window.

Next to him, Rusty's hand started to wander. "We were lucky that Levi Graham's interior decorator friend knew about this coming on the market, huh?"

As Rusty found a sensitive spot, the one in the hollow of his hip bone, Sean squirmed closer. "Uh-huh."

Sean especially liked the small fenced-in back yard. Perfect for a bar-b-que grill and a couple of lawn chairs. And a dog.

They had never talked about pets, but maybe a nice little rescue pup. It was a big commitment, but they were up to it, weren't they?

"Sean?" Rusty's hand wandered over, closer to center as he stroked a single finger around Sean's belly button.

"Yeah?"

"What do you think about us having a baby?"

The End (for now)

Thank you for reading **When Sean Loves Rusty**, the Sean and Rusty first year post-college collection (Bayou Boys #1 through #5). This story, and all my stories in the Bayou Boys series are brought to you by—you! Your purchase of an author's works enables that author to keep writing. For that, I am extremely grateful.

When Sean Loves Rusty is available both digitally and in paperback.

If you enjoyed **When Sean Loves Rusty**, please share the love.

Review
Please, share your opinion by leaving a review (and thanks in advance. Your comments mean the world to me.)

Twitter
Give a tweet, include me(@ChrisCoxWrites), and I'll RT!

Facebook
I'm a facebook junkie. Friend me at www.facebook.com/ChrisCoxWrites and/or www.facebook.com/ChrisCoxAuthor. I'd love to add a comment or a *like* if you add me to your post.

Now I'll share with you—

New Release Notification
Want to know when the next Bayou Boys story is available?
Sign up for my newsletter at www.ChrisCoxWrites.com

Sneak Peek
To get an unedited glance at Levi and Clint's story, **Down to the Studs,** turn the page.

SNEAK PEEK

Down to the Studs *(unedited)*

Coming summer 2014

"Come on, Levi, you won fair and square."

Levi Graham took his eyes off the stop and go traffic on Magazine Street only long enough to give his sister a cutting glance. "I didn't even sign up. You did it for me."

"Because you need it." Nikki shifted under her seatbelt. She had plenty of room since she was so small and his truck seat was so big.

He was the giant of the family. Almost six foot when his next closest brother was at least four inches shorter than him.

Not that he was that big, but he'd felt that way since he hit puberty. But then, he'd felt different in a lot of ways since puberty.

He braked as the car in front of him neatly slid into a parking spot his truck would have never fit into. New Orleans's Magazine Street might be renowned for upscale shopping, but it was not so famous for convenient parking.

"That promotional drawing was meant to attract future clients, not guys like me."

"Guys like you?" She gave him an exasperated look. "Guys like you have just as much rights as anyone else."

Levi couldn't help but smile as his chest loosened. He could always count on his sister, his biggest advocate, to say what he needed the most. Could she actively sense his restlessness? His loneliness? His inner conflict that flared up sometimes so high he couldn't stand himself?

Shit. What was he doing? He had a great family. Plenty of friends. Casual friends, but still willing company whenever he wanted to drink a beer and catch a game. A great place on the lake all to himself.

What else could a guy like him ask for? How long had it been since he'd even had a casual date.

Dating. It had been the only part of college he'd enjoyed. He'd fallen hard, in then out of love, before getting the message that it was all in play. Then he'd played hard, trying to prove he'd gotten the message.

LSU might be just up the road in Baton Rouge, but it had been like a whole other world to him.

Then he'd moved back home and gone to work for the family business, like he'd always known he would. And he hadn't had a date since.

Date. His stomach clenched at the thought of anyone he knew seeing and reporting back to his family.

He was so lonely. And so full of chicken shit.

But he had so much to loose. More to loose than to gain.

It was a math problem, not an emotional dilemma.

Maybe he'd hit a sports bar tonight. Beers with the boys. It wouldn't scratch his itch, but maybe it would make it bearable.

"There's a place." Nikki pointed to a parking spot right at the front door of the shop he'd been looking for.

With careful maneuvering, he could tuck his big monster in there but it would be a tight fit.

He swallowed a sigh and made himself unclench his sphincter muscle that had involuntarily tightened.

"Slow and easy," Nikki coached.

"Not helping." Wrenching his thoughts back into the proper place, he paused in his assessment and took a moment to look her in the eye, more to ground himself than to emphasize his brotherly superiority. Still, the right tone of voice came easily. "Like I'm not the one that taught you to operate heavy machinery."

"For which I shall be forever grateful."

Levi knew that was true enough. Being the only girl in a family of five boys, Nikki had been told she couldn't do things because of her gender ever since she'd been born. But Levi had never seen the logic of that. After all, a bulldozer didn't know if the person operating it was male or female.

So he'd taught her to drive every piece of equipment in his father's inventory, just like he'd been taught.

"You're a damned sight better than Steven at maneuvering anything with a motor." Their oldest brother could barely drive his tiny hybrid without running over the curb, much less anything more complicated. Good thing he was good with numbers.

Graham and Sons and Daughter needed a good accountant to take care of the influx of business they'd had for the last several years. The New Orleans area was booming again, for which they were all grateful.

"If I could only operate a backhoe like you, big brother."

With false modestly, he shrugged away the compliment. "We can't all be best at everything."

Once firmly between the lines, Levi sat and stared at the display window in front of him. All that fussiness was not his style.

"Something tells me this isn't a good idea."

"You've mentioned that a couple thousand times already." Nikki put her purse strap on her shoulder. "You need this. You can't keep living the way you do."

Levi nodded. For all the hard work he'd done on the outside, the inside was still a mess.

"Let's do it, then."

"You've committed to it anyway, so grousing about it isn't going to change anything." Nikki laughed as she opened her door and slid from the truck seat. "This could be fun if you let it. Give it a chance."

He stared at the display window full of velvet and lace. She was right. He'd lost the bet so this was going to happen. The only thing optional was his attitude.

ABOUT THE AUTHOR

Writing is one of those things I must do because it's who I am. Reading is one of those things I'm grateful you do, especially when you're reading one of my stories!

Having the freedom to write about issues that matter, as well as to write about loving relationships, gives my muse great pleasure.

The Bayou Boys series, all about Louisiana boys in love, is set around New Orleans, in my home state of Louisiana. More Bayou Boys short stories, novellas and novels are available at most places where you buy your books.

Thanks so much for buying this story. Readers buying books are what keep writers able to keep writing.

Chris

Chris Cox

Contact & Media Info:

Website: http://ChrisCoxWrites.com (sign up for new release info here)

Facebook: http://www.facebook.com/ChrisCoxWrites (lots of chatty stuff)

Facebook: http://www.facebook.com/ChrisCoxAuthor (mostly just about the writing)

Twitter: http://www.twitter.com/ChrisCoxWrites (random stuff)

Pinterest: http://www.pinterest.com/ChrisCoxWrites (inspirational story boards for past, present and future stories)

www.ingramcontent.com/pod-product-compliance
Lightning Source LLC
Chambersburg PA
CBHW032129170626
46808CB00006B/2162